FRIENDS

FRIENDS

The Crime
of My Life

The Crime of My Life

Favorite Stories
by
Presidents of the Mystery
Writers of America

Edited by
Brian Garfield

WALKER AND COMPANY, NEW YORK

M
c –

First published in the United States of America in 1984 by the Walker
Publishing Company, Inc.

Published simultaneously in Canada by John Wiley & Sons
Canada, Limited, Rexdale, Ontario.

Library of Congress Cataloging in Publication Data

Main entry under title:

The Crime of my life.

1. Detective and mystery stories, American.
I. Garfield, Brian, 1939-   . II. Mystery Writers of America.
PS648.D4C7 1984   813'.0872'08   83-40389
ISBN 0-8027-0761-0
ISBN 0-8027-7256-0 (pbk.)

Printed in the United States of America

10 9 8 7 6 5 4 3 2 1

The Crime of My Life

Contents

INTRODUCTION   *BRIAN GARFIELD*   ix

CHINOISERIE   *HELEN McCLOY*   1

PRESENT FOR
MINNA   *RICHARD MARTIN STERN*   32

HANGOVER   *JOHN D. MacDONALD*   39

THE LEOPOLD LOCKED
ROOM   *EDWARD D. HOCH*   54

GIVE THE DEVIL
HIS DUE   *LAWRENCE TREAT*   79

FRAMED FOR
MURDER   *HAROLD Q. MASUR*   96

THE MAN WHO KNEW
WOMEN   *ROBERT BLOCH*   118

THE QUESTION   *STANLEY ELLIN*   150

GALTON AND THE
YELLING BOYS   *HILLARY WAUGH*   163

MILADY BIGAMY   *LILLIAN DE LA TORRE*   175

SCRIMSHAW   *BRIAN GARFIELD*   196

BLESSED ARE THE
MEEK   *GEORGES SIMENON*   211

THE PURPLE IS
EVERYTHING *DOROTHY SALISBURY DAVIS* 255

INTRODUCTION

All the contributors to this anthology have been presidents of the Mystery Writers of America, Inc., an organization whose age (and sometimes even wit) equals that of the late but perennial Jack Benny: MWA celebrates the 39th anniversary of its founding at the time of this book's publication. And each contributor was asked to pick a favorite story from his or her own body of work.

MWA presidency is a coveted honor rather than an administrative position. It is one of the three recognitions by which MWA publicly applauds a peer. (The other two are the Grand Master Award, bestowed once in a lifetime on a writer for his or her body of work, and MWA's well-known Edgar Allan Poe Award—the annual "Edgar," the mystery's equivalent of the Oscar.) Election to the presidency is the equivalent of a salute from one's colleagues for one's work. It is without price, and I, like the 38 previous occupants of the office, am moved by the great compliment.

The tales herein represent a wide range of crime and suspense storytelling; the mystery is not a monolithic or formulaic genre. There are stories of clever detection by Edward D. Hoch (the only writer I know who makes a living by writing short stories), Harold Q. Masur (who writes so persuasively about lawyers because he is one) and Hillary Waugh (who virtually invented the police-procedural detective story). We are guided through an exotic place and time by Helen McCloy (who may put scholars to shame with her knowledge of nineteenth-century China) and through an exotic mind by Stanley Ellin (who is the reigning master of the mystery short story). We are enthralled by the trick ending of a con-game story by Robert Bloch (whose Psycho is still the touchstone of mad-killer thrillers) and we are held in suspense by John D. MacDonald (who is, I think, one of the best living American writers) and by the others represented in this collection.

To have included stories by all the past presidents of MWA would have been prohibitive—the printing costs alone for such a large volume would have put its price far beyond most readers' means. We decided therefore to limit the contents of this book to stories written by MWA presidents who are still alive and working. And the list of contributors was further shortened by the fact that some of the former presidents—the novelist Phyllis A. Whitney, for example— have never written mystery short stories.

This book contains stories by all the living MWA presidents who were able to provide them. But the volume would be incomplete without acknowledgment of and a salute to **all** the presidents.

Chronologically, here is the honor roll:

Baynard Kendrick
Ellery Queen
Hugh Pentecost
Lawrence G. Blochman
John Dickson Carr
Helen McCloy
Anthony Boucher
George Harmon Coxe
Helen Reilly
Stuart Palmer
Georges Simenon
Dorothy Salisbury Davis
Margaret Millar
Rex Stout
Raymond Chandler
Frances & Richard Lockridge
Vincent Starrett
John D. MacDonald
Howard Haycraft
Edward D. Radin

Ross Macdonald
John Creasey
Herbert Brean
James Reach
Stanley Ellin
Robert Bloch
Richard Martin Stern
Hillary Waugh
Harold Q. Masur
Aaron Marc Stein
Phyllis A. Whitney
Lawrence Treat
Mignon G. Eberhart
Robert L. Fish
Lillian de la Torre
William P. McGivern
Thomas Walsh
Edward D. Hoch
Brian Garfield

—BRIAN GARFIELD

The Crime
of My Life

"Chinoiserie" was written in 1935 when I came across a book about the first journey of the Siberian Railway. I was so fascinated by Victorian China that I went on to read every book about it that I could find in the Oriental Room of the New York Public Library. After that the story just wrote itself.

For more than thirty years "Chinoiserie" has been republished all over the world in many languages. Just before World War II it was heard as a radio play in Singapore where there is a large Chinese colony. Just after the Vietnam War it was shown as a television play in the city I still think of as Hanoi, where there are also many Chinese. These two incidents pleased me more than anything else in the history of the story because they suggested that the Chinese themselves felt it was an accurate and sympathetic portrayal of Victorian China.

—HELEN McCLOY

CHINOISERIE

HELEN McCLOY

This is the story of Olga Kyrilovna and how she disappeared in the heart of Old Pekin.

Not Peiping, with its American drugstore on Hatamen Street. Pekin, capital of the Manchu Empire. Didn't you know that I used to be language clerk at the legation there? Long ago. Long before the Boxer Uprising. Oh, yes. I was young. So young I was in love with Olga Kyrilovna . . . Will you pour the brandy for me? My hand's grown shaky the last few years. . . .

When the nine great gates of the Tartar City swung to at sunset, we were locked for the night inside a walled, medieval citadel, reached by camel over the Gobi or by boat up the Pei-ho, defended by bow and arrow and a painted representation of cannon. An Arabian Nights city where the nine gate towers on the forty-foot walls were just ninety-nine feet high so they would not impede the flight of air spirits. Where palace eunuchs kept harems of their own to "save face." Where musicians were blinded because the use of the eye destroys the subtlety of the ear. Where physicians prescribed powered jade and tigers' claws for anemia brought on by malnutrition. Where mining operations were dangerous because they opened the veins of the Earth Dragon. Where felons were slowly

1

sliced to death and beggars were found frozen to death in the streets every morning in the winter.

It was into this world of fantasy and fear that Olga Kyrilovna vanished as completely as if she had dissolved into one of the air spirits or ridden away on one of the invisible dragons that our Chinese servants saw in the atmosphere all around us.

It happened the night of a New Year's Eve ball at the Japanese Legation.

When I reached the Russian Legation for dinner, a Cossack of the Escort took me into a room that was once a Tartar general's audience hall. Two dozen candle flames hardly pierced the bleak dusk. The fire in the brick stove barely dulled the cutting edge of a North China winter. I chafed my hands, thinking myself alone. Someone stirred and sighed in the shadows. It was she.

Olga Kyrilovna . . . How can I make you see her as I saw her that evening? She was pale in her white dress against walls of tarnished gilt and rusted vermilion. Two smooth, shining wings of light brown hair. An oval face, pure in line, delicate in color. And, of course, unspoiled by modern cosmetics. Her eyes were blue. Dreaming eyes. She seemed to live and move in a waking dream, remote from the enforced intimacies of our narrow society. More than one man had tried vainly to wake her from that dream. The piquancy of her situation provoked men like Lucien de l'Orges, the French chargé.

She was just seventeen, fresh from the convent of Smolny. Volgorughi had been Russian minister in China for many years. After his last trip to Petersburg, he had brought Olga back to Pekin as his bride, and . . . well, he was three times her age.

That evening she spoke first. "Monsieur Charley . . . "

Even at official meetings the American minister called

2

me "Charley." Most Europeans assumed it was my last name.

"I'm glad you are here," she went on in French, our only common language. "I was beginning to feel lonely. And afraid."

"Afraid?" I repeated stupidly. "Of what?"

A door opened. Candle flames shied and the startled shadows leaped up the walls. Volgorughi spoke from the doorway, coolly. "Olga, we are having sherry in the study . . . Oh!" His voice warmed. "Monsieur Charley, I didn't see you. Good evening."

I followed Olga's filmy skirts into the study, conscious of Volgorughi's sharp glance as he stood aside to let me pass. He always seemed rather formidable. In spite of his grizzled hair, he had the leanness of a young man and the carriage of a soldier. But he had the weary eyes of an old man. And the dry, shriveled hands, always cold to the touch, even in summer. A young man's imagination shrank from any mental image of those hands caressing Olga . . .

In the smaller room it was warmer and brighter. Glasses of sherry and vodka had been pushed aside to make space on the table for a painting on silk. Brown, frail, desiccated as a dead leaf, the silk looked hundreds of years old. Yet the ponies painted on its fragile surface in faded pigments were the same lively Mongol ponies we still used for race meetings outside the city walls.

"The Chinese have no understanding of art," drawled Lucien de l'Orges. "Chinese porcelain is beginning to enjoy a certain vogue in Europe, but Chinese painters are impossible. In landscape they show objects on a flat surface, without perspective, as if the artist were looking down on the earth from a balloon. In portraits they draw the human face without shadows or thickness as untu-

3

tored children do. The Chinese artist hasn't enough skill to imitate nature accurately."

Lucien was baiting Volgorughi. "Pekin temper" was as much a feature of our lives as "Pekin throat." We got on each other's nerves like a storm-stayed house party. An unbalanced party where men outnumbered women six to one.

Volgorughi kept his temper. "The Chinese artist doesn't care to 'imitate' nature. He prefers to suggest or symbolize what he sees."

"But Chinese art is heathen!" This was Sybil Carstairs, wife of the English inspector general of Maritime Customs. "How can heathen art equal art inspired by Christian morals?"

Her husband's objection was more practical: "You're wastin' money, Volgorughi. Two hundred Shanghai taels for a daub that will never fetch sixpence in any European market!"

Incredible? No. This was before Hirth and Fenollosa made Chinese painting fashionable in the West. Years later I saw a fragment from Volgorughi's collection sold in the famous Salle Six of the Hotel Drouot. While the *commissaire-priseur* was bawling, *"On demande quatre cent mille francs,"* I was seeing Olga again, pale in a white dress against a wall of gilt and vermilion in the light of shivering candle flames. . . .

Volgorughi turned to her just then. "Olga, my dear, you haven't any sherry." He smiled as he held out a glass. The brown wine turned to gold in the candlelight as she lifted it to her lips with an almost childish obedience.

I had not noticed little Kiada, the Japanese minister, bending over the painting. Now he turned sleepy slant-eyes on Volgorughi and spoke blandly. "This is the work of Han Kan, greatest of horse painters. It must be the finest painting of the T'ang Dynasty now in existence."

"You think so, count?" Volgorughi was amused. He seemed to be yielding to an irresistible temptation as he went on. "What would you say if I told you I knew of a T'ang painting infinitely finer—a landscape scroll by Wang Wei himself?"

Kiada's eyes lost their sleepy look. He had all his nation's respect for Chinese art, tinctured with jealousy of the older culture. "One hears rumors now and then that these fabulous masterpieces still exist, hidden away in the treasure chests of great Chinese families. But I have never seen an original Wang Wei."

Who, or what, is Wang Wei?" Sybil sounded petulant.

Kiada lifted his glass of sherry to the light. "Madame, Wang Wei could place scenery extending to ten thousand *li* upon the small surface of a fan. He could paint cats that would keep any house free from mice. When his hour came to Pass Above, he did not die. He merely stepped through a painted doorway in one of his own landscapes and was never seen again. All these things indicate that his brush was guided by a god."

Volgorughi leaned across the table, looking at Kiada. "What would you say if I told you that I had just added a Wang Wei to my collection?"

Kiada showed even, white teeth. "Nothing but respect for your excellency's judgment could prevent my insisting that it was a copy by some lesser artist of the Yüan Dynasty—possibly Chao Méng Fu. An original Wang Wei could not be bought for money."

"Indeed?" Volgorughi unlocked a cabinet with a key he carried on his watch chain. He took something out and tossed it on the table like a man throwing down a challenge. It was a cylinder in an embroidered satin cover. Kiada peeled the cover and we saw a scroll on a roller of old milk jade.

It was a broad ribbon of silk, once white, now ripened

with great age to a mellow brown. A foot wide, sixteen feet long, painted lengthwise to show the course of a river. As it unrolled, a stream of pure lapis, jade, and turquoise hues flowed before my enchanted eyes, almost like a moving picture. Born in a bubbling spring, fed by waterfalls, the river wound its way among groves of tender, green bamboo, parks with dappled deer peeping through slender pine trees, cottages with curly roofs nestling among round hills, verdant meadows, fantastic cliffs, strange wind-distorted trees, rushes, wild geese, and at last, a foam-flecked sea.

Kiada's face was a study. He whispered brokenly, "I can hear the wind sing in the rushes. I can hear the wail of the wild geese. Of Wang Wei truly is it written—his pictures were unspoken poems."

"And the color!" cried Volgorughi, ecstasy in his eyes.

Lucien's sly voice murmured in my ear. "A younger man, married to Olga Kyrilovna, would have no time for painting, Chinese or otherwise."

Volgorughi had Kiada by the arm. "This is no copy by Chao Méng Fu! Look at that inscription on the margin. Can you read it?"

Kiada glanced—then stared. There was more than suspicion in the look he turned on Volgorughi. There was fear. "I must beg your excellency to excuse me. I do not read Chinese."

We were interrupted by a commotion in the compound. A giant Cossack, in full-skirted coat and sheepskin cap, was coming through the gate carrying astride his shoulders a young man, elegantly slim, in an officer's uniform. The Cossack knelt on the ground. The rider slipped lightly from his unconventional mount. He sauntered past the window and a moment later he was entering the study with a nonchalance just this side of insolence. To my amazement I saw that he carried a whip which he handed

6

with his gloves to the Chinese boy who opened the door.

"Princess, your servant. Excellency, my apologies. I believe I'm late."

Volgorughi returned the greeting with the condescension of a Western Russian for an Eastern Russian—a former officer of Chevaliers Gardes for an obscure colonel of Oussurian Cossacks. Sometimes I wondered why such a bold adventurer as Alexei Andreitch Liakoff had been appointed Russian military attaché in Pekin. He was born in Tobolsk, where there is Tartar blood. His oblique eyes, high cheekbones, and sallow, hairless skin lent color to his impudent claim of descent from Genghis Khan.

"Are Russian officers in the habit of using their men as saddle horses?" I muttered to Carstairs.

Alexei's quick ear caught the words. "It may become a habit with me." He seemed to relish my discomfiture. "I don't like Mongol ponies. A Cossack is just as sure-footed. And much more docile."

Olga Kyrilovna roused herself to play hostess. "Sherry, Colonel Liakoff? Or vodka?"

"Vodka, if her excellency pleases." Alexei's voice softened as he spoke to Olga. His eyes dwelt on her face gravely as he took the glass from her hand.

The ghost of mockery touched Volgorughi's lips. He despised vodka as a peasant's drink.

Alexei approached the table to set down his empty glass. For the first time, his glance fell on the painting by Wang Wei. His glass crashed on the marble floor.

"You read Chinese, don't you?" Volgorughi spoke austerely. "Perhaps you can translate this inscription?"

Alexei put both hands wide apart on the table and leaned on them, studying the ideographs. " 'Wang Wei.' And a date. The same as our A.D. 740."

"And the rest?" insisted Volgorughi.

Alexei went on. " 'At an odd moment in summer I came

across this painting of a river course by Wang Wei. Under its influence I sketched a spray of peach blossom on the margin as an expression of my sympathy for the artist and his profound and mysterious work. The words of the Emperor. Written in the Lai Ching summerhouse, 1746.' "

Kiada had been frightened when he looked at that inscription. Alexei was angry. Why I did not know.

Carstairs broke the silence. "I don't see anything mysterious about a picture of a river!"

"Everything about this picture is—mysterious." Kiada glanced at Volgorughi. "May one inquire how your excellency obtained this incomparable masterpiece?"

"From a peddler in the Chinese City." Volgorughi's tone forbade further questions. Just then his Number One Boy announced dinner.

There was the usual confusion when we started for the ball at the Japanese Legation. Mongol ponies had to be blindfolded before they would let men in European dress mount and even then they were skittish. For this reason it was the custom for men to walk and for women to drive in hooded Pekin carts. But Sybil Carstairs always defied this convention, exclaiming, "Why should I be bumped black and blue in a springless cart just because I am a woman?" She and her husband were setting out on foot when Olga's little cart clattered into the compound driven by a Chinese groom. Kiada had gone on ahead to welcome his early guests. Volgorughi lifted Olga into the cart. She was quite helpless in a Siberian cloak of blue fox paws and clumsy Mongol socks of white felt over her dancing slippers. Her head drooped against Volgorughi's shoulder drowsily as he put her down in the cart. He drew the fur cloak around her in a gesture that seemed tenderly protective. She lifted languid eyes.

"Isn't Lady Carstairs driving with me?"

"My dear, you know she never drives in a Pekin cart. You are not afraid?" Volgorughi smiled. "You will be quite safe, Olga Kyrilovna. I promise you that."

Her answering smile wavered. Then the hood hid her face from view as the cart rattled through the gateway.

Volgorughi and Lucien walked close behind Olga's cart. Alexei and I followed more slowly. Our Chinese lantern boys ran ahead of us in the darkness to light our way like the linkmen of medieval London. Street lamps in Pekin were lighted only once a month—when the General of the Nine Gates made his rounds of inspection.

The lantern light danced down a long, empty lane winding between high, blank walls. A stinging Siberian wind threw splinters of sleet in my face. We hadn't the macadamized roads of the Treaty Ports. The frozen mud was hard and slippery as glass. I tried to keep to a ridge that ran down the middle of the road. My foot slipped and I stumbled down the slope into a foul gutter of sewage, frozen solid. The lanterns turned a corner. I was alone with the black night and the icy wind.

I groped my way along the gutter, one hand against the wall. No stars, no moon, no lighted windows, no other pedestrians. My boot met something soft that yielded and squirmed. My voice croaked a question in Mandarin: "Is this the way to the Japanese Legation?" The answer came in singsong Cantonese. I understood only one word: "Alms . . ."

Like heaven itself, I saw a distant flicker of light coming nearer. Like saints standing in the glow of their own halos I recognized Alexei and our lantern boys. "What happened?" Alexei's voice was taut. "I came back as soon as I missed you."

"Nothing. I fell. I was just asking this . . ."

Words died on my lips. Lantern light revealed the

blunted lion-face, the eyeless sockets, the obscene, white stumps for hands—"mere corruption, swaddled man-wise." A leper. And I had been about to touch him.

Alexei's gaze followed mine to the beggar, hunched against the wall. "She is one of the worst I've ever seen."

"She?"

"I think it's a woman. Or, shall I say, it was a woman?" Alexei laughed harshly. "Shall we go on?"

We rounded the next corner before I recovered my voice. "These beggars aren't all as wretched as they seem, are they?"

"What put that into your head, Charley?"

"Something that happened last summer. We were in a market lane of the Chinese City—Sybil Carstairs and Olga Kyrilovna, Lucien and I. A beggar, squatting in the gutter, stared at us as if he had never seen Western men before. He looked like any other beggar—filthy, naked to the waist, with tattered blue trousers below. But his hands were toying with a little image carved in turquoise matrix. It looked old and valuable."

"He may have stolen it."

"It wasn't as simple as that," I retorted. "A man in silk rode up on a mule leading a white pony with a silver embroidered saddle. He called the beggar 'elder brother' and invited him to mount the pony. Then the two rode off together."

Alexei's black eyes glittered like jet beads in the lantern light. "Was the beggar the older of the two?"

"No. That's the queer part. The beggar was young. The man who called him 'elder brother' was old and dignified . . . . Some beggars at home have savings accounts. I suppose the same sort of thing could happen here."

Again Alexei laughed harshly, "Hold on to that idea, Charley, if it makes you feel more comfortable."

We came to a gate where lanterns clustered like a cloud of fireflies. A piano tinkled. In the compound, lantern boys were gathering outside the windows of a ballroom, tittering as they watched barbarian demons "jump" to Western music.

Characteristically, the Japanese Legation was the only European house in Pekin. Candle flames and crystal prisms. Wall mirrors and a polished parquet floor. The waltz from *Traviata*. The glitter of diamonds and gold braid. "Punch *à la Romaine.*

"Where is Princess Volgorughi?" I asked Sybil Carstairs. "Didn't she come with you and Colonel Liakoff?"

"No. Her cart followed you. We came afterward."

"Perhaps she's in the supper room." Sybil whirled off with little Kiada.

Volgorughi was standing in the doorway of the supper room with Lucien and Carstairs. "She'll be here in a moment," Carstairs was saying.

Alexei spoke over my shoulder. "Charley and I have just arrived. We did not pass her excellency's cart on the way."

"Perhaps she turned back," said Lucien.

"In that case she would have passed us," returned Alexei. "Who was with her?"

Volgorughi's voice came out in a hoarse whisper. "Her groom and lantern boy. Both Chinese. But Kiada and the Carstairses were just ahead of her; Monsieur de l'Orges and I, just behind her."

"Not all the way," amended Lucien. "We took a wrong turning and got separated from each other in the dark. That was when we lost sight of her."

"My fault." Volgorughi's mouth twisted bitterly. "I was leading the way. And it was I who told her she would be— safe."

Again we breasted the wind to follow lanterns skimming before us like will o' the wisps. Vainly we strained our eyes through the glancing lights and broken shadows. We met no one. We saw nothing. Not even a footprint or wheel rut on that frozen ground. Once something moaned in the void beyond the lights. It was only the leper.

At the gate of the Russian Legation, the Cossack guard sprang to attention. Volgorughi rapped out a few words in Russian. I knew enough to understand the man's reply. "The *baryna* has not returned, excellency. There has been no sign of her or her cart."

Volgorughi was shouting. Voices, footfalls, lights filled the compound. Alexei struck his forehead with his clenched hand. "Fool that I am! The leper!" He walked so fast I could hardly keep up with him. The lantern boys were running. A Cossack came striding after us. Alexei halted at the top of the ridge. The leper had not moved. He spoke sharply in Mandarin. "Have you seen a cart?" No answer. "When she asked me for alms, she spoke Cantonese," I told him. He repeated his question in Cantonese. Both Volgorughi and Alexei spoke the southern dialects. All the rest of us were content to stammer Mandarin.

Still no answer. The Cossack stepped down into the gutter. His great boot prodded the shapeless thing that lay there. It toppled sidewise.

Alexei moved down the slope. "Lights!" The lanterns shuddered and came nearer. The handle of a knife protruded from the leper's left breast.

Alexei forced himself to drop on one knee beside the obscene corpse. He studied it intently, without touching it.

"Murdered . . . There are many knives like that in the Chinese City. Anyone might have used it—Chinese or

12

European." He rose, brushing his knee with his gloved hand.

"Why?" I ventured.

"She couldn't see." His voice was judicious. "She must have heard—something."

"But what?"

Alexei's Asiatic face was inscrutable in the light from the paper lanterns.

Police? Extraterritorial law courts? That was Treaty Port stuff. Like pidgin English. We had only a few legation guards. No gunboats. No telegraph. No railway. The flying machine was a crank's daydream. Even cranks hadn't dreamed of a wireless telegraphy . . .

Dawn came. We were still searching. Olga Kyrilovna, her cart and pony, her groom and lantern boy, had all vanished without a trace as if they had never existed.

As character witnesses, the Chinese were baffling. "The princess's groom was a Manchu of good character," Volgorughi's Number One Boy told us. "But her lantern boy was a Cantonese with a great crime on his conscience. He caused his mother's death when he was born, which the Ancients always considered unfilial."

At noon some of us met in the smoking room of the Pekin Club. "It's curious there's been no demand for ransom," I said.

"Bandits? Within the city walls?" Carstairs was skeptical. "Russia has never hesitated to use *agents provocateurs*. They say she's going to build a railway across Siberia. I don't believe it's practical. But you never can tell what those mad Russians will do. She'll need Manchuria. And she'll need a pretext for taking it. Why not the abduction of the Russian minister's wife?"

Kiada shook his head. "Princess Volgorughi will not be

found until *The River* is restored to its companion pictures, *The Lake*, *The Sea*, and *The Cloud*."

"What do you mean?"

Kiada answered me patiently as an adult explaining the obvious to a backward child. "It is known that Wang Wei painted this series of pictures entitled *Four Forms of Water*. Volgorughi has only one of them, *The River*. The separation of one painting from others in a series divinely inspired is displeasing to the artist."

"But Wang Wei has been dead more than a thousand years!"

"It is always dangerous to displease those who have Passed Above. An artist as steeped in ancient mysteries as the pious Wang Wei has power over men long after he has become a Guest on High. Wang Wei will shape the course of our lives into any pattern he pleases in order to bring those four paintings together again. I knew this last night when I first saw *The River* and—I was afraid."

"I wonder how Volgorughi did get that painting?" mused Carstairs. "I hope he didn't forget the little formality of payment."

"He's not a thief!" I protested.

"No. But he's a collector. All collectors are mad. Especially Russian collectors. It's like gambling or opium."

Lucien smiled unpleasantly. "Art! Ghosts! Politics! Why go so far afield? Olga Kyrilovna was a young bride. And Volgorughi is—old. Such marriages are arranged by families, we all know. Women, as Balzac said, are the dupes of the social system. When they consent to marriage, they have not enough experience to know what they are consenting to. Olga Kyrilovna found herself in a trap. She has escaped, as young wives have escaped from time immemorial, by taking a lover. Now they've run off together. *Sabine a tout donné, sa beauté de colombe, et son amour . . .*"

"Monsieur de l'Orges."

We all started. Alexei was standing in the doorway. His eyes commanded the room. "What you say is impossible. Do I make myself clear?"

"Of course, Alexei. I—I was only joking." Lucien sounded piteous.

But Alexei had no pity. "A difference of taste in jokes has broken many friendships . . . . Charley, will you come back to the Russian Legation with me?"

The Tartar general's audience hall had never seemed more shabby. Volgorughi sat staring at the garish wall of red and gilt. He was wearing an overcoat, carrying hat and gloves.

"News, excellency?" queried Alexei.

Volgorughi shook his head without looking up. "I've been to the Tsungli Yamen." He spoke like a somnambulist. "The usual thing. Green tea. Melon seeds. A cold stone pavilion. Mandarins who giggle behind satin sleeves. I asked for an audience with the Emperor himself. It was offered—on the usual terms. I had to refuse—as usual. By the time a gunboat gets to the mouth of the Peiho, they may agree to open another seaport to Russian trade by way of reparation, but—I shall never see Olga Kyrilovna again. Sometimes I think our governments keep us here in the hope that something will happen to give them a pretext for sending troops into China. . . ."

We all felt that. The Tsungli Yamen, or Foreign Office, calmly assumed that our legations were vassal missions to the Emperor, like those from Tibet. The Emperor would not receive us unless we acknowledged his sovereignty by kowtowing, the forehead to strike the floor audibly nine times. Even if we had wished to go through this interesting performance for the sake of peace and trade, our governments would not let us compromise their sover-

15

eignty. But they kept us there, where we had no official standing, where our very existence was doubted. "It may be there are as many countries in the West as England, France, Germany, and Russia," one mandarin had informed me. "But the others you mention—Austria, Sweden, Spain, and America—they are all lies invented to intimidate the Chinese."

Alexei was not a man to give up easily. "Excellency, I shall find her."

Volgorughi lifted his head. "How?"

Alexei shouted. The study door opened. An old man in workman's dress came in with a young Chinese. I knew the old man as Antoine Billot, one of the Swiss clockmakers who were the only Western tradesmen allowed in Pekiñ.

"Charley," said Alexei, "tell Antoine about the fingering piece you saw in the hands of a beggar last summer."

"It was turquoise matrix, carved to represent two nude figures embracing. The vein of brown in the stone colored their heads and spotted the back of the smaller figure."

"I have seen such a fingering piece," said Antoine. "In the Palace of Whirring Phoenixes. It is in that portion of the Chinese City known as the Graveyard of the Wu family, in the Lane of Azure Thunder."

"It is the Beileh Tsai Heng who lives there," put in Antoine's Chinese apprentice. "Often have we repaired his French clocks. Very fine clocks of Limoges enamel sent to the Emperor Kang Hsi by Louis XIV. The Beileh's grandmother was the Discerning Concubine of the Emperor Tao Kwang."

"An old man?" asked Alexei.

"The Beileh has not yet attained the years of serenity. Though the name Heng means 'Steadfast,' he is impetuous as a startled dragon. He memorialized the late Emperor for permission to live in a secluded portion of the Chinese City so that he could devote his leisure to ingenious arts and pleasures."

I looked at Alexei. "You think the beggar who stared at us was a servant of this prince?"

"No. Your beggar was the prince himself. 'Elder Brother' is the correct form for addressing a Manchu prince of the third generation."

"It is the latest fad among our young princes of Pekin," explained the apprentice, "to haunt the highways and taverns dressed as beggars, sharing the sad life of the people for a few hours. They vie with each other to see which can look the most dirty and disreputable. But each one has some little habit of luxury that he cannot give up, even for the sake of disguise. A favorite ring, a precious fan, an antique fingering piece. That is how you can tell them from the real beggars."

Alexei turned to me. "When a taste for the exquisite becomes so refined that it recoils upon itself and turns into its opposite—a taste for the ugly—we call that decadence. Prince Heng is decadent—bored, curious, irresponsible, ever in search of a new sensation." Alexei turned back to the apprentice. "Could the Beileh be tempted with money?"

"Who could offer him anything he does not already possess?" intoned the young Chinese. "His revered father amassed one hundred thousand myriad snow white taels of silver from unofficial sources during his benevolent reign as governor of Kwantung. In the Palace of Whirring Phoenixes even the wash bowls and spitting basins are curiously wrought of fine jade and pure gold, for this prince loves everything that is rare and strange."

Alexei hesitated before his next question. "Does the Beileh possess any valuable paintings?"

"His paintings are few but priceless. Four landscape scrolls from the divine brush of the illustrious Wang Wei."

Volgorughi started to his feet. "What's this?"

"You may go, Antoine." Alexei waited until the door had closed. "Isn't it obvious, sir? Your Wang Wei scroll was stolen."

Volgorughi sank back in his chair. "But—I bought it. From a peddler in the Chinese City. I didn't ask his name."

"How could a nameless peddler acquire such a painting from such a prince honestly?" argued Alexei. "Your peddler was a thief or a receiver. Such paintings have religious as well as artistic value to the Chinese. They are heirlooms, never sold even by private families who need the money. Last night, the moment I saw the marginal note written by the Emperor Ch'ien Lung I knew the picture must have been stolen from the Imperial Collection. I was disturbed because I knew that meant trouble for us if it were known you had the painting. That's why I didn't want to read the inscription aloud. It's easy to see what happened. The thief was captured and tortured until he told Heng you had the painting. Heng saw Olga Kyrilovna with Charley and Lucien in the Chinese City last summer. He must have heard then that she was your wife. When he found you had the painting, he ordered her abduction. Now he is holding her as hostage for the return of the painting. All this cannot be coincidence."

Volgorughi buried his face in his hands. "What can we do?"

"With your permission, excellency, I shall go into the Chinese City tonight and return the painting to Heng. I shall bring back Olga Kyrilovna—if she is still alive."

Volgorughi rose, shoulders bent, chin sunk on his chest. "I shall go with you, Alexei Andreitch."

"Your excellency forgets that special circumstances make it possible for me to go into the Chinese City after dark when no other European can do so with safety. Alone I have some chance of success. With you to protect, it would be impossible."

"You will need a Cossack escort."

"That would strip the legation of guards. And it would antagonize Heng. Olga Kyrilovna might be harmed before I could reach her. I prefer to go alone."

Volgorughi sighed. "Report to me as soon as you get back . . . . You are waiting for something?"

"The painting, excellency."

Volgorughi walked with a shuffling step into the study. He came back with the scroll in its case. "Take it. I never want to see it again."

At the door I looked back. Volgorughi was slumped in his seat, a figure of utter loneliness and despair.

Alexei glanced at me as we crossed the compound. "Something is puzzling you, Charley. What is it?"

"If this Beileh Heng is holding Olga Kyrilovna as a hostage for the painting, he wants you to know that he has abducted her. He has nothing, to conceal. Then why was the leper murdered if not to conceal something?"

Alexei led the way into a room of his own furnished with military severity. I'm flad Volgorughi didn't think of that question, Charley. It has been troubling me, too."

"And the answer?"

"Perhaps I shall find it in the Palace of Whirring Phoenixes. Perhaps it will lead me back to one of the men who dined with us yesterday evening. Except for the Carstairses, we were all separated from each other at one time or another in those dark streets—even you and I. . . ."

Alexei was opening a cedar chest. He took out a magnificent robe of wadded satin in prismatic blues and greens.

When he had slipped it on he turned to face me. The
Tartar cast of his oblique eyes and sallow skin was more
pronounced than I had ever realized. Had I passed him
wearing this costume in the Chinese City, I should have
taken him for a Manchu or a Mongol.

He smiled. "Now will you believe I have the blood of
Temudjin Genghis Khan in my veins?"

"You've done this before!"

His smile grew sardonic. "Do you understand why I am
the only European who can go into the Chinese City after
dark?"

My response was utterly illogical. "Alexei, take me with
you tonight!"

He studied my face. "You were fond of Olga Kyrilovna,
weren't you?"

"Is there no way?" I begged.

"Only one way. And it's not safe. You could wear the
overalls of a workman and carry the tools of a clockmaker.
And stay close to me, ostensibly your Chinese employer."

"If Antoine Billot will lend me his clothes and tools . . ."

"That can be arranged." Alexei was fitting a jeweled nail
shield over his little finger.

"Well? Is there any other objection?"

"Only this." He looked up at me intently. His pale face
and black eyes were striking against the kingfisher blues
and greens of his satin robe. "We are going to find
something ugly at the core of this business, Charley. You
are younger than I and—will you forgive me if I say you
are rather innocent? Your idea of life in Pekin is a series of
dances and dinners, race meetings outside the walls in
spring, charades at the English Legation in winter, snipe
shooting at Hai Ten in the fall. Your government doesn't
maintain an intelligence service here. So you can have no
idea of the struggle that goes on under the surface of this
pleasant social life. Imperialist ambitions and intrigues,

the alliance between politics and trade, even the opium trade—what do you know of all that? Sometimes I think you don't even know much about the amusements men like Lucien find in the Chinese City. . . . Life is only pleasant on the surface, Charley. And now we're going below the surface. Respectability is as artificial as the clothes we wear. What it hides is as ugly as our naked bodies and animal functions. Whatever happens tonight, I want you to remember this: under every suit of clothes, broadcloth or rags, there is the same sort of animal."

"What are you hinting at?"

"There are various possibilities. You said Heng stared at your party as if he had never seen Western men before. Are you sure he wasn't staring at Olga Kyrilovna as if he had never seen a Western woman before?"

"But our women are physically repulsive to Chinese!"

"In most cases. But the Chinese are not animated types. They are individuals, as we are. Taste is subjective and arbitrary. Individual taste can be eccentric. Isn't it possible that there are among them, as among us, men who have romantic fancies for the exotic? Or sensual fancies for the experimental? I cannot get those words of Antoine's apprentice out of my mind: *this prince loves everything that is rare and strange. . . .*"

A red sun was dipping behind the Western Hills when we passed out a southern gate of the Tartar City. In a moment all nine gates would swing shut and we would be locked out of our legations until tomorrow's dawn. It was not a pleasant feeling. I had seen the head of a consul rot on a pike in the sun. That was what happened to barbarian demons who went where they were not wanted outside the Treaty Ports.

The Chinese City was a wilderness of twisting lanes, shops, taverns, theaters, tea houses, opium dens, and brothels. Long ago conquering Manchu Tartars had driven conquered Chinese outside the walls of Pekin proper, or the Tartar City, to this sprawling suburb where the conquered catered to the corruption of the conqueror. The Chinese City came to life at nightfall when the Tartar City slept behind its walls. Here and there yellow light shone through blue dusk from a broken gateway. Now and then we caught the chink of porcelain cups or the whine of a *yuehkin* guitar.

Alexei seemed to know every turn of the way. At last I saw why he was Russian military attaché at Pekin. Who else would learn so much about China and its people as this bold adventurer who could pass for a Manchu in Chinese robes? When we were snipe shooting together, he seemed to know the Peichih-li Plain as if he carried a military map of the district in his head. Years afterward, when the Tsar's men took Port Arthur, everyone learned about Russian Intelligence in China. I learned that evening. And I found myself looking at Alexei in his Chinese dress as if he had suddenly become a stranger. What did I know of this man whom I had met so casually at legation parties? Was he ruthless enough to stab a beggar already dying of leprosy? Had he had any reason for doing so?

We turned into a narrower lane—a mere crack between high walls. Alexei whispered, "The Lane of Azure Thunder."

A green tiled roof above the dun-colored wall proclaimed the dwelling of a prince. Alexei paused before a vermilion gate. He spoke Cantonese to the gatekeeper. I understood only two words—"Wang Wei." There were some moments of waiting. Then the gate creaked open and we were ushered through that drab wall into a wonderland of fantastic parks and lacquered pavilions blooming with all the colors of Sung porcelain.

I was unprepared for the splendor of the audience hall. The old palaces we rented for legations were melancholy places, decaying and abandoned by their owners. But here rose, green, and gold rioted against a background of dull ebony panels, tortured by a cunning chisel into grotesquely writhing shapes. There were hangings of salmon satin embroidered with threads of gold and pale green, images of birds and flowers carved in jade and coral and malachite. The slender rafters were painted a poisonously bright jade green and on them tiny lotus buds were carved and gilded. There was a rich rustle of satin and the Beileh Heng walked slowly into the room.

Could this stately figure be the same rude fellow I had last seen squatting in the gutter, half naked in the rags of a beggar? He moved with the deliberate grace of the grave religious dancers in the Confucian temples. His robe was lustrous purple—the "myrtle-red" prescribed for princes of the third generation by the Board of Rites. It swung below the paler mandarin jacket in sculptured folds, stiff with a sable lining revealed by two slits at either side. Watered in the satin were the Eight Famous Horses of the Emperor Mu Wang galloping over the Waves of Eternity. His cuffs were curved like horseshoes in honor of the cavalry that set the Manchu Tartars on the throne. Had that cavalry ridden west instead of south, Alexei himself might have owed allegiance to this prince. Though one was Chinese and one Russian, both were Tartar.

Heng's boots of purple satin looked Russian. So did his round cap faced with a band of sable. His skin was a dull ivory, not as yellow as the southern Chinese. His cheeks were lean, his glance searching and hungry. He looked like a purebred descendant of the "wolf-eyed, lantern-jawed Manchus" of the Chinese chronicles. A conqueror who would take whatever he wanted, but who had learned from the conquered Chinese to want only the precious and fanciful . . .

Something else caught my eye. There was no mistake.

23

This was the beggar. For pale against his purple robe gleamed the fingering piece of turquoise matrix which his thin, neurotic fingers caressed incessantly.

No ceremonial tea was served. We were being received as enemies during a truce. But Alexei bowed profoundly and spoke with all the roundabout extravagance of mandarin politeness.

"An obscure design of Destiny has brought the property of your highness, a venerable landscape scroll painted by the devout Wang Wei, into the custody of the Russian minister. Though I appear Chinese in this garb, know that I am Russian and my minister has sent me in all haste and humility to restore this inestimable masterpiece to its rightful owner."

Heng's eyes were fixed on a point above our heads, for, Chinese or barbarian, we were inferiors, unworthy of his gaze. His lips scarcely moved. "When you have produced the scroll, I shall know whether you speak truth or falsehood."

"All your highness's words are unspotted pearls of perpetual wisdom." Alexei stripped the embroidered case from the jade roller. Like a living thing, the painted silk slipped out of his grasp and unwound itself at the Beileh's feet.

Once again a faery stream of lapis, jade, and turquoise hues unrolled before my enchanted eyes. Kiada was right. I could hear the wind sing in the rushes and the wail of the wild geese, faint and far, a vibration trembling on the outer edge of the physical threshold for sound.

The hand that held the fingering piece was suddenly still. Only the Beileh's eyeballs moved, following the course of Wang Wei's river from its bubbling spring to its foam-flecked sea. Under his cultivated stolidity, I saw fear and, more strangely, sorrow.

At last he spoke. "This painting I inherited from my august ancestor, the ever glorious Emperor Ch'ien Lung, who left his words and seal upon the margin. How has it come into your possession?"

Alexei bowed again. "I shall be grateful for an opportunity to answer that question if your highness will first condescend to explain to my mean intelligence how the scroll came to leave the Palace of Whirring Phoenixes?"

"Outside barbarian, you are treading on a tiger's tail when you speak with such insolence to an Imperial Clansman. I try to make allowances for you because you come of an inferior race, the Hairy Ones, without manners or music, unversed in the Six Fine Arts and the Five Classics. Know then that it is not your place to ask questions or mine to answer them. You may follow me, at a distance of nine paces, for I have something to show you."

He looked neither to right nor left as he walked soberly through the audience hall, his hands tucked inside his sleeves. At the door he lifted one hand to loosen the clasp of his mandarin jacket, and it slid from his shoulders. Before it had time to touch the ground, an officer of the Coral Button sprang out of the shadows to catch it reverently. The Beileh did not appear conscious of this officer's presence. Yet he had let the jacket fall without an instant's hesitation. He knew that wherever he went at any time there would always be someone ready to catch anything he let fall before it was soiled or damaged.

We followed him into a garden, black and white in the moonlight. We passed a pool spanned by a crescent bridge. Its arc of stone matched the arc of its reflection in the ice-coated water, completing a circle that was half reality, half illusion. We came to another pavilion, its roof curling up at each corner, light filtering through its doorway. Again we heard the shrill plaint of a guitar. We rounded a devil-screen of gold lacquer and the thin sound ended on a high, feline note.

I blinked against a blaze of lights. Like a flight of particolored butterflies, a crowd of girls fluttered away from us, tottering on tiny, mutilated feet. One who sat apart from the rest rose with dignity. A Manchu princess, as I saw by her unbound feet and undaunted eyes. Her hair was piled high in the lacquered coils of the Black Cloud Coiffure. She wore hairpins, earrings, bracelets, and tall heels of acid-green jade. Her gown of seagreen silk was sewn with silver thread worked in the Pekin stitch to represent the Silver-Crested Love Birds of Conjugal Peace. But when she turned her face, I saw the sour lines and sagging pouches of middle age.

Princess Heng's gaze slid over us with subtle contempt and came to rest upon the Beileh with irony. "My pleasure in receiving you is boundless and would find suitable expression in appropriate compliments were the occasion more auspicious. As it is, I pray you will forgive me if I do not linger in the fragrant groves of polite dalliance, but merely inquire why your highness has seen fit to introduce two male strangers, one a barbarian, into the sanctity of the Inner Chamber?"

Heng answered impassively. "Even the Holy Duke of Yen neglected the forms of courtesy when he was pursued by a tiger."

A glint of malice sparkled in the eyes of the Beileh's Principal Old Woman. "Your highness finds his present situation equivalent to being pursued by a tiger? To my inadequate understanding that appears the natural consequence of departing from established custom by attempting to introduce a barbarian woman into the Inner Chamber."

Heng sighed. "If the presence of these far-traveled

26

strangers distresses you and my Small Old Women you have permission to retire."

Princess Heng's jade bangles clashed with the chilly ring of ice in a glass as she moved toward the door. The Small Old Women, all girls in their teens, shimmered and rustled after the Manchu princess, who despised them both as concubines and as Chinese.

Heng led us through another door.

"Olga!"

The passion in Alexei's voice was a shock to me. In my presence he had always addressed her as "excellency" or "princess." She might have been asleep as she lay there on her blue fox cloak, her eyes closed, her pale face at peace, her slight hands relaxed in the folds of her white tulle skirt. But the touch of her hands was ice and faintly from her parted lips came the sweet sickish odor of opium.

Alexei turned on Heng. "If you had not stolen her, she would not have died!"

"Stolen?" It was the first word that had pierced Heng's reserve. "Imperial Clansmen do not steal women. I saw this far-traveled woman in a market lane of the Chinese City last summer. I coveted her. But I did not steal her. I offered money for her, decently and honorably, in accord with precepts of morality laid down by the Ancients. Money was refused. Months passed. I could not forget the woman with faded eyes. I offered one of my most precious possessions. It was accepted. The painting was her price. But the other did not keep his side of the bargain. For she was dead when I lifted her out of her cart."

The lights were spinning before my eyes. "Alexei, what is this? Volgorughi would not . . ."

Alexei's look stopped me.

"You . . ." Words tumbled from my lips. "There was a lover. And you were he. And Volgorughi found out. And he watched you together and bided his time, nursing his hatred and planning his revenge like a work of art. And finally he punished you both cruelly by selling her to Heng. Volgorughi knew that Olga would drive alone last night. Volgorughi had lived so long in the East that he had absorbed the Eastern idea of women as well as the Eastern taste in painting. The opium must have been in the sherry he gave her. She was already drowsy when he lifted her into the cart. No doubt he had planned to give her only a soporific dose that would facilitate her abduction. But at the last moment he commuted her sentence to death and let her have the full, lethal dose. He gave her good-bye tenderly because he knew he would never see her again. He promised her she would be safe because death is, in one sense, safety—the negation of pain, fear and struggle. . . .

"There was no peddler who sold him the painting. That was his only lie. He didn't prevent your coming here tonight because he wanted you to know. That was your punishment. And he saw that you could make no use of your knowledge now. Who will believe that Olga Kyrilovna, dead of a Chinese poison in the Chinese City, was killed by her own husband? Some Chinese will be suspected—Heng himself, or his jealous wife, or the men who carry out his orders. No European would take Heng's story seriously unless it were supported by at least one disinterested witness. That was why the leper had to die last night, while Volgorughi was separated from Lucien by a wrong turning that was Volgorughi's fault. The leper must have overheard some word of warning or instruction from Volgorughi to Olga's lantern boy that revealed the whole secret. That word was spoken in Cantonese. Olga's lantern boy was Cantonese. Volgorughi spoke that dialect. The leper knew no other tongue. And Lucien, the only person who walked with Volgorughi, was as ignorant of Cantonese as all the rest of us, save you."

Heng spoke sadly in his own tongue. "The treachery of the Russian minister in sending this woman to me dead deserves vengeance. But one thing induces me to spare him. He did not act by his own volition. He was a blind tool in the skillful hand of the merciless Wang Wei. Through this woman's death *The River* has been restored to its companion pictures, *The Lake, The Sea*, and *The Cloud*. And I, who separated the pictures so impiously, have had my own share of suffering as a punishment. . . ."

. . .Yes, I'll have another brandy. One more glass. Olga? She was buried in the little Russian Orthodox cemetery at Pekin. Volgorughi was recalled. The breath of scandal clung to his name the rest of his life. The Boxer Uprising finally gave the West its pretext for sending troops into China. That purple-satin epicurean, the Beileh Heng, was forced to clean sewers by German troops during the occupation and committed suicide from mortification. The gay young bloods of Pekin who had amused themselves by playing beggars found themselves beggars in earnest when the looting was over. Railways brought Western businessmen to Pekin and before long it was as modern as Chicago.

Alexei? He became attentive to the wife of the new French minister, a woman with dyed hair who kept a Pekinese sleeve dog in her bedroom. I discovered the distraction that can be found in study of the early Chinese poets. When I left the service, I lost track of Alexei. During the Russian Revolution, I often wondered if he were still living. Did he join the Reds, as some Cossack officers did? Or was he one of the Whites who settled in Harbin or Port

Arthur? He would have been a very old man then, but I think he could have managed. He spoke so many Chinese dialects . . .

The scroll? Any good reference book will tell you that there are no Wang Wei scrolls in existence today, though there are some admirable copies. One, by Chao Méng Fu, in the British Museum, shows the course of a river. Scholars have described this copy in almost the same words I have used tonight to describe the original. But they are not the same. I went to see the copy. I was disappointed. I could no longer hear the song of the wind in the rushes or the wail of the wild geese. Was the change in the painting? Or in me?

*The first thing that comes to my mind about "Present for Minna"
is that it was based on a true event, told to me by a friend who in his
youth had shipped out as an ordinary seaman on a freighter bound
for the Med and return. (I believe I made him a present of Old
Fitzgerald when* This Week *bought the tale.) I might add that after
publication, I had two or three letters from retired Customs agents
saying that the story rang true and may very well have happened to
them. I might also add that, like Andy, the protagonist, I am fond of
cats—and brandy.*

—RICHARD MARTIN STERN

PRESENT FOR MINNA

RICHARD MARTIN STERN

Andy sat on the edge of his bunk, his big feet set wide and his thick hands clasped and his face furrowed with thought, with worry. And four or five of the crew sat around watching him, waiting for Carl to start it up again on this, the last night out. Carl was leaning against the bulkhead smiling a little in his sharp way. "You got it figured out yet?" he said. "Got the arithmetic all straight?"

Andy opened his hands. He studied their palms. He closed them again. He said nothing. He smiled in a helpless sort of way.

"A case of brandy you got," Carl said. "Good French brandy. Cost you twenty bucks in Marseilles. A bargain, you said. You an' the missus like brandy, a little nip after dinner." He waited until the laughter died. "You got any idea what the duty'll be?"

"Well," Andy said. He shook his head slowly. "Not much, maybe." He sat there like a great bear at the baiting, taking his punishment, wishing it would stop, knowing no way in which to avoid it. "Maybe not much," he said again.

"The stuff sells for six, seven bucks a bottle," Carl said. "You paid less than two. The difference is duty. Say five bucks on twelve bottles, sixty bucks. You got sixty bucks for that?"

Andy was thinking of the little apartment out in Brooklyn, of Minna, of money in the savings account, of a television set some day, a real good one, with a large clear picture so that Minna, on the long lonely nights when he was at sea, could watch and listen, maybe laugh and forget for a time that she was alone.

And maybe a small sip of brandy at bedtime, just a sip, to lie pleasantly on the stomach in the empty darkness. They understood one another, he and Minna, and waiting, he knew, is the hard part of life, and small things help, small things like brandy, and television, and the other things he had managed to bring to her. But he had had no idea that on twenty dollars' worth of brandy—

Carl said, "You got sixty bucks so's the missus can have her snort after dinner?"

"No," Andy said, and he listened to the laughter again.

"I tell you," Carl said. "I'll give you an idea." The laughter died down. Andy lifted his head and watched and waited. "I've been thinkin'," Carl said, "an' I got the answer." He paused. He smiled. "Smuggle it through Customs, that's all you have to do. Just smuggle the case right through. Then you won't have to pay nothin'!"

He had thought of it, of course. He smiled at Carl and shook his great head slowly. "That wouldn't be honest," he said. "If they got a law—" The laughter smothered the rest of it, and he sat there patiently waiting for it to die. His thick hands were clasped again. There was no use trying to explain.

"Wouldn't be honest!" Carl was saying. "That's the only reason! You hear him? Wouldn't be honest! I'll tell you what I'll do. I'll lay you ten to one you couldn't get that case through Customs if you tried. How's that? Ten to one. You think it over."

Andy sat alone on the edge of his bunk, and stared

down at his hands, at his feet, at the deck itself. And two of the many ship's cats came in and saw him and eyed one another warily and climbed up onto his great knees and sat there singing at him. He rubbed them idly and spoke to them in a low voice, taking pleasure from their companionship, while his mind walked slowly around and around his problem, thinking of Minna, of brandy, of Customs, of Carl and of Carl's bet.

And the cats, his friends, sang on, as if they were talking to him, telling him something, telling him— His big hands stopped in their stroking. He stared at the cats. They sang on, and Andy was smiling, and his mind was at last at rest. . . .

They docked in the morning. They finished their jobs. In the fo'c's'le, Carl cornered him again, and the rest of the crew gathered around, grinning. "Gonna take my bet?" Carl said. "Ten to one? And some of the other guys want in, too. How 'bout it?"

"Well," Andy said. His hands were deep in his pockets. He looked at Carl and he looked at the others, and he looked at the case of brandy on his bunk. Slowly he nodded. He pulled out a small leather purse. "I got fifty dollars," he said.

The bosun held the stakes. Ashore, in the bar across the street from the Customs shed. And they all crowded against the window to watch Andy, with sea bag and suitcase, in shore clothes, come ponderously down for his inspection. And they waited, hearing nothing of the talk.

The Customs man went through the sea bag. He patted Andy. He reached for the suitcase. Andy said, "I can't open that."

"So?" The Customs man was smiling.

"Well," Andy said, "it's full of cats." His big face was crinkled with the effort of explanation. "I mean, we got too many on board, an' the skipper says get rid of some of them."

"Good story," the Customs man said. "One of the best I've heard."

"It's true," Andy said. "The crew, they wanted to toss them over the side. But I like cats, an' I thought if I could take them ashore maybe I could find homes for them." He was sweating; his big face shone.

"I like cats," he said again. "Don't open it, please." His voice shook.

"Look, Mac," the Customs man said. He was undoing the straps. "It won't work, see? It's a good try, but it won't work." He undid the latch and opened the case.

There were six cats, although it seemed like quite a few more. They came out in a rush, clawing and snarling and spitting with rage. They circled the Customs shed, gathering speed, and then they streaked back out the wharf and up the gangplank and disappeared onto the ship.

Andy closed the empty suitcase. He strapped it carefully. He gave the Customs man one long, mournful look. Then he plodded back aboard ship.

In the bar, the bosun was laughing so hard he cried into his drink. And the crew was laughing, too. All but Carl. Carl said, "He can't get away with it! Not that big dumb—"

"You made a bet," the bosun said. "An' that's how it goes."

It was forty minutes before Andy was back to the Customs shed again. He had the suitcase in his hand, and he leaned a little against its weight. He set it down at the Customs man's feet. He wiped his broad face. "You want to open it this time?" he said. "They was awful hard to catch again."

The Customs man stared at the suitcase. He stared at

Andy. He opened his mouth and then he closed it again, and Andy waited, quivering inside. "Go on," the Customs man said. "Get the hell outa here."

So there it was. Andy's face showed nothing. "Yes, sir," he said, and he picked up the suitcase and his sea bag and walked slowly across the street and into the bar. He was thinking of Minna, and of a television set, and maybe, although he didn't know what such things cost, of one of those mechanical washing machines that took clothes and a little soap and did everything, all by itself. Minna, he thought, would like that; she could sip her brandy, and laugh at the television screen and listen to the machine doing her work for her. The concept pleasured him.

He let the prospect of these simple delights curl inside him and warm the smile with which he greeted his crew-mates. They crowded around him, pummeling his shoulders. All, that is, except Carl, who sourly watched the bosun take out a sheaf of bills.

Andy stood among them, massive and solid, smiling his helpless sort of smile, while the bosun counted the money into his hand. From time to time the bosun stopped his counting to wipe his eyes. "Them cats," he said. "Squallin' an' snortin' through that shed!"

"Well," Andy said, "I fed them real good when I went back on board. I don't hardly think they mind any more." Minna would like that part of it; Minna liked cats, just as he did. He folded the money and put it carefully into his purse. He smiled at everybody, including Carl. He picked up his sea bag. "Well," he said.

"How about a drink?" the bosun said.

Andy shook his head. "I got to go."

"The old lady?" the bosun said. "She'd never know."

Andy shook his head again. "It wouldn't be honest."

Carl snorted. "Honest!" He slapped the suitcase with his open hand. It gurgled gently. "Honest, he says!"

Andy nodded. "An' I got to tell the man, too."

"What man?" the bosun said. "Tell him what?"

"Why," Andy said, "the Customs man. I got to tell him I got this brandy here. For my wife." And he pulled out the small purse. "An' I got money to pay duty on it." He paused there. "The way the law says."

This twenty-seven-year-old story seems to hang around in one of the back closets of my mind, and I am continually surprised at how often people remember it out of the hundreds I have written. Its ambience does not seem dated, at least to me, and every one of us who has at one time or another drunk to excess will recall that time of dreadful speculation about what could have happened. (You mean to tell me I was driving!)

—JOHN D. MacDONALD

HANGOVER

JOHN D. MacDONALD

He dreamed that he had dropped something, lost something of value in the furnace, and he lay on his side trying to look down at an angle through a little hole, look beyond the flame down into the dark guts of the furnace for what he had lost. But the flame kept pulsing through the hole with a brightness that hurt his eyes, with a heat that parched his face, pulsing with an intermittent husky rasping sound.

With his awakening the dream became painfully explicable—the pulsing roar was his own harsh breathing, the parched feeling was a consuming thirst, the brightness was transmuted into pain intensely localized behind his eyes. When he opened his eyes a long slant of early-morning sun dazzled him and he shut his eyes quickly again.

This was a morning time of awareness of discomfort so acute that he had no thought for anything beyond the appraisal of the body and its functions. Though he was dimly aware of psychic discomforts which might later exceed the anguish of the flesh, the immediacy of bodily pain localized his attentions. Even without the horizontal brightness of the sun he would have known it was early. Long sleep would have muffled the beat of the taxed heart to a softened, sedate, and comfortable rhythm. But it was early and the heart knocked sharply, with a violence and in a cadence almost hysterical, so that no matter how he turned his head he could feel it, a tack hammer chipping away at his immortality.

His thirst was monstrous, undiminished by the random and fretful nausea that teased at the back of his throat. His hands and feet were cool, yet where his thighs touched he was sweaty. His whole body felt clotted, and he knew that he had perspired heavily during the evening, an oiled perspiration that left an unpleasant residue after it dried. The pain behind his eyes was a slow bulging and shrinking, in contrapuntal rhythm to the clatter of his heart.

He sat on the edge of the bed, head bowed, eyes squeezed shut, cool trembling fingers resting on his bare knees. He felt tremblingly weak, nauseated, acutely depressed.

This was the great joke. This was a hangover. Thing of sly wink, of rueful guffaw. This was death in the morning.

He stood on trembling legs and walked into the bathroom. He turned the cold water on as far as it would go. He drank a full glass greedily. He was refilling the glass when the first spasm came. He turned to the toilet, half-falling, cracking one knee painfully on the tile floor, and knelt there and clutched the edge of the bowl in both hands, hunched, miserable, naked. The water ran in the sink for a long time while he remained there, retching, until nothing more came but flakes of greenish bile. When he stood up he felt weaker, but a little bit better. He mopped his face with a damp towel, then drank more water, drank it slowly and carefully, and in great quantity, losing track of the number of glasses. He drank the cold water until his belly was swollen and he could hold no more, but he felt as thirsty as before.

40

Putting the glass back on the rack he looked at himself in the mirror. He took a quick, overly casual look, the way one glances at a stranger, the eye returning for a longer look after it is seen that the first glance aroused no undue curiosity. Though his face was grayish, eyes slightly puffy, jaws soiled by beard stubble, the long face with its even, undistinguished features looked curiously unmarked in relation to the torment of the body.

The visual reflection was a first step in the reaffirmation of identity. You are Hadley Purvis. You are thirty-nine. Your hair is turning gray with astonishing and disheartening speed.

He turned his back on the bland image, on the face which refused to comprehend his pain. He leaned his buttocks against the chill edge of the sink and a sudden unbidden image came into his mind, as clear and supernaturally perfect as a colored advertisement in a magazine. It was a shot glass full to the very brim with dark brown bourbon.

By a slow effort of will he caused the image to fade away. Not yet, he thought, and immediately wondered about his instinctive choice of mental phrase. Nonsense. This was a part of the usual morbidity of hangover—to imagine oneself slowly turning into an alcoholic. The rum sour on Sunday mornings had become a ritual with him, condoned by Sarah. And that certainly did not speak of alcoholism. Today was, unhappily, a working day, and it would be twelve-thirty before the first martini at Mario's. If anyone had any worries about alcoholism it was Sarah, and her worries resulted from her lack of knowledge of his job and its requirements. After a man has been drinking for twenty-one years he does not suddenly become a legitimate cause for the sort of annoying concern Sarah had been showing lately.

41

In the evening when they were alone before dinner they would drink, and that certainly did not distress her. She liked her few knocks as well as anyone. Then she had learned somehow that whenever he went to the kitchen to refill their glasses from the martini jug in the deep freeze, he would have an extra one for himself, opening his throat for it, pouring it down in one smooth, long, silvery gush. By mildness of tone she had trapped him into an admission, then had told him that the very secrecy of it was "significant." He had tried to explain that his tolerance for alcohol was greater than hers, and that it was easier to do it that way than to listen to her broad hints about how many he was having.

Standing there in the bathroom he could hear the early morning sounds of the city. His hearing seemed unnaturally keen. He realized that it was absurd to stand there and conduct mental arguments with Sarah and become annoyed at her. He reached into the shower stall and turned the faucets and waited until the water was the right temperature before stepping in, just barely warm. He made no attempt at first to bathe. He stood under the roar and thrust of the high nozzle, eyes shut, face tilted up.

As he stood there be began, cautiously, to think of the previous evening. He had much experience in this sort of reconstruction. He reached out with memory timorously, anticipating remorse and self-disgust.

The first part of the evening was, as always, easy to remember. It had been an important evening. He had dressed carefully yesterday morning, knowing that there would not be time to come home and change before going directly from the office to the hotel for the meeting, with its cocktails, dinner, speeches, movie and unveiling of the new model. Because of the importance of the evening he had taken it very easy at Mario's at lunchtime, limiting himself to two martinis before lunch, conscious of virtue—only to have it spoiled by Bill Hunter's coming into his office at three in the afternoon, staring at him with both relief and approval and saying, "Glad you didn't have one of those three-hour lunches, Had. The old man was a little dubious about your joining the group tonight."

Hadley Purvis had felt suddenly and enormously annoyed. Usually he liked Bill Hunter, despite his aura of opportunism, despite the cautious ambition that had enabled Hunter to become quite close to the head of the agency in a very short time.

"And so you said to him, 'Mr. Driscoll, if Had Purvis can't go to the party, I won't go either.' And then he broke down."

He watched Bill Hunter flush. "Not like that, Had. But I'll tell you what happened. He asked me if I thought you would behave yourself tonight. I said I was certain you realized the importance of the occasion, and I reminded him that the Detroit people know you and like the work you did on the spring campaign. So if you get out of line, it isn't going to do me any good either."

"And that's your primary consideration, naturally."

Hunter looked at him angrily, helplessly. "Damn it, Had . . ."

"Keep your little heart from fluttering. I'll step lightly."

Bill Hunter left his office. After he was gone Hadley tried very hard to believe that it had been an amusing little interlude. But he could not. Resentment stayed with him. Resentment at being treated like a child. And he suspected that Hunter had brought it up with Driscoll, saying very casually, "Hope Purvis doesn't put on a floor show tonight."

It wasn't like the old man to have brought it up. He felt that the old man genuinely liked him. They'd had some laughs together. Grown-up laughs, a little beyond the capacity of a Boy Scout like Hunter.

He washed up at five, then went down and shared a cab with Davey Tidmarsh, the only one of the new kids who had been asked to come along. Davey was all hopped up about it. He was a nice kid. Hadley liked him. Davey demanded to know what it would be like, and in the cab, Hadley told him.

"We'll be seriously outnumbered. There'll be a battalion from Detroit, also the bank people. It will be done with enormous seriousness, and a lot of expense. This is a pre-preview. Maybe they'll have a mockup there. The idea is that they get us all steamed up about the new model. Then, all enthused, we whip up two big promotions. The first promotion is a carnival deal they will use to sell the new models to the dealers and get them all steamed up. That'll be about four months from now. The second promotion will be the campaign to sell the cars to the public. They'll make a big fetish of secrecy, Davey. There'll be uniformed company guards. Armed."

It was as he had anticipated, only a bit bigger and gaudier than last year. Everything seemed to get bigger and gaudier every year. It was on the top floor of the hotel, in one of the middle-sized convention rooms. They were carefully checked at the door and each was given a badge to wear, a numbered badge. On the left side of the room was sixty feet of bar. Along the right wall was the long table where the buffet would be. There was a busy rumble of male conversation, a blue haze of smoke. Hadley nodded and smiled at the people he knew as they worked their way toward the bar. With drink in hand he went into the next room, after being checked again at the door, to look at the mockup.

Hadley had to admit that it had been done very neatly. The mockup was one-third actual size. It revolved slowly on a chest-high pedestal, a red and white convertible with the door open, with the model of a girl in a swimming suit standing beside it, both model girl and model car bathed in an excellent imitation of sunlight. He looked at the girl first, marveling at how cleverly the sheen of suntanned girl had been duplicated. He looked at the mannequin's figure and thought at once of Sarah and felt a warm wave of tenderness for her, a feeling that she was his luck and, with her, nothing could ever go wrong.

He looked at the lines of the revolving car and, with the glibness of long practice, he made up phrases that would be suitable for advertising it. He stood aside for a time and watched the manufactured delight on the faces of those who were seeing the model for the first time. He finished his drink and went out to the bar. With the first drink the last traces of irritation at Bill Hunter disappeared. As soon as he had a fresh drink he looked Bill up and said, "I'm the man who snarled this afternoon."

"No harm done," Hunter said promptly and a bit distantly. "Excuse me, Had. There's somebody over there I have to say hello to."

Hadley placed himself at the bar. He was not alone long. Within ten minutes he was the center of a group of six or seven. He relished these times when he was sought out for his entertainment value. The drinks brought him quickly to the point where he was, without effort, amusing. The sharp phrases came quickly, almost without thought. They laughed with him and appreciated him. He felt warm and loved.

He remembered that at that time there had been small

warnings in the back of his mind, but he had ignored them. He would know when to stop. He told the story about Jimmy and Jackie and the punch card over at Shor's, and knew he told it well, and knew he was having a fine time, and knew that everything was beautifully under control.

But, beyond that point, memory was faulty. It lost continuity. It became episodic, each scene bright enough, yet separated from other scenes by a grayness he could not penetrate.

He was still at the bar. The audience had dwindled to one, a small man he didn't know, a man who swayed and clung to the edge of the bar. He was trying to make the small man understand something. He kept shaking his head. Hunter came over to him and took his arm and said, "Had, you've got to get something to eat. They're going to take the buffet away soon."

"Smile, pardner, when you use that word 'got.' "

"Sit down and I'll get you a plate."

"Never let it be said that Hadley Purvis couldn't cut his own way through a solid wall of buffet." As Hunter tugged at his arm, Hadley finished his drink, put the glass on the bar with great care and walked over toward the buffet, shrugging his arm free of Hunter's grasp. He took a plate and looked at all the food. He had not the slightest desire for food. He looked back. Hunter was watching him. He shrugged and went down the long table.

Then, another memory. Standing there with plate in hand. Looking over and seeing Bill Hunter's frantic signals. Ignoring him and walking steadily over to where Driscoll sat with some of the top brass from Detroit. He was amused at the apprehensive expression on Driscoll's face. But he sat down and Driscoll had to introduce him.

Then, later. Dropping something from his fork. Recapturing it and glancing up to trap a look of distaste on the face of the most important man from Detroit, a bald, powerful-looking man with a ruddy face and small bright blue eyes.

He remembered that he started brooding about that look of distaste. The others talked and he ate doggedly. They think I'm a clown. I'm good enough to keep them laughing, but that's all. They don't think I'm capable of deep thought.

He remembered Driscoll's frown when he broke into the conversation, addressing himself to the bald one from Detroit, and taking care to pronounce each word distinctly, without slur.

"That's a nice-looking mockup. And it is going to make a lot of vehicles look old before their time. The way I see it, we're in a period of artificially accelerated obsolescence. The honesty has gone out of the American product. The great God is turnover. So all you manufacturers are straining a gut to make a product that wears out, or breaks, or doesn't last or, like your car, goes out of style. It's the old game of rooking the consumer. You have your hand in his pocket, and we have our hand in yours."

He remembered his little speech vividly, and it shocked him. Maybe it was true. But that had not been the time or place to state it, not at this festive meeting where everybody congratulated each other on what a fine new sparkling product they would be selling. He felt his cheeks grow hot as he remembered his own words. What a thing to say in front of Driscoll. The most abject apologies were going to be in order.

He could not remember the reaction of the man from Detroit, or Driscoll's immediate reaction. He had no further memories of being at the table. The next episode was back at the bar, a glass in his hand, Hunter beside him speaking so earnestly you could almost see the tears in his eyes. "Good Lord, Had! What did you say? What did you do? I've never seen him so upset."

"Tell him to go do something unspeakable. I just gave them a few clear words of ultimate truth. And now I intend to put some sparkle in that little combo."

"Leave the music alone. Go home, please. Just go home, Had."

There was another gap, and then he was arguing with the drummer. The man was curiously disinclined to give up the drums. A waiter gripped his arm.

"What's your trouble?" Hadley asked him angrily. "I just want to teach this clown how to stay on top of the beat."

"A gentleman wants to see you, sir. He is by the cloakroom. He asked me to bring you out."

Then he was by the cloakroom. Driscoll was there. He stood close to Hadley. "Don't open your mouth, Purvis. Just listen carefully to me while I try to get something through your drunken skull. Can you understand what I'm saying?"

"Certainly I can—"

"Shut up! You may have lost the whole shooting match for us. That speech of yours. He told me he wasn't aware of the fact that I hired Commies. He said that criticisms of the American way of life make him physically ill. Know what I'm going back in and tell him?"

"No."

"That I got you out here and fired you and sent you home. Get this straight. It's an attempt to save the contract. Even if it weren't, I'd still fire you, and I'd do it in person. I thought I would dread it. I've known you a long time. I find out, Purvis, that I'm actually enjoying it. It's such a damn relief to get rid of you. Don't open your mouth. I wouldn't take you back if you worked for free. Don't come back. Don't come in tomorrow. I'll have a girl pack your personal stuff. I'll have it sent to you by messenger, along with your check. You'll get both tomorrow, before noon. You're a clever man, Purvis, but the town is full of clever men who can hold liquor. Goodbye."

Driscoll turned on his heel and went back into the big room. Hadley remembered that the shock had penetrated the haze of liquor. He remembered that he had stood there, and he had been able to see two men setting up a projector, and all he could think about was how he would tell Sarah and what she would probably say.

And, without transition, he was in the Times Square area, on his way home. The sidewalk would tilt unexpectedly and each time he would take a lurching step to regain his balance. The glare of the lights hurt his eyes. His heart pounded. He felt short of breath.

He stopped and looked in the window of a men's shop that was still open. The sign on the door said Open Until Midnight. He looked at his watch. It was a little after eleven. He had imagined it to be much later. Suddenly it became imperative to him to prove both to himself and to a stranger that he was not at all drunk. If he could prove that, then he would know that Driscoll had fired him not for drinking, but for his opinions. And would anyone want to keep a job where he was not permitted to have opinions?

He gathered all his forces and looked intently into the shop window. He looked at a necktie. It was a gray wool tie with a tiny figure embroidered in dark red. The little embroidered things were shaped like commas. He decided that he liked it very much. The ties in that corner of the window were priced at three-fifty. He measured his stability, cleared his throat, went into the shop.

"Good evening, sir."

"Good evening. I'd like that tie in the window, the gray one on the left with the dark red pattern."

"Would you please show me which one, sir?"

"Of course." Hadley pointed it out. The man took a duplicate off a rack.

"Would you like this in a box, or shall I put it in a bag?"

"A bag is all right."

"It's a very handsome tie."

He gave the man a five dollar bill. The man brought him his change. "Thank you, sir. Good night."

"Good night." He walked out steadily, carrying the bag. No one could have done it better. A very orderly purchase. If he ever needed proof of his condition, the clerk would remember him. "Yes, I remember the gentleman. He came in shortly before closing time. He bought a gray tie. Sober? Perhaps he'd had a drink or two. But he was as sober as a judge."

And somewhere between the shop and home, all memory ceased. There was a vague something about a quarrel with Sarah, but it was not at all clear. Perhaps because the homecoming scene had become too frequent for them.

He dried himself vigorously on a harsh towel and went into the bedroom. When he thought of the lost job he felt quick panic. Another one wouldn't be easy to find. The same sort might be impossible. It was a profession that fed on gossip.

Maybe it was a good thing. It would force a change on them. Maybe a new city, a new way of life. Maybe they could regain something that they had lost in the last year

50

or so. But he knew he whistled in the dark. He was afraid. This was the worst of all mornings-after.

Yet even that realization was diffused by the peculiar aroma of unreality that clung to all his hangover mornings. Dreams were always vivid, so vivid that they became confused with reality. With care he studied the texture of the memory of Driscoll's face and found therein a lessening of his hope that it could have been dreamed.

He went into his bedroom and took fresh underwear from the drawer. He found himself thinking about the purchase of the necktie again. It seemed strange that the purchase should have such retroactive importance. The clothing he had worn was where he had dropped it beside his bed. He picked it up. He emptied the pockets of the suit. There was a skein of dried vomit on the lapel of the suit. He could not remember having been ill. There was a triangular tear in the left knee of the trousers, and he noticed for the first time an abrasion on his bare knee. He could not remember having fallen. The necktie was not in the suit pocket. He began to wonder whether he had dreamed about the necktie. In the back of his mind was a ghost image of some other dream about a necktie.

He decided that he would go to the office. He did not see what else he could do. If his memory of what Driscoll had said was accurate, maybe by now Driscoll would have relented. When he went to select a necktie, after he had shaved carefully, he looked for the new one on the rack. It was not there. As he was tying the one he had selected he noticed a wadded piece of paper on the floor beside his wastebasket. He picked it up, spread it open, read the name of the shop on it and knew that the purchase of the tie had been real.

By the time he was completely dressed it still was not eight o'clock. He felt unwell, though the sharpness of the

51

headache was dulled. His hands were shaky. His legs felt empty and weak.

It was time to face Sarah. He knew that he had seen her the previous evening. Probably she had been in bed, had heard him come in, had gotten up as was her custom and, no doubt, there had been a scene. He hoped he had not told her of losing the job. Yet, if it had been a dream, he could not have told her. If he had told her it would be proof that it had not been a dream. He went through the bathroom into her bedroom, moving quietly. Her bed had been slept in, turned back where she had gotten out.

He went down the short hall to the small kitchen. Sarah was not there. He began to wonder about her. Surely the quarrel could not have been so bad that she had dressed and left. He measured coffee into the top of the percolator and put it over a low gas flame. He mixed frozen juice and drank a large glass. The apartment seemed uncannily quiet. He poured another glass, drank half of it and walked up the hallway to the living room.

Stopping in the doorway, he saw the necktie, recognized the color of it, recognized the small pattern. He stood there, glass in hand, and looked at the tie. It was tightly knotted. And above the knot, resting on the arm of the chair, was the still, unspeakable face of Sarah, a face the shiny hue of fresh eggplant.

I suppose I'm no different from most other writers in choosing my favorite from among those stories which have received the most acclaim. Though it was nominated for no awards, "The Leopold Locked Room" sold to television soon after it was published in Ellery Queen's Mystery Magazine *and appeared as an episode of NBC-TV's "McMillan & Wife." Since then it has been reprinted in several anthologies, including Ellery Queen's twenty-volume* Masterpieces of Mystery *and Jan Broberg's six-volume* Mystery Masters in Sweden. *It was the only mystery chosen for inclusion in a recent college literature textbook. (One science fiction story, by Arthur C. Clarke, was also included.)*

Writers' opinions of their stories are constantly changing, and I always hope the next story out of the typewriter will become my favorite. But for the present this is it, and I hope others like it as much as I do.

—EDWARD D. HOCH

THE LEOPOLD LOCKED ROOM

EDWARD D. HOCH

Captain Leopold had never spoken to anyone about his divorce, and it was a distinct surprise to Lieutenant Fletcher when he suddenly said, "Did I ever tell you about my wife, Fletcher?"

They were just coming up from the police pistol range in the basement of headquarters after their monthly target practice, and it hardly seemed a likely time to be discussing past marital troubles. Fletcher glanced at him sideways and answered, "No, I guess you never did, Captain."

They had reached the top of the stairs and Leopold turned in to the little room where the coffee, sandwich, and soft-drink machines were kept. They called it the lunchroom, but only by the boldest stretch of the imagination could the little collection of tables and chairs qualify as such. Rather it was a place where off-duty cops could sit and chat, which was what Leopold and Fletcher were doing now.

Fletcher bought the coffee and put the steaming paper cups on the table between them. He had never seen Leopold quite this open and personal before, anxious to talk about a life that had existed far beyond the limits of Fletcher's friendship. "She's coming back," Leopold said

54

simply, and it took Fletcher an instant to grasp the meaning of his words.

"You wife is coming back?"

"My ex-wife."

"Here? What for?"

Leopold sighed and played with the little bag of sugar that Fletcher had given him with his coffee. "Her niece is getting married. Our niece."

"I never knew you had one."

"She's been away at college. Her name is Vicki Nelson, and she's marrying a young lawyer named Moore. And Monica is coming back east for the wedding."

"I never even knew her name," Fletcher observed, taking a sip of his coffee. "Haven't you seen her since the divorce?"

Leopold shook his head. "Not for fifteen years. It was a funny thing. She wanted to be a movie star, and I guess fifteen years ago lots of girls still thought about being movie stars. Monica was intelligent and very pretty—but probably no prettier than hundreds of other girls who used to turn up in Hollywood every year back in those days. I was just starting on the police force then, and the future looked pretty bright for me here. It would have been foolish of me to toss up everything just to chase her wild dream out to California. Well, pretty soon it got to be an obsession with her, really bad. She'd spend her afternoons in movies theaters and her evenings watching old films on television. Finally, when I still refused to go west with her, she just left me."

"Just walked out?"

Leopold nodded. "It was a blessing, really, that we didn't have children. I heard she got a few minor jobs out there—as an extra, and some technical stuff behind the scenes. Then apparently she had a nervous breakdown.

55

About a year later I received the official word that she'd divorced me. I heard that she recovered and was back working, and I think she had another marriage that didn't work out."

"Why would she come back for the wedding?"

"Vicki is her niece and also her godchild. We were just married when Vicki was born, and I suppose Monica might consider her the child we never had. In any event, I know she still hates me and blames me for everything that's gone wrong with her life. She told a friend once a few years ago she wished I were dead."

"Do you have to go to this wedding, too, Captain?"

"Of course. If I stayed away it would be only because of her. At least I have to drop by the reception for a few minutes." Leopold smiled ruefully. "I guess that's why I'm telling you all this, Fletcher. I want a favor from you."

"Anything, Captain. You know that."

"I know it seems like a childish thing to do, but I'd like you to come out there with me. I'll tell them I'm working and that I can only stay for a few minutes. You can wait outside in the car if you want. At least they'll see you there and believe my excuse."

Fletcher could see the importance of it to Leopold, and the effort that had gone into the asking. "Sure," he said. "Be glad to. When is it?"

"This Saturday. The reception's in the afternoon, at Sunset Farms."

Leopold had been to Sunset Farms only once before, at the wedding of a patrolman whom he'd especially liked. It was a low rambling place at the end of a paved driveway, overlooking a wooded valley and a gently flowing creek. If it had ever been a farm, that day was long past; but for wedding receptions and retirement parties it was the ideal place. The interior of the main building was, in reality, one huge square room, divided by accordion doors to make up to four smaller square rooms.

For the wedding of Vicki Nelson and Ted Moore three quarters of the large room was in use, with only the last set of accordion doors pulled shut its entire width and locked. The wedding party occupied a head table along one wall, with smaller tables scattered around the room for the families and friends. When Leopold entered the place at five minutes of two on Saturday afternoon, the hired combo was just beginning to play music for dancing.

He watched for a moment while Vicki stood, radiant, and allowed her new husband to escort her to the center of the floor. Ted Moore was a bit older than Leopold had expected, but as the pair glided slowly across the floor, he could find no visible fault with the match. He helped himself to a glass of champagne punch and stood ready to intercept them as they left the dance floor.

"It's Captain Leopold, isn't it?" someone asked. A face from his past loomed up, a tired man with a gold tooth in the front of his smile. "I'm Immy Fontaine, Monica's stepbrother."

"Sure," Leopold said, as if he'd remembered the man all along. Monica had rarely mentioned Immy, and Leopold recalled meeting him once or twice at family gatherings. But the sight of him now, gold tooth and all, reminded Leopold that Monica was somewhere nearby, that he might confront her at any moment.

"We're so glad you could come," someone else said, and he turned to greet the bride and groom as they came off the dance floor. Up close, Vicki was a truly beautiful girl, clinging to her new husband's arm like a proper bride.

"I wouldn't have missed it for anything," he said.

"This is Ted," she said, making the introductions.

Leopold shook his hand, silently approving the firm grip and friendly eyes.

"I understand you're a lawyer," Leopold said, making conversation.

"That's right, sir. Mostly civil cases, though. I don't tangle much with criminals."

They chatted for a few more seconds before the pressure of guests broke them apart. The luncheon was about to be served, and the more hungry ones were already lining up at the buffet tables. Vicki and Ted went over to start the line, and Leopold took another glass of champagne punch.

"I see the car waiting outside," Immy Fontaine said, moving in again. "You got to go on duty?"

Leopold nodded. "Just this glass and I have to leave."

"Monica's in from the West Coast."

"So I heard."

A slim man with a mustache jostled against him in the crush of the crowd and hastily apologized. Fontaine seized the man by the arm and introduced him to Leopold. "This here's Dr. Felix Thursby. He came east with Monica. Doc, I want you to meet Captain Leopold, her ex-husband."

Leopold shook hands awkwardly, embarrassed for the man and for himself. "A fine wedding," he mumbled. "Your first trip east?"

Thursby shook his head. "I'm from New York. Long ago."

"I was on the police force there once," Leopold remarked.

They chatted for a few more minutes before Leopold managed to edge away through the crowd.

"Leaving so soon?" a harsh unforgettable voice asked.

"Hello, Monica. It's been a long time."

He stared down at the handsome, middle-aged woman who now blocked his path to the door. She had gained a little weight, especially in the bosom, and her hair was graying. Only the eyes startled him, and frightened him just a bit. They had the intense wild look he'd seen before on the faces of deranged criminals.

"I didn't think you'd come. I thought you'd be afraid of me," she said.

"That's foolish. Why should I be afraid of you?"

The music had started again, and the line from the buffet tables was beginning to snake lazily about the room. But for Leopold and Monica they might have been alone in the middle of a desert.

"Come in here," she said, "where we can talk." She motioned toward the end of the room that had been cut off by the accordion doors. Leopold followed her, helpless to do anything else. She unlocked the doors and pulled them apart, just wide enough for them to enter the unused quarter of the large room. Then she closed and locked the doors behind them, and stood facing him. They were two people, alone in a bare unfurnished room.

They were in an area about thirty feet square, with the windows at the far end and the locked accordion doors at Leopold's back. He could see the afternoon sun cutting through the trees outside, and the gentle hum of the air-conditioner came through above the subdued murmur of the wedding guests.

"Remember the day we got married?" she asked.

"Yes. Of course."

She walked to the middle window, running her fingers along the frame, perhaps looking for the latch to open it. But it stayed closed as she faced him again. "Our marriage was as drab and barren as this room. Lifeless, unused!"

"Heaven knows I always wanted children, Monica."

"You wanted nothing but your damned police work!" she shot back, eyes flashing as her anger built.

"Look, I have to go. I have a man waiting in the car."

"Go! That's what you did before, wasn't it? *Go, go!* Go out to your damned job and leave me to struggle for myself. Leave me to—"

"You walked out on me, Monica. Remember?" he reminded her softly. She was so defenseless, without even a purse to swing at him.

"Sure I did! Because I had a career waiting for me! I had all the world waiting for me! And you know what happened because you wouldn't come along? You know what happened to me out there? They took my money and my self-respect and what virtue I had left. They made me into a tramp, and when they were done they locked me up in a mental hospital for three years. Three years!"

"I'm sorry."

"Every day while I was there I thought about you. I thought about how it would be when I got out. Oh, I thought. And planned. And schemed. You're a big detective now. Sometimes your cases even get reported in the California papers." She was pacing back and forth, caged, dangerous. "Big detective. But I can still destroy you just as you destroyed me!"

He glanced over his shoulder at the locked accordion doors, seeking a way out. It was a thousand times worse than he's imagined it would be. She was mad—mad and vengeful and terribly dangerous. "You should see a doctor, Monica."

Her eyes closed to mere slits. "I've seen doctors." Now she paused before the middle window, facing him. "I came all the way east for this day, because I thought you'd be here. It's so much better than your apartment, or your office, or a city street. There are one hundred and fifty witnesses on the other side of those doors."

"What in hell are you talking about?"

Her mouth twisted in a horrible grin. "You're going to know what I knew. Bars and cells and disgrace. You're going to know the despair I felt all those years."

"Monica—"

At that instant perhaps twenty feet separated them. She lifted one arm, as if to shield herself, then screamed in terror. "No! Oh, God, no!"

Leopold stood frozen, unable to move, as a sudden gunshot echoed through the room. He saw the bullet strike her in the chest, toppling her backward like the blow from a giant fist. Then somehow he had his own gun out of its belt holster and he swung around toward the doors.

They were still closed and locked. He was alone in the room with Monica.

He looked back to see her crumple on the floor, blood spreading in a widening circle around the torn black hole in her dress. His eyes went to the windows, but all three were still closed and unbroken. He shook his head, trying to focus his mind on what had happened.

There was noise from outside, and a pounding on the accordion doors. Someone opened the lock from the other side, and the gap between the doors widened as they were pulled open. "What happened?" someone asked. A women guest screamed as she saw the body. Another toppled in a faint.

Leopold stepped back, aware of the gun still in his hand, and saw Lieutenant Fletcher fighting his way through the mob of guests. "Captain, what is it?"

"She—Someone shot her."

Fletcher reached out and took the gun from Leopold's hand—carefully, as one might take a broken toy from a child. He put it to his nose and sniffed, then opened the cylinder to inspect the bullets. "It's been fired recently,

Captain. One shot." Then his eyes seemed to cloud over, almost to the point of tears. "Why the hell did you do it?" he asked. "Why?"

Leopold saw nothing of what happened then. He only had vague and splintered memories of someone examining her and saying she was still alive, of an ambulance and much confusion. Fletcher drove him down to headquarters, to the commissioner's office, and he sat there and waited, running his moist palms up and down his trousers. He was not surprised when they told him she had died on the way to Southside Hospital. Monica had never been one to do things by halves.

The men—the detectives who worked under him—came to and left the commissioner's office, speaking in low tones with their heads together, occasionally offering him some embarrassed gesture of condolence. There was an aura of sadness over the place, and Leopold knew it was for him.

"You have nothing more to tell us, Captain?" the commissioner asked. "I'm making it as easy for you as I can."

"I didn't kill her," Leopold insisted again. "It was someone else."

"Who? How?"

He could only shake his head. "I wish I knew. I think in some mad way she killed herself, to get revenge on me."

"She shot herself with *your* gun, while it was in *your* holster, and while *you* were standing twenty feet away?"

Leopold ran a hand over his forehead. "It couldn't have been my gun. Ballistics will prove that."

"But your gun had been fired recently, and there was an empty cartridge in the chamber."

"I can't explain that. I haven't fired it since the other day at target practice, and I reloaded it afterwards."

"Could she have hated you that much, Captain?" Fletcher asked. "To frame you for her murder?"

"She could have. I think she was a very sick woman. If I did that to her—if I was the one who made her sick—I suppose I deserve what's happening to me now."

"The hell you do," Fletcher growled. "If you say you're innocent, Captain, I'm sticking by you." He began pacing again and finally turned to the commissioner. "How about giving him a paraffin test, to see if he's fired a gun recently?"

The commissioner shook his head. "We haven't used that in years. You know how unreliable it is, Fletcher. Many people have nitrates or nitrites on their hands. They can pick them up from dirt, or fertilizers, or fireworks, or urine, or even from simply handling peas or beans. Anyone who smokes tobacco can have deposits on his hands. There are some newer tests for the presence of barium or lead, but we don't have the necessary chemicals for those."

Leopold nodded. The commissioner had risen through the ranks. He wasn't simply a political appointee, and the men had always respected him. Leopold respected him. "Wait for the ballistics report," he said. "That'll clear me."

So they waited. It was another forty-five minutes before the phone rang and the commissioner spoke to the ballistics man. He listened, and grunted, and asked one or two questions. Then he hung up and faced Leopold across the desk.

"The bullet was fired from your gun," he said simply. "There's no possibility of error. I'm afraid we'll have to charge you with homicide."

The routines he knew so well went on into Saturday evening, and when they were finished Leopold was escorted from the courtroom to find young Ted Moore waiting for him. "You should be on your honeymoon," Leopold told him.

"Vicki couldn't leave till I'd seen you and tried to help. I don't know much about criminal law, but perhaps I could arrange bail."

"That's already been taken care of," Leopold said. "The grand jury will get the case next week."

"I—I don't know what to say. Vicki and I are both terribly sorry."

"So am I." He started to walk away, then turned back. "Enjoy your honeymoon."

"We'll be in town overnight, at the Towers, if there's anything I can do."

Leopold nodded and kept on walking. He could see the reflection of his guilt in young Moore's eyes. As he got to his car, one of the patrolmen he knew glanced his way and then quickly in the other direction. On a Saturday night no one talked to wife-murderers. Even Fletcher had disappeared.

Leopold decided he couldn't face the drab walls of his office, not with people avoiding him. Besides, the commissioner had been forced to suspend him from active duty pending grand-jury action and the possible trial. The office didn't even belong to him anymore. He cursed silently and drove home to his little apartment, weaving through the dark streets with one eye out for a patrol car. He wondered if they'd be watching him, to prevent his jumping bail. He wondered what he'd have done in the commissioner's shoes.

The eleven-o'clock news on television had it as the lead item, illustrated with a black-and-white photo of him taken during a case last year. He shut off the television without listening to their comments and went back outside, walking down to the corner for an early edition of the Sunday paper. The front-page headline was as bad as he'd expected: DETECTIVE CAPTAIN HELD IN SLAYING OF EX-WIFE.

On the way back to his apartment, walking slowly, he tried to remember what she'd been like—not that afternoon, but before the divorce. He tried to remember her face on their wedding day, her soft laughter on their honeymoon. But all he could remember were those mad vengeful eyes. And the bullet ripping into her chest.

Perhaps he had killed her after all. Perhaps the gun had come into his hand so easily he never realized it was there.

"Hello, Captain."

"I—Fletcher! What are you doing here?"

"Waiting for you. Can I come in?"

"Well . . ."

"I've got a six-pack of beer. I thought you might want to talk about it."

Leopold unlocked his apartment door. "What's there to talk about?"

"If you say you didn't kill her, Captain, I'm willing to listen to you."

Fletcher followed him into the tiny kitchen and popped open two of the beer cans. Leopold accepted one of them and dropped into the nearest chair. He felt utterly exhausted, drained of even the strength to fight back.

"She framed me, Fletcher," he said quietly. "She framed me as neatly as anything I've ever seen. The thing's impossible, but she did it."

"Let's go over it step by step, Captain. Look, the way I see it there are only three possibilities: Either you shot her, she shot herself, or someone else shot her. I think we can rule out the last one. The three windows were locked on the outside and unbroken, the room was bare of any

65

hiding place, and the only entrance was through the accordion doors. These were closed and locked, and although they could have been opened from the other side, you certainly would have seen or heard it happen. Besides, there were one hundred and fifty wedding guests on the other side of those doors. No one could have unlocked and opened them and then fired the shot, all without being seen."

Leopold shook his head. "But it's just as impossible that she could have shot herself. I was watching her every minute. I never looked away once. There was nothing in her hands, not even a purse. And the gun that shot her was in my holster, on my belt. I never drew it till *after* the shot was fired."

Fletcher finished his beer and reached for another can. "I didn't look at her close, Captain, but the size of the hole in her dress and the powder burns point to a contact wound. The medical examiner agrees, too. She was shot from no more than an inch or two away. There were grains of powder in the wound itself, though the bleeding had washed most of them away."

"But she had nothing in her hand," Leopold repeated. "And there was nobody standing in front of her with a gun. Even I was twenty feet away."

"The thing's impossible, Captain."

Leopold grunted. "Impossible—unless I killed her."

Fletcher stared at his beer. "How much time do we have?"

"If the grand jury indicts me for first-degree murder, I'll be in a cell by next week."

Fletcher frowned at him. "What's with you, Captain? You almost act resigned to it! Hell, I've seen more fight in you on a routine holdup!"

"I guess that's it, Fletcher. The fight is gone out of me.

She's drained every drop out of me. She's had her revenge."

Fletcher sighed and stood up. "Then I guess there's really nothing I can do for you, Captain. Good night."

Leopold didn't see him to the door. He simply sat there, hunched over the table. For the first time in his life he felt like an old man.

Leopold slept late Sunday morning and awakened with the odd sensation that it had all been a dream. He remembered feeling the same way when he'd broken his wrist chasing a burglar. In the morning, on just awakening, the memory of the heavy cast had always been a dream, until he moved his arm. Now, rolling over in his narrow bed, he saw the Sunday paper where he'd tossed it the night before. The headline was still the same. The dream was a reality.

He got up and showered and dressed, reaching for his holster out of habit before he remembered he no longer had a gun. Then he sat at the kitchen table staring at the empty beer cans, wondering what he would do with his day. With his life.

The doorbell rang and it was Fletcher. "I didn't think I'd be seeing you again," Leopold mumbled, letting him in.

Fletcher was excited, and the words tumbled out of him almost before he was through the door. "I think I've got something, Captain! It's not much, but it's a start. I was down at headquarters first thing this morning, and I got hold of the dress Monica was wearing when she was shot."

Leopold looked blank. "The dress?"

Fletcher was busy unwrapping the package he'd brought. "The commissioner would have my neck if he knew I brought this to you, but look at this hole!"

Leopold studied the jagged, blood-caked rent in the fabric. "It's large," he observed, "but with a near-contact wound the powder burns would cause that."

"Captain, I've seen plenty of entrance wounds made by a thirty-eight slug. I've even caused a few of them. But I never saw one that looked like this. Hell, it's not even round!"

"What are you trying to tell me, Fletcher?" Suddenly something stirred inside him. The juices were beginning to flow again.

"The hole in her dress is much larger and more jagged than the corresponding wound in her chest, Captain. That's what I'm telling you. The bullet that killed her couldn't have made this hole. No way! And that means maybe she wasn't killed when we thought she was."

Leopold grabbed the phone and dialed the familiar number of the Towers Hotel. "I hope they slept late this morning."

"Who?"

"The honeymooners." He spoke sharply into the phone, giving the switchboard operator the name he wanted, and then waited. It was a full minute before he heard Ted Moore's sleepy voice answering on the other end. "Ted, this is Leopold. Sorry to bother you."

The voice came alert at once. "That's all right, Captain. I told you to call if there was anything—"

"I think there is. You and Vicki between you must have a pretty good idea of who was invited to the wedding. Check with her and tell me how many doctors were on the invitation list."

Ted Moore was gone for a few moments and then he returned. "Vicki says you're the second person who asked her that."

"Oh? Who was the first?"

"Monica. The night before the wedding, when she arrived in town with Dr. Thursby. She casually asked if he'd get to meet any other doctors at the reception. But Vicki told her he was the only one. Of course we hadn't invited him, but as a courtesy to Monica we urged him to come."

"Then after the shooting, it was Thursby who examined her? No one else?"

"He was the only doctor. He told us to call an ambulance and rode to the hospital with her."

"Thank you, Ted. You've been a big help."

"I hope so, Captain."

Leopold hung up and faced Fletcher. "That's it. She worked it with this guy Thursby. Can you put out an alarm for him?"

"Sure can," Fletcher said. He took the telephone and dialed the unlisted squad-room number. "Dr. Felix Thursby? Is that his name?"

"That's it. The only doctor there, the only one who could help Monica with her crazy plan of revenge."

Fletcher completed issuing orders and hung up the phone. "They'll check his hotel and call me back."

"Get the commissioner on the phone, too. Tell him what we've got."

Fletcher started to dial and then stopped, his finger in mid-air. "What *have* we got, Captain?"

The commissioner sat behind his desk, openly unhappy at being called to headquarters on a Sunday afternoon, and listened bleakly to what Leopold and Fletcher had to tell him. Finally he spread his fingers on the desktop and said, "The mere fact that this Dr. Thursby seems to have left town is hardly proof of his guilt, Captain. What you're saying is that the woman wasn't killed until later—that

Thursby killed her in the ambulance. But how could he have done that with a pistol that was already in Lieutenant Fletcher's possession, tagged as evidence? And how could he have fired the fatal shot without the ambulance attendants hearing it?"

"I don't know," Leopold admitted.

"Heavens knows, Captain, I'm willing to give you every reasonable chance to prove your innocence. But you have to bring me more than a dress with a hole in it."

"All right," Leopold said. "I'll bring you more."

"The grand jury gets the case this week, Captain."

"I know," Leopold said. He turned and left the office, with Fletcher tailing behind.

"What now?" Fletcher asked.

"We go talk to Immy Fontaine, my ex-wife's stepbrother."

Though he'd never been friendly with Fontaine, Leopold knew where to find him. The tired man with the gold tooth lived in a big old house overlooking the Sound, where on this summer Sunday they found him in the back yard, cooking hot dogs over a charcoal fire.

He squinted into the sun and said, "I thought you'd be in jail, after what happened."

"I didn't kill her," Leopold said quietly.

"Sure you didn't."

"For a stepbrother you seem to be taking her death right in stride," Leopold observed, motioning toward the fire.

"I stopped worrying about Monica fifteen years ago."

"What about this man she was with? Dr. Thursby?"

Immy Fontaine chuckled. "If he's a doctor I'm a plumber! He has the fingers of a surgeon, I'll admit, but when I asked him about my son's radius that he broke skiing, Thursby thought it was a leg bone. What the hell, though, I was never one to judge Monica's love life. Remember, I didn't even object when she married you."

"Nice of you. Where's Thursby staying while he's in town?"

"He was at the Towers with Monica."

"He's not there anymore."

"Then I don't know where he's at. Maybe he's not even staying for her funeral."

"What if I told you Thursby killed Monica?"

He shrugged. "I wouldn't believe you, but then I wouldn't particularly care. If you were smart you'd have killed her fifteen years ago when she walked out on you. That's what I'd have done."

Leopold drove slowly back downtown, with Fletcher grumbling beside him. "Where are we, Captain? It seems we're just going in circles."

"Perhaps we are, Fletcher, but right now there are still too many questions to be answered. If we can't find Thursby I'll have to tackle it from another direction. The bullet, for instance."

"What about the bullet?"

"We're agreed it could not have been fired by my gun, either while it was in my holster or later, while Thursby was in the ambulance with Monica. Therefore, it must have been fired earlier. The last time I fired it was at target practice. Is there any possibility—any chance at all—that Thursby or Monica could have gotten one of the slugs I fired into that target?"

Fletcher put a damper on it. "Captain, we were both firing at the same target. No one could sort out those bullets and say which came from your pistol and which from mine. Besides, how would either of them gain access to the basement target range at police headquarters?"

"I could have an enemy in the department," Leopold said.

"Nuts! We've all got enemies, but the thing is still

impossible. If you believe people in the department are plotting against you, you might as well believe that the entire ballistics evidence was faked."

"It was, somehow. Do you have the comparison photos?"

"They're back at the office. But with the narrow depth of field you can probably tell more from looking through the microscope yourself."

Fletcher drove him to the lab, where they persuaded the Sunday-duty officer to let them have a look at the bullets. While Fletcher and the officer stood by in the interests of propriety, Leopold squinted through the microscope at the twin chunks of lead.

"The death bullet is pretty battered," he observed, but he had to admit that the rifling marks were the same. He glanced at the identification tag attached to the test bullet: *Test slug fired from Smith & Wesson .38 Revolver, serial number 2420547.*

Leopold turned away with a sigh, then turned back.

2420547.

He fished into his wallet and found his pistol permit. *Smith & Wesson 2421622.*

"I remembered those two's on the end," he told Fletcher. "That's not my gun."

"It's the one I took from you, Captain. I'll swear to it!"

"And I believe you, Fletcher. But it's the one fact I needed. It tells me how Dr. Thursby managed to kill Monica in a locked room before my very eyes, with a gun that was in my holster at the time. And it just might tell us where to find the elusive Dr. Thursby."

By Monday morning Leopold had made six long-distance calls to California, working from his desk telephone while Fletcher used the squad-room phone. Then, a little before noon, Leopold, Fletcher, the commissioner, and a man from the district attorney's office took a car and drove up to Boston.

"You're sure you've got it figured?" the commissioner asked Leopold for the third time. "You know we shouldn't allow you to cross the state line while awaiting grand-jury action."

"Look, either you trust me or you don't," Leopold snapped. Behind the wheel Fletcher allowed himself a slight smile, but the man from the D.A.'s office was deadly serious.

"The whole thing is so damned complicated," the commissioner grumbled.

"My ex-wife was a complicated woman. And remember, she had fifteen years to plan it."

"Run over it for us again," the D.A.'s man said.

Leopold sighed and started talking. "The murder gun wasn't mine. The gun I pulled after the shot was fired, the one Fletcher took from me, had been planted on me sometime before."

"How?"

"I'll get to that. Monica was the key to it all, of course. She hated me so much that her twisted brain planned her own murder in order to get revenge on me. She planned it in such a way that it would have been impossible for anyone but me to have killed her."

"Only a crazy woman would do such a thing."

"I'm afraid she was crazy—crazy for vengeance. She set up the entire plan for the afternoon of the wedding reception, but I'm sure they had an alternate in case I hadn't gone to it. She wanted some place where there'd be lots of witnesses."

"Tell them how she worked the bullet hitting her," Fletcher urged.

"Well, that was the toughest part for me. I actually saw her shot before my eyes. I saw the bullet hit her and I saw the blood. Yet I was alone in a locked room with her. There was no hiding place, no opening from which a person or even a mechanical device could have fired the bullet at her. To you people it seemed I must be guilty, especially when the bullet came from the gun I was carrying.

"But I looked at it from a different angle—once Fletcher forced me to look at it at all! I *knew* I hadn't shot her, and since no one else physically could have, I knew no one did! If Monica was killed by a thirty-eight slug, it must have been fired *after* she was taken from that locked room. Since she was dead on arrival at the hospital, the most likely time for her murder—to me, at least—became the time of the ambulance ride, when Dr. Thursby must have hunched over her with careful solicitousness."

"But you *saw* her shot!"

"That's one of the two reasons Fletcher and I were on the phones to Hollywood this morning. My ex-wife worked in pictures, at times in the technical end of movie-making. On the screen there are a number of ways to simulate a person being shot. An early method was a sort of compressed-air gun fired at the actor from just off-camera. These days, especially in the bloodiest of the Western and war films, they use a tiny explosive charge fitted under the actor's clothes. Of course the body is protected from burns, and the force of it is directed outward. A pouch of fake blood is released by the explosion, adding to the realism of it."

"And this is what Monica did?"

Leopold nodded. "A call to her Hollywood studio confirmed the fact that she worked on a film using this device. I noticed when I met her that she'd gained weight around the bosom, but I never thought to attribute it to the padding and the explosive device. She triggered it when she raised her arm as she screamed at me."

"Any proof?"

"The hole in her dress was just too big to be an entrance hole from a thirty-eight, even fired at close range—too big and too ragged. I can thank Fletcher for spotting that. This morning the lab technicians ran a test on the bloodstains. Some of it was her blood, the rest was chicken blood."

"She was a good actress to fool all those people."

"She knew Dr. Thursby would be the first to examine her. All she had to do was fall over when the explosive charge ripped out the front of her dress."

"What if there had been another doctor at the wedding?"

Leopold shrugged. "Then they would have postponed it. They couldn't take that chance."

"And the gun?"

"I remembered Thursby bumping against me when I first met him. He took my gun and substituted an identical weapon—identical, that is, except for the serial number. He'd fired it just a short time earlier, to complete the illusion. When I drew it I simply played into their hands. There I was, the only person in the room with an apparently dying woman, and a gun that had just been fired."

"But what about the bullet that killed her?"

"Rifling marks on slugs are made by the lands in the rifled barrel of a gun causing grooves in the lead of a bullet. A bullet fired through a smooth tube has no rifling marks."

"What in hell kind of gun has a smooth tube for a barrel?" the commissioner asked.

"A homemade one, like a zip gun. Highly inaccurate,

but quite effective when the gun is almost touching the skin of the victim. Thursby fired a shot from the pistol he was to plant on me, probably into a pillow or some other place where he could retrieve the undamaged slug. Then he reused the rifled slug on another cartridge and fired it with his homemade zip gun, right into Monica's heart. The original rifling marks were still visible and no new ones were added."

"The ambulance driver and attendant didn't hear the shot?"

"They would have stayed up front, since he was a doctor riding with a patient. It gave him a chance to get the padded explosive mechanism off her chest, too. Once that was away, I imagine he leaned over her, muffling the zip gun as best he could, and fired the single shot that killed her. Remember, an ambulance on its way to a hospital is a pretty noisy place—it has a siren going all the time."

They were entering downtown Boston now, and Leopold directed Fletcher to a hotel near the Common. "I still don't believe the part about switching the guns," the D.A.'s man objected. "You mean to tell me he undid the strap over your gun, got out the gun, and substituted another one—all without your knowing it?"

Leopold smiled. "I mean to tell you only one type of person could have managed it—an expert, professional pickpocket. The type you see occasionally doing an act in nightclubs and on television. That's how I knew where to find him. We called all over southern California till we came up with someone who knew Monica and knew she'd dated a man named Thompson who had a pick-pocket act. We called Thompson's agent and discovered he's playing a split week at a Boston lounge, and is staying at this hotel."

"What if he couldn't have managed it without your catching on? Or what if you hadn't been wearing your gun?"

"Most detectives wear their guns off-duty. If I hadn't been, or if he couldn't get it, they'd simply have changed their plan. He must have signaled her when he'd safely made the switch."

"Here we are," Fletched said. "Let's go up."

The Boston police had two men waiting to meet them, and they went up in the elevator to the room registered in the name of Max Thompson. Fletcher knocked on the door, and when it opened, the familiar face of Felix Thursby appeared. He no longer wore the mustache, but he had the same slim surgeonlike fingers that Immy Fontaine had noticed. Not a doctor's fingers, but a pickpocket's.

"We're taking you in for questioning," Fletcher said and the Boston detectives issued the standard warnings of his legal rights.

Thursby blinked his tired eyes at them and grinned a bit when he recognized Leopold. "She said you were smart. She said you were a smart cop."

"Did you have to kill her?" Leopold asked.

"I didn't. I just held the gun there and she pulled the trigger herself. She did it all herself, except for switching the guns. She hated you that much."

"I know," Leopold said quietly, staring at something far away. "But I guess she must have hated herself just as much."

I've always liked a touch of whimsy in a story, but I hate being slapped with the impossible. To balance a story so that you can either sprout wings along with it or else keep your feet on good, solid concrete—that's the trick, and I hope that in this one I've pulled it off. As for psychiatrists, they're supposed to perform miracles, aren't they?

—LAWRENCE TREAT

GIVE THE DEVIL HIS DUE

LAWRENCE TREAT

When Dr. Ira Frost, psychiatrist, returned to his office on that particular Tuesday, he was amazed to find blisters on his hands, but he was even more amazed to find a stranger sitting in the chair at his own desk.

"Who," he said, "are you? And how did you get in here?"

The stranger stood up. "Didn't mean to scare you," he said. "As to who I am—well, I have a great many names, and since people are pretty informal these days you can call me Lou. It's as good a name as any. As for how I got in, I'm afraid you wouldn't believe it even if I told you."

"Try me."

Lou shrugged. "If you wish. But, strictly speaking, I didn't get here at all. I"—and his mouth twisted up into a wry, sardonic smile—"I materialized."

"You bet I don't believe you," Ira said. "You're nothing but a damn hallucination. I guess I've been working too hard."

"Just like people these days to try and find an ordinary, prosaic explanation. Okay, then, explain this." He put his hand on the desk, which shot forth a spear of flame. The odor of brimstone was sharp and acrid.

"Lou?" Ira exclaimed. "Why, you're Lucifer!"

"Exactly. But you look a trifle pale, so why don't you sit down and relax? Then we can talk in comfort."

Warily Ira circled his desk and lowered himself into his chair. The seat was cold as ice, and he gave an involuntary shudder.

Lou laughed. "An old trick of mine—to startle people when they refuse to believe in me. But you seem to be taking things in stride, so I think we can get down to business."

"Which is?"

"Oh, come now, Dr. Faust. You realize—"

"Faust?" Ira said, interrupting. "My name's Frost."

"Of course. Just a slip of the tongue, Doctor." Lou eased himself onto the couch. "I was starting to say that this book you've been writing, about the devil in twentieth-century literature—you've missed the boat."

"Impossible! I've been working on it for three years, I read two hundred and eighty-seven books. My bibliography is exhaustive, but it's true the publishers won't buy it. Why? Why?"

"Maybe I don't want it published," Lou said.

"Why not? What have you got against it?" Ira asked.

"You misrepresent me. You know what my main interest is, don't you?"

"Evil."

"Exactly. Evil and corruption. I buy souls. I match wits with humans who are in trouble or who think they're smarter than I am. But when you psychiatrists deny the whole doctrine of evil and replace it with some nonsensical notion of mental sickness, you're attacking my very existence."

"Good," Ira said. "You're on your way out."

"Not a bit of it. I haven't been getting much publicity lately because I was busy making a departmental overhaul and computerizing my business. Now that it's done I can get away from the office. And frankly I wish I never had to go back."

"What's the trouble?"

"The world's too impersonal. Right up into the nineteenth century I used to come and go freely. People saw me all the time, I was a well-known figure around town, and people gave me credit for every kind of disaster. But now I'm becoming anonymous."

"I'd put it differently," Ira said. "You're becoming obsolete."

"Nonsense!" Lou said sharply. "A war that killed off a few million, a world that's being ruined by Pollution, Overpopulation, and Drugs—POD. That's my POD program and I'm doing an outstanding job."

"I'll admit that the world is in pretty bad shape, but it doesn't follow that you're responsible for it. Give me one good reason for thinking that you are."

"You make my point nicely. Doctor, the whole trouble is that people no longer believe in evil. They want reasons for everything, they're full of scientific explanations. People aren't immoral any more, they're psychologically sick. And they aren't stupid, they're underprivileged and mentally retarded. A whole profession—and a very prosperous one, as you well know—has been built on just that concept. So I thought I'd enjoy coming here and facing it out with a psychiatrist."

"Okay, but why me?"

"Because of that book of yours. It's full of scientific jargon that nobody but another psychiatrist can possibly understand. You make me look like a stuffed shirt, and I resent it."

"I didn't think I characterized you in such terms."

"You didn't characterize me at all. There's not a single

sentence in the whole book that reflects my true point of view. You almost make sin seem unattractive."

"And that upsets you?"

"You bet it does. I'm a personality boy and I hate abstractions. While it's nice seeing rivers that nobody can drink from and beaches lined with oil slick, and while it's exhilarating to see people cough just from the air they breathe, I miss the person-to-person relationship, and that's why I'm here."

"I suppose," Ira said, "that you have some kind of proposition."

"Certainly. Doctor, do you believe you have a soul?"

"Me, fall for that religious claptrap? I gave it up while I was still in high school."

"I'm sorry about that," Lou said. "If you believed you had a soul, our conversation would get places much faster. The highest stake a human being can play for is the hereafter."

"You can have it," Ira said drily.

Lou leaped up from the couch. "Exactly!" he said. "That's what I'm aiming at. You get the now—anything you want in it—and I get the hereafter. Nicely put, Doctor. Occasionally you do manage to state things clearly, which is pretty rare in your trade."

"My profession, you mean."

"Have it your way," Lou said. "Anyhow, here's my offer: I give you three wishes, and in return you give me your soul."

"I have no soul."

"Your unconscious or superego or whatever you want to call it. I'll give you three wishes, and you give me your psyche. Is it a bargain?"

"I can't give you my psyche. By very definition my psyche is me. I can't separate it out, as if it were a thing."

"You're making it hard for me," Lou said. "I'm offering you three wishes. What will you give me in return?"

"Nothing."

"Wonderful!" Lou exclaimed. "You give me nothing. But if I can turn nothing into everything, then I win."

"Pure sophistry," Ira said.

"No matter. Is it a deal?"

"Sure," Ira said. "Do we shake on it?"

Lou recoiled in horror. "Hell, no—if you'll pardon the expression. If you touched me I'd burn your hand off. I don't need anything as silly as that. Just give me your word, that's all I need."

"Good. You have my word, but—" Ira shook his head. "Wait a minute. Suppose I get my three wishes, and then I die the next day—you're perfectly capable of pulling a trick like that."

"I solemnly promise you at least fifty years of life, after the granting of your three wishes."

"In reasonably good health?" Ira asked.

"Agreed. And on your side there are a couple of conditions. You can't ask to live forever, and you can't try to help someone else. You have to be selfish."

"That's easy."

"Fine. Now there's no hocus-pocus about this. All you do is sit here in your office and state each wish, one week apart and at exactly the same time of the day. It's now one-fifty-eight and you can start with the first wish. What is it?"

"Well," Ira said, "you probably know that my marriage to Margot was the biggest mistake I ever made, and that I don't get along with her. She's extravagant, nagging, vindictive—"

"I'm not interested in her character analysis," Lou said. "Just tell me what you want."

"I want to get rid of her," Ira said.

Lou cracked his fingers. As Ira stared, the figure of Lou seemed gradually to fade away, and Ira found himself staring at the mauve wall opposite his desk. He continued to stare for the next two minutes. Then, as the hour struck two, he heard the doorbell ring and his first afternoon patient came in.

Ira was singularly unstrung all afternoon. It was difficult for him to concentrate, and he was convinced that he'd experienced some kind of debilitating hallucination. He sat with a pad on his lap, as he always did, but instead of making notes he merely doodled. When his patient stopped talking, he remarked absently, "Go ahead. This is all very interesting and I'm listening to every word. Just keep on." But later he had no idea of what the patient had said.

At five o'clock, shortly before his last patient was due, he called his home in the suburbs. There was no answer. He called again at six, and again there was no answer.

Coincidence, he decided. Margot was taking a bath or she was working in the garden; but she'd be home as usual when he arrived on the 6:42.

She wasn't. Instead there was a typed note in his study. It read: "Ira, I can't stand it any more. I've found someone I can be happy with and I'm leaving. You can get a divorce on grounds of desertion, and I only hope I'll never see you again."

He stared at the note. It was like her and her sloppy-mindedness to leave the note unsigned, and he decided to rectify the omission, in case he had to produce the note at some future time. It was easy to find a batch of returned checks with her signature, and he practised copying it. When he felt he was reasonably proficient, he wrote it at the bottom of the sheet of paper, put the sheet in a drawer, and went out to a restaurant. He had two martinis and then a small bottle of wine with his steak. He felt drowsy from the liquor and wine, and he went home and to bed. He slept heavily.

The week was uneventful. He told his closer friends that Margot had left him. As the news got around, dinner invitations began to pile up. He was, to a certain extent, a social lion, but he found he was no longer geared to living alone. In particular, the weekend was utterly dreary.

Shortly before two P.M. on the following Tuesday he sat at his desk and watched a familiar shape step through the closed door.

"So you're real," Ira said. "I was beginning to doubt our whole conversation."

"People always start by doubting me," Lou said, "especially these days. With all that scientific nonsense going around, I have to make things seem reasonable. If I promise somebody a fortune, I not only have to produce it, but I have to make it look perfectly natural. For instance, one of my favorite methods is to set up an oil strike in somebody's back yard, although that's not feasible everywhere. I come up against some pretty tough problems."

"I'm sure you have no real trouble," Ira said. "A man of your talents can do practically anything he wants."

"In a way you're right, but there are difficulties. For instance, for a while I arranged all the lotteries. You didn't know they were rigged, did you?"

"By you?"

Lou nodded. "Naturally, but I've more or less given up the lottery business. If somebody wants a fortune and I promise to let him win a hundred thousand or so, what happens? Taxes! He ends up with less than half his winnings. If people get the idea that I'm a welsher, then where am I? Nobody will sell his soul to a devil who doesn't keep his word. I may be clever and tricky, but I have to project an image of absolute reliability."

"I never thought of it that way."

"Nobody does. To coin a phrase, nobody gives the devil his due." Lou apparently thought he'd uncorked a witticism, and he chuckled. "But did you ever stop to think that I have no prejudices whatsoever? Rich or poor, black or brown or white—I corrupt whoever comes along. If I have any bias at all, it's that I particularly like to corrupt a saint, although nowadays there are damn few of them around. And anyhow, that certainly has nothing to do with you."

Lou glanced at the clock, which showed 1:55. "Those electric gadgets," he said, "they practically run the world, but no clock can run me." He opened his lips and let out a jet of fire straight at the clock, which promptly shattered. "There," he said comfortably. "That's out of the way, so let's call it one fifty-eight, so we can get on with our business. Ready with your second wish?"

"I've been thinking of nothing else all week. Lou, I want a meaningful relationship with a lovely woman. I want her to fall in love with me. I can't marry her yet, but I want to live with her as man and wife, in harmony and peace and—"

"Don't get corny. All you really want is a bedmate, and I knew it even before I came here. So—blonde or brunette?"

"Redheaded," Ira said, out of sheer contrariness.

"So be it," Lou said. "See you next week. Same time, same place."

Then the phone rang and Ira answered it, to be told that his two o'clock patient couldn't come today. When he put the phone down, Lucifer had disappeared.

A few minutes later the doorbell rang and Ira went out to the waiting room and to the front door. The woman standing there was small, slender, and blue-eyed. She had red hair that curled along the nape of her neck, and she glanced up timorously.

"Dr. Frost?" she said, and she stood there, tongue-tied and unable to conceal her adoration of him.

"I'm Dr. Frost," Ira said. "Come in, won't you?"

"Yes. And I hope you don't mind my coming here without an appointment. If you're too busy—"

"No, no—please. I just happened to get a cancellation."

"How lucky!" she said. "For me."

"For both of us," he said gallantly.

In the next few minutes he learned that her name was Sara Mowberry, that she was 31 years old and divorced, that she'd never really been in love and had never had a satisfying affair.

Once he had her vital statistics and had set up her file, he suggested that she lie down on the couch and tell him about herself. She obeyed self-consciously, as if she suspected he had an ulterior motive, but after she'd settled down, she began talking freely. Her words came in a torrent, as if she wanted Ira, and Ira alone, to know all about her—her problems as a child, the ache of growing up, the marriage she should never have embarked on.

"I want to tell you everything," she said. "Everything." And as she uttered the words she moved provocatively and Ira kept telling himself that fate had brought her here.

Fate? More likely the devil. And he interrupted her.

"Sara, did you ever meet Lou?"

She hesitated. "Lou who?"

"I don't know his last name. Lou something. Did he suggest that you come here?"

"Lou? No. Nobody by that name. It was somebody I met at a party—he spoke highly of you but I can't remember his name. It began with an A. Astor—Astoria—something like that."

"Asmodeus?"

"Maybe, I'm not sure. Why?"

"I do referral work, and I can't remember anybody just walking in, the way you did."

"I didn't just walk in. Somehow I had to. As if—"

"As if you were drawn by an invisible thread?"

Her laughter tinkled as she shook her head.

He got up, walked over to the couch, and sat down next to her. "Sara," he said, "I know a lot of people think that psychiatrists take advantage of their patients and make love to them, but I'm not like that. Not at all."

He gazed into her eyes, liquid and somehow drawing him. "I think I'm falling in love," he said.

"I *am* in love," she said.

They had dinner together that evening, and he spent the night in her apartment in the city. He saw her every night for the balance of the week, and on Saturday she came to the country with him.

"I love it here," she said. "I don't want to go back to the city. I want to garden and sit in the sun and breathe fresh air, and wait for you to come home every night. Do you mind?"

"Mind?" he said. "That's like asking a starving man if he'd like something to eat. But the only thing I'm concerned about is you. The neighbors know that my wife left me, and some of them, I'm sure, would disapprove of your living here with me."

Her bubbling laugh dismissed the problem as unimportant. "It doesn't matter," she said. "I love you and I don't care if it's legal or not, just so you love me and keep me near you."

"Forever," he said. And she gave him a peculiar look.

In his own mind he had decided what his third wish would be. Lou had promised him fifty years of life after the third wish had been granted, and Ira expected every year and every day of each year to be as perfect as this past week. Even if he believed in this ridiculous fantasy of Lucifer, even if he believed he had a soul and had sold it, the bargain would be well worth it.

Fifty years, Ira thought, and he smiled.

At breakfast on Tuesday morning he gave Sara a fond glance. "Do you realize," he said, "that it's exactly one week since we met?"

"A hundred and sixty-two hours," she said. "Ira, I can hardly believe it!"

"I called off my afternoon appointments," he said. "I thought we'd go somewhere and celebrate."

"Oh, Ira, what a wonderful idea! I'll garden this morning, and then I'll come to the city and meet you at your office. At what time?"

"A little after two," he said. "No earlier. I have a rather unusual patient who stays until two, and he doesn't like to be seen in the office. You know how some people are."

"I understand," she said, and she got up, circled the table, and kissed him gently on the forehead. "Ira!" she murmured.

After lunch later that day he was sitting at his desk when Lou appeared. This time he seemed to walk through the wall. In fact, it seemed to Ira that Lou strutted, as if to show off his tricks.

"Doors—walls—windows," Lou remarked. "All the same to me. Except that I don't like heights. Some of the people I have to see live on the fortieth floor or so, and while I'm not actually afraid of falling—I did that once, and from much higher than the fortieth floor—still, I'm never quite comfortable high up."

"Acrophobia," Ira said. "I get it, too, and why not? Because if I fell, it would be all over, whereas you probably wouldn't even get bruised."

"You'd be surprised," Lou said. He glanced at the ruins

89

of the clock. "I meant to ask you—did I short-circuit the building last week?"

"Not that I know of."

"Good. I don't like to create minor inconveniences. I leave that to elves and gnomes and poltergeists. But since we still have a minute or two, tell me how things are going."

"Wonderfully. Sara is perfect, she's almost too good to be believed."

"You can believe in her all right. No doubts there. She's as human as anybody."

"I found that out," Ira remarked. "But Lou, everything that's happened so far can be explained without giving you any credit. Margot left me because she had somebody else. Sara came here because she needed help."

"I told you the other day that I try to stay away from even the appearance of miracles. This is the age of science and technology, and I try to conform to contemporary mores. But now—your last wish."

"I suppose it's obvious," Ira said. "I want money. Plenty of it. I'm not greedy, and I've been thinking of how much I need, and I want one hundred thousand a year. Figuring a five percent return that comes to two million. No more and no less, but remember—tax-free."

"Trust me," Lou said, sighing. "But you might give me a little help. Have you ever, for instance, invested in a gold mine and were told that it had petered out? Or bought some bonds of a Latin American country for a few cents each, and then forgotten all about it? Things like that can suddenly be worth a fortune, and your tax is only on a capital-gains basis."

"I have never made any speculative investments," Ira said. "I'm much too conservative."

"I should have realized that, but the truth is that I read

your dossier several weeks ago, and not too carefully. After all, when you're a few thousand years old, your memory isn't what it used to be."

"It's hard to realize you're a few thousand years old," Ira said. "You certainly don't look it."

"Of course not. I lead a healthy life and go in for none of your food fads. No TV dinners for me, no *haute cuisine*. And in the old days I never attended any of those Roman banquets. Just plain simple food, and only the best."

"You *eat?*"

"Not for nourishment, just for the pleasure. Tell me, did you ever taste a morel mushroom?"

"Morel? What's that?"

"Skip it. I had you mixed up with somebody else. But I'm afraid I have to go now."

"In the usual way?" Ira asked.

Lou nodded and backed toward the wall. "I'll say goodbye for the present," he remarked. "It's been nice knowing you, and I don't mind telling you that our relationship has been exceedingly pleasant. You're so easy to handle."

"Me?" Ira said. But he was speaking to a blank wall.

He kept staring at the wall until the phone rang. He picked it up and said, "Hello?"

Sara spoke up. "Ira, it's me. I'm still home, and I developed the most splitting headache. I get them sometimes. I'm so sorry, I wanted us to have the afternoon together."

"I'm sorry on your account," he said. "Is there anything I can do?"

"No, nothing. I get these migraines occasionally, and I just have to go to bed and wait them out. Please forgive me."

"Feel better," he said. "That's all I want."

91

After he'd put the phone down, he tapped his fingers on the desk and wondered if he'd made a mistake in not asking Lou for a woman who was never sick. He'd covered himself on his own health without even using an extra wish, but he'd forgotten to include Sara.

Ira straightened up in his chair. Ridiculous. There was no devil and no Lou. Everything that had happened thus far was perfectly natural. Margot had been having an affair—Ira had known that for a long time. Sara had walked into his office just when he, and she, needed each other. It was as simple as that, and nothing was magical and nothing would be, unless money somehow materialized in his pocket.

Which was impossible. He'd get his money in a normal way. Or maybe he'd get none, and then he'd be back face to face with normal, prosaic events.

With a long afternoon ahead of him he decided to do some of the work he'd been neglecting during this past week. But first, he went to the door to pick up his afternoon mail.

The long envelope with the return address—Evans, Bromfield & Evans, Attorneys at Law—attracted him immediately and he slit it open. The letter informed him that a former patient of his, a Mrs. Brandon, had died and left the bulk of her estate to him. According to the attorneys the amount was substantial—at least $2,000,000.

Marveling, open-mouthed, Ira reread the letter. He remembered Mrs. Brandon as an eccentric whom he'd treated a couple of years ago. Her cure had been complete.

Lou?

Ira found it hard to contain his excitement. Three wishes, and now he had all that a man could possibly desire: a woman who loved him, plenty of money and no encumbrances, and a guarantee of fifty years of life ahead of him. He felt creative, at the peak of his powers, and a multitude of ideas and projects raced through his mind. He saw for the first time precisely what was wrong with that book of his and what he could do to make it marketable.

Marketable? That was the understatement of the year. He'd have himself a best-seller, he was on the road to fame, he'd be at the top of his profession. And he'd make his recent experiences the basis of articles for the psychiatric journals. His mind raced and he jotted down phrases and notes, and at the end of an hour he had the entire project outlined.

He stood up then. He experienced a freshness of spirit and a mental clarity that were extraordinary. He decided he ought to be with Sara, that something of his buoyant energy might transfer itself to her. Migraines? Maybe he could find out precisely why she got them and effect a cure.

It was midafternoon when he reached his house, unlocked the door, and walked in.

"Sara?" he called.

A man's voice answered him. "She's not here, Doctor."

Ira stared into the dimness of the hallway and saw two men in police uniforms. "What happened?" he asked anxiously. "What's wrong?"

"Would you mind stepping out to the garden with us?" one of the cops said.

Ira moved forward. His throat was dry and his lips felt parched. "I don't understand. What do you want?"

"If you'll be good enough," the officer said. He took Ira by the arm and edged him outside. There, close to the garden wall, Ira gazed down at the partly excavated body of his wife, Margot.

He shuddered violently. "I had nothing to do with

this!" he exclaimed. "I don't know who killed her. She went away and left me a note, it's upstairs, I can show it to you."

"We have it," the cop said drily. "Forged signature and all."

Ira gasped, and from somewhere behind him he seemed to hear the rumbling sound of satanic laughter, and he shivered. Then for the first time he looked at the face of the cop who was arresting him.

It was Lou's.

The original notion for this story grew out of a reluctant visit to the Museum of Modern Art and struck me as a fresh variation for the fictional lawyer Scott Jordan who has supported me most of my adult life. A monumental ignorance about the Impressionists compelled some research which helped to enrich a very limited sense of art appreciation—for which I am grateful. Beyond that, the finished product so intrigued me that I expanded it into a full-length novel which was recently published and well-received in England. What author does not enjoy the additional exploitation of a single idea?

—HAROLD Q. MASUR

FRAMED FOR MURDER

HAROLD Q. MASUR

A 49-cent ballpoint pen saved my life. Literally. It still writes, but I do not use it. I keep it as a talisman, a reminder to count my blessings in times of adversity.

The pen was in my attaché case when a taxi deposited me in front of the Gotham Trust late Monday morning. Carl Steiner arrived on foot at the same time. "Counselor," he greeted me. "Prompt as usual."

"Hello, Carl."

Steiner represented the sovereign State of New York through its Department of Taxation and Finance. We shook hands, entered the bank, and marched past the tellers' windows toward the desk of branch manager Walter Knox. With his usual air of Olympian detachment, Knox was explaining something to a woman. She turned suddenly, her face shocked; she blinked in recognition and came stumbling toward me.

"My God!" she whispered. "He's dead, Mr. Jordan. The man says Victor is dead."

"Yes, Angela. He died Friday evening. Hadn't you heard?"

She shook her head. "I was out of town, drove back last night. How did it happen?"

"Coronary occlusion. During dinner, at his hotel in

Chicago. There was nothing they could do. He was gone when the ambulance arrived."

She looked stunned, marooned in a private world of grief or despair. Angela Lowe was Victor Rosemont's assistant at the Rosemont Gallery. And according to Rosemont's estranged wife she was something more than an assistant.

"What brought you to the bank?" I asked.

"I'm here at Victor's request. He needed some papers in Chicago. I have a power of attorney for the safe-deposit box and I was supposed to fly them out to him this afternoon. But now the man says Victor's box is sealed."

"What kind of papers?"

"He found a customer for the Picasso and wanted to show him the authenticating documents."

"When did he call you?"

"He didn't. He couldn't reach me. So he called his wife and told her it was urgent and asked her to give me the message. When she finally got through to me on Friday, it was after 3:00 o'clock and too late for the bank. So I phoned Victor and told him I would do it today, Monday. Now Mr. Knox won't let anyone open the box without a court order."

"Customary procedure, Angela. Look, go back to the gallery and hold the fort. I'll stop by later."

Her steps were slow and tentative—she was a forlorn figure. I opened my attaché case and handed a paper to Walter Knox. It was an order from the Surrogate directing the Gotham Trust to open the box of Victor Rosemont, deceased, for the purpose of removing his Last Will and Testament and filing it for probate.

As Rosemont's lawyer I had drawn his will and knew that he had named me as executor. The drill was a familiar one. Strict compliance with all rules was mandatory.

That's why Carl Steiner was present. When a man dies, New York wants its full share of estate taxes. To make sure nobody secretly disposes of any property, they send a representative to itemize all the box's contents when it is first opened. A bank official also attends and he is charged with delivering the will safely to court.

Knox cast his jaundiced eye over the order, found it satisfactory, and led the way down a flight of marble stairs to the vault area. He spoke briefly to the man behind the steel bars. Keys changed hands. The attendant produced a large metal box, convoyed us to a small conference room, and discreetly withdrew.

We sat. Steiner got out paper and pencil and smiled in anticipation. My attaché case yielded a legal pad and the ballpoint pen, so I could make my own list as Steiner announced the contents.

Knox slid the box to me and as I passed it across to Steiner, my ballpoint rolled to the floor. I had to duck under the table to retrieve it, hearing Steiner say jovially, "All right, gentlemen, let's see what we have here."

They were the last words he ever spoke.

The world blew apart. There was a blinding flash, an ear-shattering concussion. I felt as if an elephant had stepped on my back. Wood splintered, plaster fell, acrid smoke choked the air. And then a deep dead silence.

I stumbled to my feet, dazed, coughing. The room was a shambles. A jagged hole gaped open on the corridor. The door hung askew on a single hinge. I saw Carl Steiner and turned away. Sitting over the booby-trapped box, he had caught the full brunt. Walter Knox lay hunched in the debris, comatose and bleeding.

Faces materialized in the corridor. The vault attendant, a retired cop, picked his way through the wreckage and got me out of there. "Knox may still be alive," I mumbled. "Somebody call an ambulance."

A diligent young resident at Manhattan General did a quick workup and found me sound. He put four stitches in my cheek and said I was lucky. He suggested 24 hours of bed rest. Detective Lieutenant John Nola, waiting outside the Emergency Room, offered me a lift.

In the police car he told me that Carl Steiner was dead and that Walter Knox was in surgery, his condition critical. Of the three men in the bank's conference room I was the only one presently capable of speech and Nola wanted my version.

Nola was an old friend, precise and incorruptible, so I dealt off the top. I told him about Victor Rosemont's fatal heart attack in Chicago, about Rosemont's will and my appointment at the bank with Carl Steiner of the Estate Tax Section. How somebody must have planted a bomb in Rosemont's safe-deposit box. And about Angela Lowe's narrow escape when she failed to gain access earlier that morning. I painted a brief profile of Rosemont, a prominent art dealer operating out of a highly prestigious gallery on Madison Avenue.

"The Lowe woman," Nola said, "what was she looking for?"

"Certain papers Rosemont needed. He was in Chicago on business and as usual he carried transparencies of various paintings. One of them was a Picasso and apparently he'd interested a prospective customer. But of course he could not complete a sale of any important canvas without the provenance."

"Without the what?"

"Provenance—documents detailing the origin and background of a painting to establish its authenticity. Collectors seldom pay large sums of money without proof that the work is genuine. He wanted Miss Lowe to get those documents from his safe-deposit box and fly them out to Chicago. When he failed to reach her, he called his wife and asked her to relay the message."

"Hold it, Counselor. You just told me that Rosemont and his wife were separated."

"Temporarily. Margot Rosemont is a very possessive and jealous woman. She suspected her husband of some extracurricular activity with Miss Lowe. She wanted the woman booted out of the gallery. He refused and she left him. This is the third time. But she always came back."

"Any basis for her suspicions?"

"Probably. Angela Lowe is a very attractive dish and Rosemont was an incurable chaser. Margot knew that angle of his personality—she used to be his assistant at the gallery herself, before they were married. Anyway, they stayed in touch, even though she'd walked out. And since it was inconvenient to keep making long-distance calls, Rosemont got through to Margot, and she reached Miss Lowe last Friday, too late for the bank. So Angela went there this morning to follow instructions. She'd been out of town and did not know that Rosemont was dead."

"And she had a power of attorney for his safe-deposit box?"

"Yes. Because Rosemont traveled extensively, searching for art treasures, Angela remained here, in charge of the gallery. In case of a sale the provenance had to be available. And those papers were too valuable to be lying around loose."

"The wife also had a power of attorney?"

"Probably."

Nola reflected thoughtfully for a moment. "So we have

a very jealous wife, with access, who calls her husband's mistress, with access, and directs her to open a box that's been wired with lethal explosives."

"You're suggesting that Margot planted the bomb?"

"It's a possibility."

"I can't buy it, Lieutenant. Suppose Margot was unable to reach Miss Lowe. Suppose Rosemont flew back and went to the box himself."

"You drew his will. Who's his chief legatee?"

"His wife."

"So he opens the box and goodbye husband. They're only separated. She inherits his money, his gallery, his paintings, the works. Either way, she can't lose."

Cynicism. An occupational hazard. Even so, I pondered the notion. If Rosemont had not suffered a fatal heart attack, if the box had not been sealed, Angela Lowe instead of Carl Steiner would now be lying in the morgue, with nobody available to testify that Margot had phoned and prompted Angela's visit to the bank.

I shook my head. "The bomb was in Rosemont's box. I think he was the primary target."

"Who else had access?"

"Me."

"How come?"

"Rosemont gave me a power of attorney six months ago when both he and Miss Lowe flew off to Japan. The art market there is wide open."

"You having any problems with Rosemont?"

"That's a dry hole, Lieutenant. Don't waste time drilling it."

"Well, now, Counselor, let's give it a thought. Three men are in a small conference room at the bank. A bomb explodes. One man is killed, one is critically wounded, and the third walks away alive and kicking. He just happens to the under a heavy table at precisely the right moment."

"I thought you were my friend."

"A policeman investigating homicide has no friends."

"But I haven't been near Rosemont's safe-deposit box in over five months. You can check the vault records."

"I already have. It's a bum system. You sign a slip, the attendant matches signatures, then discards the form. No records. They say they don't want to bury themselves in paper." He looked at me. "I'm going to visit the widow now. I want you to come along."

Margot Rosemont admitted us to her temporary quarters at the Sutton Towers. She had style and presence and a deceptive look of vulnerability. Her husband's body had been flown back from Chicago on Saturday and buried on Sunday. We had agreed that I should proceed at once to probate his will so that business affairs could be carried on without delay.

"Scott!" she exclaimed. "What happened to your face?"

She gaped in dismay when I told her about the explosion, adding, "This is Lieutenant John Nola, in charge of the investigation."

Nola said, "Jordan believes the bomb must have been intended for your husband. Did he have any enemies?"

Her fingers were a bowknot of distress at her throat. "All successful businessmen have enemies. But I don't see how any of them could have got into his safe-deposit box to plant the bomb."

"Well, a number of people had access, Mrs. Rosemont. You. Miss Lowe. The counselor here."

"Please, Lieutenant. I was not one of Victor's enemies."

"You left his room and board. There must have been some friction."

She smiled minimally. "Show me a married couple who do not have friction. Oh, yes, we fought, we separated, but always there was a reconciliation. As a matter of fact, he phoned me Friday afternoon before he died."

"We know. He wanted you to contact Miss Lowe and direct her to remove some papers from his vault."

"Yes. He couldn't reach her. She was not at the gallery."

"I take it you are not charmed by Miss Lowe."

"I detest her."

"Is it your impression that she was trying to steal your husband?"

"If she could, yes."

"And you would have done anything to prevent that?"

"Within reason."

"If she had followed your instructions and opened his safe-deposit box, any relationship between them would have been effectively terminated."

"She was lucky, wasn't she?"

"Two other people were not so lucky. Do you have any proof that your husband actually phoned you on Friday?"

Her eyes opened wide. "Do you doubt my word?"

"Skepticism is a tool of my trade."

"And a very unbecoming one. Of course I have no proof. I did not record his call on tape, if that's what you need."

"Then we have only your word."

She studied him in a wintry silence. "Lieutenant, I have just been through several very difficult days. I'm really not prepared to cope with such innuendoes at this time."

"A suggestion," I said. "The switchboard operator at Rosemont's hotel in Chicago should have a record of any long-distance calls he made. It's easy enough to check."

Nola walked over to her telephone and made a note of the number. He would check it from his office later.

Margot turned to me. "You told me that under the circumstances the court will probably accept your copy of Victor's will. And if they don't, I'll inherit the estate anyway, as his widow. Isn't that true?"

"It is."

"Then the gallery is mine. I want that woman off the premises. I want Miss Lowe fired. Today. This afternoon."

I shook my head. "Not so fast. As Victor's executor, I need her on the job. She's familiar with all current and pending deals. When the estate is settled, do as you wish."

She thought about it and shrugged. "All right. But it seems wasteful to pay rent for two apartments. Is there any reason I can't move back into our own place?"

Nola had no objection and neither did I.

"Then I'll do it tomorrow," she said.

Outside, Nola and I parted. He was anxious to question the Bomb Squad. Sifting through the rubble, they might have found a clue he could work on. I headed west toward Madison Avenue.

The Rosemont Gallery was an elegantly appointed showplace, with an air of high-priced exclusivity. Victor's specialty had been the Impressionists and Post-Impressionists: Monet, Cézanne, Gauguin, Degas, and all the rest of that brilliantly innovative crew. He had been a surpassing salesman, a man with an imperious presence who spoke in sonorous Shakespearean cadences that both charmed and intimidated important collectors. Dealers fortunate enough to acquire one of the modern masters had willingly split their commissions with Rosemont, knowing that his ability and his connections would invariably command astronomical prices.

Angela Lowe was supervising a rumpled, gnomish figure in the arrangement of new pictures. She came over to me. When I explained the bandage on my face, she blanched, her eyes huge.

"Mr. Knox is critically injured," I said, "and Steiner, the tax man, is dead."

"It—it could have been me," she whispered.

"Yes. We were both lucky."

She closed her eyes. "Who could have done such a thing?"

"I don't know. But we have to carry on."

"Yes. There's so much to do. We're opening a new Klaus Helman exhibit this week. Klaus," she called, "come here for a moment and meet Mr. Rosemont's lawyer. This is Scott Jordan."

He had a sallow face and paint-stained fingers. "My second show in twenty years," he told me. "Sold one small canvas that time. Forty dollars. Mr. Rosemont was a genius, a man who could recognize talent. The only dealer in this whole crazy business willing to gamble on me. Only names they want. Famous names." He leveled a scornful look. "Because it's a good investment, not because it's beautiful. Imbeciles. Excuse me, please. I have much to do."

Angela watched him for a moment. "Victor had been planning this exhibit for a long time. He pulled strings. He wanted the major critics to see Helman's work. We sent out notices weeks ago. I know he'd want us to open on schedule."

I surveyed the man's work. A landscape, a still life, a figure study, water colors, oils, gouaches, all extravagantly colored and skillfully rendered, but to my eye somehow derivative, reminiscent of the Fauves, those so-called wild beasts of the famous Paris exhibition in the Salon d'Automne around the turn of the century.

Angela and I went back to Rosemont's private office.

She seemed preoccupied, unable to concentrate, burdened by the responsibility of managing the gallery on her own, and shaken by her narrow escape from the bomb in Rosemont's safe-deposit box.

"Such a strange way to commit a murder," she said.

I nodded. "Someone wanted to eliminate Victor. So even without that heart attack his days were numbered."

Understandably she was concerned about her job, anticipating her dismissal when Margot took over. I did not disabuse her. There was a knock on the door; it was Klaus Helman asking for her advice on the placement of a canvas.

Alone, I sat back, wondering if the gallery could survive without Rosemont's expertise. It had been so essentially a one-man operation. The phone rang and I answered it. A high-pitched excited voice assaulted my eardrum.

"Mr. Losemont, you are a cluhk. I speak to my royer. He say you must give back the money or go to plisson."

"Who is this?" I asked.

"You know me too damn well. Sama Kosuri. Kosuri Electronics, Osaka, Japan. I come now for a check, yes? I give you back your no-good Vraminck, yes?"

"Mr. Kosuri, what seems to be the problem?"

"Plobrem is fake Vraminck. Give back money and my royer don't sue. But soon. Day after tomollow I fry back to Osaka."

"There seems to be some misunderstanding. You are not talking to Mr. Rosemont. My name is—"

"No more tlicks." His voice scaled a full octave. "Hundled and twenty thousand dollah too much money for fake."

Angela opened the door, saying, "Did I hear the phone?"

"A Mr. Sama Kosuri," I said, offering the handset.

She took it, pronounced her name and listened, lips compressed. "Now, Mr. Kosuri," she said in a conciliating tone. "I don't think that would be wise. In twenty years no one has ever impugned the integrity or the reputation of this gallery. We allowed you to take that Vlaminck and to have it examined by experts at both the Metropolitan and the Muesum of Modern Art, establishments of such international eminence that nobody would presume to question their judgment or their probity. They inspected the provenance and the painting and vouched for its authenticity. Are you now charging *them* with fraud? Of collusion with us? That would be foolhardy, Mr. Kosuri. Your so-called expert is mistaken. And for your information I might add that Mr. Rosemont is no longer with us. He died several days ago."

He hung up on her. She gestured helplessly. "These Japanese! They're so bright. They make such marvelous products and we've bought so many television sets and cameras and motorcycles from them they seem to have more dollars than they can handle. So they've been investing in art, mostly the Impressionists.

"About a month ago Mr. Kosuri walked into the gallery. We had a perfectly splendid Vlaminck, a major work, priced at one hundred and twenty thousand dollars. Mr. Kosuri fell in love with it, but Victor insisted that he have it authenticated. When Kosuri was satisfied, he brought us a certified check for the full amount. He thought the frame was all wrong, so after Victor had another one made he personally delivered the painting to Mr. Kosuri's suite at the Hilton."

She made a face. "Now the man wants his money back. He's found some buffoon who claims the Vlaminck is a forgery. Which is absurd. The Met itself would have bought the painting if they hadn't been short of cash."

I sighed. I had more than enough to handle without the added headache of a potential lawsuit for fraud, whatever its merits. A lawsuit could tie up the estate for months.

"Are you positive the Vlaminck is genuine?"

"Absolutely."

"Do you have copies of the original provenance?"

"Of course. Every important document is Xeroxed in triplicate."

"Let me have a set."

I borrowed an envelope because my attaché case had been shredded in the explosion. The only part of me that did not seem to ache at the moment were my sideburns. Nevertheless, I went back to my office. I found a stack of messages and a reporter from the *News*, eager for information. I referred him to Lieutenant Nola. One of the messages surprised me. Phone Mr. Stanley Kemper on a matter of considerable urgency.

Kemper is a fussy and humorless lawyer, a nitpicker, a corrosive misanthrope. I filed the message in my wastebasket and twenty minutes later his strident voice was on the line.

"Jordan? I understand you're the attorney for Victor Rosemont's estate."

"Correct."

"Rosemont was a crook."

"You're slandering a dead man, Kemper."

"With justification. He defrauded one of my clients. A Mr. Sama Kosuri. Sold him a fake painting, a forged Vlaminck."

"We deny the allegation."

"I have a sworn affidavit from a recognized expert."

"Tell him to see a good optometrist. And take another look at the provenance. What more does Kosuri want?"

"He wants his money. One hundred and twenty thousand dollars."

"I hope he knows how to whistle."

"We'll sue the estate."

"Your privilege, Kemper. That's what the courts are for."

He struggled for control. "Let's take the painting to any expert you name and see what he says."

Well, I thought, why not? Anything reasonable to avoid litigation. "Agreed," I told him. "Set up an appointment at MOMA and let me know." MOMA is not a lady. It is the acronym for the Museum of Modern Art.

He called back in half an hour saying that arrangements had been made for the following afternoon. I promised to be there. I knew that I would accomplish nothing constructive that afternoon. What I needed was rest, so I decided to take the doctor's advice and go home to bed.

A new day had dawned when the telephone awakened me. In my ear the widow Rosemont's voice sounded thin and tense. "Please come quickly," she said. "I'm in Victor's apartment."

Twenty minutes later I was at the entrance of a renovated town house with my finger on the bell. Margot Rosemont drew me in and pointed, her face white. Utter chaos. The place had been sacked and ransacked by vandals. And in the midst of all the carnage lay a rumpled figure. Alongside the ruined skull was a Giacometti bronze.

"Klaus Helman," I said. "You found him like this?"

"Yes."

"When?"

"Two minutes before I called you."

"Tell me about him, Margot."

"He's an artist, not very successful. I remember we tried to sell some of his work at the gallery, but no one seemed interested. He was always begging Victor to give him a one-man show."

"He'll have it posthumously," I told her. "It was being arranged yesterday."

She stared. "At the gallery? That's insane. There won't be a single customer."

"It was Victor's decision, not Angela Lowe's."

She seemed at a loss. "I don't understand. It was not Victor's style to indulge people. And anyway, who killed him? What was he doing here? Can't you have the body removed?"

"Not me. It's a job for the police. I want you to call them after I leave. Don't tell them I was here. And then make a full inventory. Did Victor keep any valuable artwork in the place?"

"Very little. The insurance was too high. Almost everything was at the gallery, protected by all sorts of alarms and devices."

"All right, Margot. I'll be in touch later. Can you take care of it?"

She nodded indecisively and watched me leave.

It was time to meet Stanley Kemper and I headed for the Museum of Modern Art. He was waiting in the lobby, Kosuri's Vlaminck wrapped in heavy kraft under his arm. We nodded but did not shake hands. The resident expert was J. Zachary Barnett, bearded and smugly assured; he told us to be seated and took the painting to another room. Time spent alone with Kemper is about as rewarding as watching deodorant commercials. I listened to a dozen semantic fandangos on the laws of consumer fraud.

At last the MOMA expert returned. He shook his head

sadly. "Gentlemen, you've been taken. This is not a Vlaminck. Vlaminck's style, yes. A genuine Vlaminck, no. It is definitely a fake, but a remarkably good one. What the forger did here is most interesting. He found some vintage canvas, probably in Paris. I would say that he mixed his own pigments and copied from the original. And then, apparently, he sprayed the finished work with a special restorer's varnish that helps to dry the oils more quickly and produces a craqueleur, as you can see here, these tiny veined cracks generally found in old paintings." Barnett shook his head in admiration. "I would truly like to meet this man. Behind bars, of course. He's a menace. God alone knows how many gullible dealers and collectors he must have duped. At a rough guess I would say this painting is worth at most maybe a hundred dollars."

"You see. You see." Kemper was jumping triumphantly. "What did I tell you? Rosemont was a crook."

I ignored him and said to Barnett, "Less than a month ago you people authenticated this very same Vlaminck."

"No, sir. We authenticated one that looked like it. Not this one."

"What are you going to do about it?" Kemper demanded.

I gave him a pitying look. "Your Mr. Kosuri is a lulu, Kemper. He digs up a fake, hides the genuine Vlaminck, and then demands a refund."

It brought him so close to apoplexy that I almost relented. Instead, I walked out of the room. He dogged my heels, yapping outside a telephone booth while I called my office and learned that Lieutenant Nola wanted to see me without delay. I lost sight of Kemper's rancorous face when a taxi carried me off.

At the precinct Lieutenant Nola sat behind his desk and regarded me for a long moment, his dark eyes speculative, his mouth tight. "Well, Counselor," he said finally, "we've got another one. A new corpse. Laid out in Rosemont's apartment. The widow found him. Little fella. Some kind of an artist. Klaus Helman. Know the name?"

"I met him once, briefly. What happened? Heart attack?"

"You could say that. Brought on by a cracked skull.

"When?"

"Some time last night. Mrs. Rosemont moved back this morning and there he was. Somebody had torn the place apart. She was in no condition to talk. And, incidentally, there is no record of any call from Rosemont's hotel room in Chicago to his wife. Was this Helman a good painter?"

"I'm not an art critic, Lieutenant."

"We checked his studio. Very unusual. Three locks on the outside, a police lock on the inside. And a strange cache of artwork."

"Strange how?"

"One of my lab men, this new breed, college fella, he's an art buff. Said it looked as if someone had looted the Louvre." Nola consulted his notes. "Pictures that looked like Matisse, Gauguin, Degas, Cézanne. And hidden away in a closet we found a steel box with papers, some of them made out to the Rosemont Gallery—records of sale, certificates, affidavits. What was that word you used?"

"Provenance."

"Yeah. A lot of them. So we have to run a check on this Helman."

My mind was racing. "By all means," I said.

A small card in the window cordially invited the public to view the work of Klaus Helman starting on Saturday the 19th. But Angela Lowe was not especially sanguine about sales. She looked harried. "Klaus didn't come in today. Nothing has been hung in the back room yet and I can't seem to reach him at his studio. Usually he's very dependable."

"Helman won't be in at all," I told her. "He's dead."

Sudden distress flashed across her face. "Oh, no," she moaned. "I can't take much more of this. First Victor and now Klaus. What happened?"

She listened and then fled to the office. Nola shrugged. We gave her a couple of minutes to compose herself. She was sitting behind Rosemont's desk, staring into space.

"Angela," I said quietly, "we need your help."

She swallowed and nodded.

"How long have you known?" I asked.

"How long have I know what?"

"That Klaus Helman was an expert art forger. That he'd been counterfeiting the Impressionists for some time. That he knew every trick in the book. That he connived with Victor to supply the gallery with spurious works of art. That somehow Victor had lost his moral compass and exploited his reputation to deceive and defraud his customers. Did you know from the beginning?"

After a long moment she found her voice. "I never really knew for certain, Mr. Jordan. But recently I began to suspect that something seemed out of focus. And then after Mr. Kosuri complained about his Vlaminck, it began to explain a number of strange incidents."

"Such as?"

"Giving Helman a one-man show when he knew it was doomed from the start, just to keep Klaus happy."

"Do you have any idea how many forgeries may have been sold?"

She gestured helplessly. "It's a mess, Mr. Jordan. Victor had customers all over the world. Two months ago he sold a Degas pastel to a West German banker. And before that a Renoir water color to one of the oil sheiks from Kuwait. He sometimes accepted cash and the transactions never appeared on our books."

"So Victor must have salted away quite a bit of money."

"I suppose."

"And you, Angela? How about you? Have you put away a lot of money?"

She blinked at me. "I beg your pardon."

"Money, Angela. True, at first you only suspected a conspiracy between Victor and Helman. And then, somehow, you stumbled onto hard evidence. And you began to shake him down. Because you realized that he would never divorce Margot to marry you, so you demanded a piece of the action. Security for your future."

Her face was stiff with restraint. "You're insane. That's absolute nonsense."

"Ah, Angela, such righteous indignation! And such brash conduct. You should have known that Victor would never hold still for blackmail. He'd know that it never ends, that no matter how much he shelled out you might still blow the whistle on him someday. He really had only one solution. Nullify the danger by eliminating you. And since he was a devious man he cooked up an elaborate scheme.

"It was Victor himself who put the bomb in his safe-deposit box. The implication, of course, would be that someone had tried to kill him. But it was really meant for you, Angela. He called his wife from Chicago and asked her to instruct you to open his box. But he used a pay phone booth so there would be no record of the call. And if his wife talked, he would deny phoning her. Margot had access to the box. It was common knowledge that she blamed you for her separation. Which would make her a prime suspect. She might even be tried and convicted. To Rosemont everyone was expendable."

"What tipped you?" Nola demanded.

"Your discovery that Rosemont's authentication papers were hidden in Helman's studio. Victor was a greedy man. Those documents were too valuable. He would not allow them to be destroyed in the explosion. So he removed them from the safe-deposit box. He had no reason to do that if he hadn't arranged the booby-trap himself."

"He trusted Helman?"

"Sure. They were partners in the conspiracy. They needed each other."

"Why was Helman killed?"

"Because he had forged a Vlaminck, copying an original that had already been authenticated and sold. Rosemont substituted the forgery for the genuine painting while he was arranging for a new frame. Then Rosemont suffered a heart attack. Helman knew that the real Vlamnick was probably hidden in Rosemont's apartment and decided to retrieve it for himself. It was, after all, worth a lot of money.

"But someone else had the same idea. Our friend Angela. She guessed what had happened when the buyer of the Vlaminck complained. And as a special friend of the boss, she had a key to Rosemont's apartment. She probably got there before Helman and took cover when she heard him at the door. Then she sneaked up from behind and brained him."

She appealed to Nola. "Make him stop. He doesn't know what he's talking about."

I said, "What about those fingerprints you found on the Giacometti, Lieutenant?"

"Listen," she said frantically. "I rearranged that statue on Victor's mantel many times."

"Yes, but will you be able to convince a jury?" I asked. "Or explain how you managed to get possession of the Vlaminck? The police know how to search, Angela.

They'll take your place apart. And they'll find the painting. They'll find witnesses who must have seen you in the neighborhood. They'll find unexplained sums of money you extorted from Victor."

She seemed to shrink before our eyes, suddenly ill. Nola took a slip of paper from his pocket and began to read the lady her rights. Then he turned to me. "I'm curious, Counselor. You had no idea what kind of rank specimen you were representing in this Rosemont?"

I looked at him, aggrieved. "If I had known, would I have accepted the fee he paid me last year? For twelve months of legal services. Claimed he was short of cash and offered me a small Modigliani nude. Which I grabbed before he could change his mind." I shook my head in disgust. "Probably something Helman knocked out one morning before breakfast. Worth maybe fourteen dollars. Why, the damn frame cost me more than that."

As an ardent champion of women's rights, I strongly believe that women are entitled to equal consideration in the annals of crime.

No fair-minded person can claim that lethal ladies like Lucrezia Borgia, Countess Bathory or Lady Macbeth are any less monstrous than their spouses. Indeed, a strong case can be argued for Rudyard Kipling's statement that the female of the species is more deadly than the male.

Males, in fact, are often far more vulnerable—as the mate of any praying mantis or black widow spider can attest, if he lives to tell the tale.

My own tale, which follows, is a personal favorite. Read it and cherchez la femme!

—ROBERT BLOCH

THE MAN WHO KNEW WOMEN

ROBERT BLOCH

Before he left his motel room, Luis Manuel took a good look in the mirror. He wanted to make sure that Lou Manning was there.

His reflection reassured him. Lou Manning was very much present.

Actually, Luis Manuel was allergic to mirrors. He didn't like the sight of himself—a little, balding, swarthy man with a greying mustache and ill-fitting false teeth made by a prison dentist.

But Lou Manning was something to look at. He was at least two inches taller than Luis, thanks to the elevator shoes. The cheap choppers had long since been replaced by gleaming platework, and the bald forehead completely concealed with a curly brown hairpiece. A pair of scissors and a bit of dye transformed the straggly grey mustache into a black and virile symbol of masculinity.

Luis smiled and adjusted his silk tie. He admired his new tropical gabardine suit, his open-weave shirt, his over-size zircon ring. He didn't take pride in them for their own sake—it was the effect they created. The effect of Lou Manning. He was proud of the way Lou Manning looked, and proud of what Lou Manning could do.

In the past month, Lou Manning had done a lot. He had written all those letters to the Romance Club and carefully scanned the replies. He had selected Bessie Carmody as a likely prospect and given her a real snow job. To such good effect that before the month was up, he was out of the snow of Boston and down here in the warmth of Daytona Beach.

And the past week had seen even greater progress. Once he found out that Bessie Carmody really *was* a childless widow with an $8,000 bank-account, Lou Manning really went to work on her. The old bat (she was fifty-three, just a trifle older than Luis Manuel) was flattered at the attentions of dashing, debonair Lou. And she was tired of working as a clerk at one of the Boardwalk motels. The idea of marrying a wealthy promoter was irresistible.

Lou Manning shrugged at his image. He was a promoter, all right, but he wasn't wealthy—yet. That's why he was promoting; he could use that $8,000 in a hurry. He'd gambled his last few hundred dollars to come down here, invest in a new outfit, and pitch a little woo at fat, foolish Bessie Carmody.

Well, the gamble had paid off. Before the week was out the marriage would go through.

So Lou Manning had every reason to be proud of himself. He knew how to handle women. It was like being an actor, he often rationalized. That's what he really was; an actor who played the role of Lou Manning.

This was quite a rationalization, for most people would consider Lou Manning a bad actor, in the slang sense of the term. He didn't play his part for applause, and although he had had several captive audiences in the past, they all seemed to have disappeared.

But there was no need to worry about that now. Lou Manning picked up the corsage and the box of candy.

119

Another eight bucks shot—but what the hell, he was shooting for eight *thousand* bucks. It was a good investment. Bessie Carmody would be pleased with the corsage and her fat jowls would quiver over the candy.

And that's the way it worked out. When Lou left his shabby little motel and walked over to the lobby of the big $40-a-day establishment on the ocean side of the boardwalk, Bessie was waiting for him. She did coo over the corsage and she did quiver over the candy, and it was all Lou could do to keep from laughing as he watched the plump, overdressed, middle-aged widow simpering girlishly and fluttering her eyelashes.

He planned, now, to take her out for dinner and a few drinks. That would cost him another twelve bucks or so, but it would be money spent for a purpose. He'd soften her up, make a date to get the marriage license tomorrow, and discuss where to spend their honeymoon. Lou had it all planned.

But there was one thing he hadn't planned on. When he kissed her on the forehead and said, "Well, shall we go now?" Bessie shook her head.

"Just a minute, dear," she told him. "I've got company. He'll be down right away."

"*He?*"

"Oh, here he comes now."

And sure enough, this character came walking down the stairs—this little, thin, dried-up, baldheaded guy with the rimless glasses and the pasty white complexion. He was wearing a light gray suit and a loud purple shirt—a real creep outfit. Lou Manning didn't like his looks and he didn't like his actions. He went right up to Bessie, smiled, and kissed her on the mouth. Lou wanted to clobber him.

Instead, he waited for the introduction.

It came. Bessie simpered and said, "Dear, I have a surprise for you. This is my brother, Bert Jackson."

This was a surprise, all right. She'd never mentioned a brother before. And what in hell was he doing here?

Lou didn't have to ask the question, because Bert Jackson was already supplying the answer.

"Take five," he said, holding out his hand. It was cold and small and soft, like a dead sardine. But he pumped Lou's arm up and down, and his voice was loud and hearty. "The kid wrote me about you last week," he said. "Told me you were going to make an honest woman out of her, so I didn't bother to bring my shotgun. So I figured I'd lay off for a week and take a run down here to get acquainted. After all, she's the only family I've got."

"You're not married, eh?" Lou asked.

"No, but I'm all for it. Marriage is a great institution—no family should be without it." Bert Jackson uttered a barking laugh and dug Lou in the ribs. "That's an old Cantor gag," he said.

Bessie smiled indulgently at her brother. "Bert used to be in vaudeville years ago," she explained. "He was one of the best—"

"What do you mean, *used* to be?" Bert demanded. "I'm still working the same routine, only now they call it television. Of course, mainly I play club dates these days. My agent keeps me booked solid, and it's sure a lot better than the old five-a-day. Or even the two-a-day."

Bessie took her brother's arm. "I hope you didn't give up a good job just to run down here."

"You know I always head south at least once a year for a change and a rest," Bert Jackson said. He grinned at Lou. "The bellboys get the change and the bookies get the rest."

Lou kept the forced smile in place. This fink and his corny chatter—was he going to be hanging around now?

Apparently so, because Bessie was saying, "I thought Bert could join us tonight for dinner."

121

There was nothing else to do but go along with the gag; go along with the gagster. And that's the way it worked out. Lou had planned to eat at a Chinese place with a bar attached, and he took them there. But the rest of his plans—including lining up the trip to the license bureau tomorrow—went by the board. He had no chance to talk to Bessie alone. In fact, he scarcely got a chance to talk at all. Bert Jackson took over in that department.

A few drinks put him in a reminiscent mood. Bessie herself had never been in what Bert Jackson insisted on calling "show biz" but apparently she'd followed her brother's career, because he addressed himself mainly to her.

"Remember when I got my first big break on Orpheum time? Those were the days. Lou Holtz was doing a single in blackface; they were still imitating Tinney, you know. Only a few comics who didn't work that old heckling routine with the orchestra leader. Old Herb Williams used to sock the leader over the head with a baseball bat. He had another great sight gag—got himself a gimmick axe and hit the leader with that instead. But it backfired on him—looked too gruesome, see? So he had to cut it out."

Lou listened and wondered how it would be if he could hit Bert Jackson over the head with an axe. He wouldn't bother to use a fake one, either, if he had the chance. But all he could do was sit and smile.

"Of course, for my money, the real comics were the ones who didn't force the laugh. Bert Wheeler and the apple-eating bit, and old Raymond Hitchcock in his baggy street-clothes with the hair hanging down in his eyes. I'll bet Will Rogers copied that getup from him. I was on a bill with Will once in Scranton, when he was still doing the rope act. He tried to teach it to Fred Stone. There was an all-round trouper for you, that Stone! Reminds me of Joe

Cook, another guy who could do anything. Of course they all got into musical comedy or legit in the twenties. I was only a kid, and by the time things started breaking for me, vaude was on its last legs. Oh, we had good people working—Fred Sanborn and his xylophone, Fanny and Kitty Watson, old Johnny Burke and his rookie mono- logue, Senator Murphy, and even some of the flash acts like Kellerman and the Gus Edwards gang. But you could see the end coming—"

Lou wished he could see the end coming. But he had to sit there and be polite, nodding at the mention of names that meant nothing to him. What did he know about Cross and Dunn or Savoy and Brennan or Jones and Hare? And what did he care about Lowe, Hite and Stanley or Willie West and McGinty or Herman Timberg, Jr.?

The more he drank, the more the little man talked. And Lou found himself drinking just in order to keep going. There came a time when he was grateful for that. Because somehow the conversation had shifted from vaudeville and gotten around to Lou Manning—what he'd done in the old days, where he'd come from, what he did for a living now.

Only it wasn't a case of "somehow"; Lou suddenly realized that Bert Jackson had deliberately led up to this. Quite a clever little operator, this old-time vaudevillian! On the other hand, since when was a two-a-day ham any match for a professional actor? And Lou Manning consid- ered himself to be just that. Oh, he didn't give his per- formances on the legitimate stage—but in his own field, the illegitimate theatre, he was supreme. He knew how to build up a characterization, all right.

And he built one now. He parried all the questions Bert Jackson could throw at him. The drinks gave him confi- dence, and so did Bessie's plump hand resting on his wrist as he talked. He smiled at the little bald-headed brother and poured it on. He talked about his mining interests out west, and about his poor dead wife Florence, and about his hopes for the future.

The orphan from the Orpheum circuit ate it all up. How did he know that the closest Lou ever came to mining out west was a stretch on the rockpile, or that he never had a wife named Florence? There'd been one named Mae, and one named Ellen, and one named Dorinda, but never a Florence. And as to those hopes for the future—Lou carefully omitted all mention of the eight grand.

It worked out all right. Walking home after leaving brother and sister at their motel, Lou congratulated himself. Until he remembered that he hadn't managed to talk to Bessie in private or discuss their plans. Bert Jackson had seen to that. All he had was a vague promise to see her tomorrow, after work.

Lou figured he had to do something about it, so he called her the next morning and arranged for a private get-together. To his surprise, Bessie offered no objections. In fact, she didn't even mention her brother.

That came later. It came when they met in the evening and sat on a bench overlooking the boardwalk, watching the waves roll in. Lou had his arm around her and he was talking about the marriage license when he felt her stiffen. He knew enough about women to realize that something was wrong.

"What's the matter, honey?" he asked. "You aren't getting cold feet, are you?"

"No." Bessie stared out at the water. "It's just that— well, maybe we're rushing things a little."

"How can you say that? Only two days ago you were all set. You told me yourself how tired you were of living alone."

"I know. But I didn't have any choice, then."

"Don't tell me somebody else has come along to beat my time?"

Bessie giggled, but her heart wasn't in it. "Oh, nothing like that! It's just Bert."

"Bert? What about Bert?"

"Well—" She shifted uneasily, then faced him. "Bert says I should come and live with him. Says he's thinking of settling down in a place of his own, doing a little local TV work and maybe just playing the Borscht Circuit in summer. And he'd like me to keep house for him. It'll be just like being married, only—" Bessie hesitated, but Lou picked it right up.

"Only what?" he demanded.

"Nothing."

"Nothing, my eye!" Lou put his hand on her arm. "Bert doesn't want you to marry me, does he? I could tell that last night. He's got something against me."

Oh, no!" Bessie's denial was emphatic. "He was very honest about that, dear—he hasn't got a single, solitary thing against you. It's just that he feels we haven't known each other long enough. He has an idea you're sort of rushing me into this."

Lou laughed. "*I'm* rushing you into this? What about him? He hasn't seen you for years and all at once he pops up down here and within twenty-four hours he's trying to promote you for a free housekeeper." Lou hesitated, then decided to take the risk. "And I'll bet he even suggested you go in with him and help pay for the house."

From the expression on Bessie's fat face, Lou knew his hunch had paid off. He bored in. "Sure," he said. "It's the Big Brother act, isn't it? He wants to protect you. Hah!" Suddenly he made his voice soften. "Don't get me wrong, honey. I'm not trying to knock the guy. But the way he struck me, from seeing him last night, is that Bert's not the type who'll ever really settle down. He never got married, did he? He's used to moving around, spending his money as fast as he earns it, and I'll bet he likes to take a little drink every now and then, too. I know these actors, honey—they're always out for a good time and a lot of laughs. But Bert isn't getting any younger, is he? And all of a sudden he realizes maybe it would be nice to have a home of his own and somebody to look after him."

"What's so wrong about that?" Bessie demanded.

"Nothing. For Bert, it's perfect. But he's thinking about himself. And I'm thinking about you."

Lou's voice got even softer as he slid his arm around Bessie's waist. "You want your own home, don't you?" he said. "The kind of home you used to have, when Clarence was still alive. Remember, how you told me about it? How nice it was to know that there was somebody to be with you, every night, somebody to love? You're still a young woman, Bessie. You don't need a brother—you need a husband."

It made Lou sick to have to talk this way; almost as sick as it did to put his arm around the old bag. But this was the kind of pitch that paid off. He kept on for quite a while, until Bessie started sobbing.

"You—you *do* love me, don't you, darling?" she wheezed. "I mean, it isn't just an act of some kind?"

"How can you even imagine such a thing?" Lou whispered. "No—don't answer me. You couldn't imagine it, I know. It would take Bert to think of an idea like that. Tell me the truth, now, Bessie. What other ideas has he been putting in your head?"

Bessie sobbed a little louder. She could scarcely get the words out. "He said he thought you were a—a phoney. And he said—" The words came in a rushing gurgle. "He said that you wore a *toupee*."

It sounded so damned funny Lou could scarcely choke back the laugh. On the other hand, it was damned serious, too. Women had the screwiest ideas sometimes. Lou debated his reply for a moment.

"All right," he said. "Your brother is a pretty shrewd observer. I *do* wear a *toupee*. But that's nothing to be ashamed of, is it? Is it?"

"N-no."

"But that's as far as it goes, dear. I'm not going to try and defend myself against Bert's suspicions. I don't think I have to. My actions speak for themselves. Have I ever done anything to make you think I'm a phoney, as he puts it? Have I ever stepped out of line in any way? Answer me, Bessie—have I?"

"Of course not."

"All I've ever done is make you an honorable offer of marriage. Because I love you, and I want to take care of you. I don't want to see you slaving away in a motel, or spending the rest of your life keeping house for your selfish brother. You deserve a *real* home; a nice place out on the West Coast, maybe, with one of those Japanese maids. Of course, we'll probably want to do a lot of traveling—Mexico, Hawaii, places like that—"

Lou poured it on now, and she took it all in; she wanted to take it all in. She didn't care about the lousy toupee any more. He could have told her he had a wooden leg and a truss and she'd still buy the deal. So he put the deal to her now.

"No sense starting any family argument," he said. "I don't want to see you quarreling with your brother. And that's just the way it's going to be, if you go back and tell him what I said. Nothing's liable to make him change his mind. He'll have to see for himself that things are different. We'll just write him a postcard from Miami Beach."

"Miami Beach?"

"Sure. Isn't that a nice place for a honeymoon?" Lou squeezed her close. "I had the plans all made before Bert showed up—even wired for reservations. I figured we'd get married Saturday and take off right away. Spend a couple of weeks just lying around in the sun—maybe fly over to Havana for a while, if you like." He squeezed harder. "But now I've got an even better idea. You and I aren't going to get married here at all. We're going to elope—tomorrow."

"Elope?"

"That's right, honey. You aren't going to go through any big scene with that brother of yours."

"But I'd have to give notice—there's a million and one things to do."

"Never mind. I want you to go back to your place and pack up now. We'll take the morning plane out." Lou smiled at her. "From now on, this is my show."

2

The rest was easy. There wasn't even any hitch about the money; Bessie was the one who suggested she go down and draw it out of the bank before they took off.

Lou stuck close to her all the way. Once she'd gotten out of the motel without her brother seeing her, his troubles were over.

The following afternoon they were in Miami. Bessie had a fresh corsage and Lou had the eight grand in a cashier's check nestling in his wallet. Right after they were married Bessie wanted him to open a joint account.

Lou knew his women, all right. He played it very straight. He never touched Bessie, never made a suggestion. They took their tests, waited, and went in the following week for a civil ceremony.

Apparently Bert Jackson hadn't been able to figure out their destination, because he never followed them. Lou took the precaution of registering under a phoney name, but just the same he sweated it out until the marriage was performed. He didn't want that wise little creep to stick his nose in and queer the pitch.

After the ring was on Bessie's finger he allowed her to send two wires. One went to the motel in Daytona and the other to her brother's regular address in Newark, just in case he'd returned home.

A few days later, he even allowed Bessie to sit down and write a long letter to Bert Jackson at the Newark address, telling him how happy she was and inviting him to pay them a visit when they got established in a place of their own.

Again Lou sweated, worrying about the off chance of having the guy suddenly show up to spoil the honeymoon. But he must have decided he was licked, because he didn't answer and he didn't appear.

So the honeymoon wasn't spoiled, after all.

It was nice to put up at a swanky joint, eat at the best places, and do the town at night. Of course, steering this old tub around was no picnic, but Lou knew how to handle her. He kept pouring drinks and it worked. Bessie wasn't used to liquor, but she got so she liked it. Lou tried to keep her stoned at night and he saw to it that she attracted attention when he dragged her back to the hotel. This all cost dough, but it was necessary. Every day was eating further into the eight grand, and yet he had to stall for time.

He waited until well into the second week before he sat down and sent off his own letter to Bert Jackson. It was a little masterpiece—it ought to be, because he rewrote it four times, one morning while Bessie slept off a hangover.

Let bygones be bygones, forgive and forget, we're all one family now—that sort of thing. And then, the plant, just a touch, about how Bessie was very happy but she had to take things a little easy on account of the old ticker.

That was enough for Bert, Lou figured. The next step was to spread the word around. Whenever Bessie slept late, he made a point of showing up in the lobby downstairs. He told the maids and Room Service not to disturb his wife, because she wasn't well.

Once, as a master-stroke, he even managed to give *her* the needle. During the course of a particularly bad hangover he convinced her that she should see the house physician.

He was a young squirt who didn't know his stethoscope from second base. All he did was examine her and give her a couple of pills. But his visit gave Lou a chance to take him aside privately and put on the old act.

"I don't know what to think, Doc," he said. "It scares me, sometimes. We're just married, you know—and I never realized that she—well—" He allowed his voice to trail off in embarrassment. "Don't you have some kind of pills that sort of take away the craving?"

The house physician gave him some advice on how to keep Bessie away from the sauce and even promised to come back again and talk to her about it when she felt better.

Lou thanked him, and then he went to work.

He got the digitalis at a drug store way out in the sticks. As a matter of fact, *he* didn't get it; Luis Manuel got it. Luis Manuel, the baldheaded little guy, wearing big horn-rims and driving a rented car.

But it was Lou Manning who arranged for the Saturday night binge at the nitery down the street. It was Lou Manning who brought Bessie back to the hotel, stewed to

the eyeballs, and poured her a nightcap when she got to
bed.

It was Lou Manning who gave her the digitalis, got rid
of the bottle, cleaned and refilled the glass, and saw that
she put her own fingerprints all over it again. It was Lou
Manning who ran the shower to cover up the sound of her
groans.

Bessie didn't have to do anything but die.

When she stopped threshing around and her eyeballs
rolled up and the gasping ceased, he knew it was safe to
call the house physician.

There were no problems.

He told his story about the sudden attack, and the death
certificate read "cardiac collapse during acute gastro-en-
teritis." Everybody was very sorry, and the cemetery lot
was easy to buy, and nobody came to the funeral to
comment on the cheap casket or the lack of flowers. That's
because, in his grief and confusion, Lou forgot to wire
Bert Jackson until the day before the funeral. So Bert
couldn't possibly have made it down there in time.

But those things happen and must be forgiven. And it
was perfectly understandable that the stricken husband
wouldn't stay at the hotel any longer. If Bert Jackson did
show up later, they could explain it to him.

As for Lou Manning, he didn't wait around. The day
after Bessie was planted he checked out. Fortunately, he
had over seven thousand of Bessie's money in cash. He
bought himself a ticket to Havana.

He figured he deserved a little vacation.

3

There was a girl named Encarnacion and there was a
thing called a Silver Punch and there was a gambling

casino. Lou Manning didn't quite know where to place the blame. All he knew was that a month later he was back in New York with less than a grand left in his pocket.

He'd blown the wad. It was a damned fool thing to have done, but there it was.

But easy come, easy go. And there was always plenty more where that came from.

Lou checked into a small East Side hotel, went around to a cheap printer and got some letterheads made up, and batted out another inquiry to the Romance Club. He enclosed the usual fee.

After that, there was nothing else to do but wait.

It took several weeks for the first replies to come in, and at first nothing looked good. Some Polack waitress out in Montana with two kids—a dame in Chicago who claimed she owned a big estate but who wrote on cheap stationery which gave her away immediately as a phoney. Lou Manning could smell a phoney a thousand miles away.

So he sweated it out, cutting down his expenses to thirty bucks a week. Sooner or later the right one would come along. He'd been through this before. There was nothing to worry about, because when the right one came, he'd handle her. Lou knew women.

Sure enough, he got a break.

The break's name was Mrs. Amy Goodrich.

She said she was forty-one and sent a picture to prove it, but that meant nothing. Usually they cut about fifteen years off their ages and used an old snapshot. Lou Manning didn't care about that, one way or another.

What interested him was the eight-unit apartment building left to her by her late husband. It was too much for her to handle alone; she had no relatives and few close friends. That's why she had written to the Romance Club, she told him in her second letter. It made her feel just a wee bit foolish and ashamed, but she needed a friend.

Lou Manning liked her letters. They were neatly typed and the grammar was good but not *too* good—which was perfect, because you had to watch out for the brainy types. Lou liked her setup, too. There was just one thing wrong with the deal, though.

Mrs. Amy Goodrich lived in Miami Beach.

Normally, he'd have arranged to rush right down, but this was a special problem. Miami Beach was entirely too close to Miami.

So he tried to work the angles. He wrote, assuring her that he was the friendly type. And it just so happened that he had some experience in property management and real estate. As soon as he disposed of his own holdings in New York, he was going to California. Right now he couldn't possibly get away until the deal was cleaned up. But why didn't she try to sell her place and fly into town for a visit so that they could get better acquainted?

Of course he didn't lay it on the line cold like that, and he didn't crowd all his suggestions in at once. There was plenty of padding and sweet-talk in between, and he managed to stretch his proposal over four letters. He built up a very convincing picture of himself as a well-to-do widower, and he was really in there pitching at the end. He had to, because he was down to a little over six hundred dollars.

But Amy Goodrich wouldn't buy—or, rather, she wouldn't sell. Lou realized, too late, that he'd outsmarted himself.

If he had experience in handling property (she wrote) then why didn't he come down and pay *her* a visit? Maybe he could help handle the deal and get a better price. Or perhaps he might decide it would be a good idea to keep the apartments, which really brought high rentals in season. She was telling him these things assuming that she could trust him and that he was serious about his intentions. Of course, there was only one way to find out and that was to get acquainted personally. His letters sounded charming, but a lonely woman has to be sure of things before she entrusts her future to a stranger. She hoped they'd be compatible, because she didn't want to spend the rest of her life alone. And she was relieved to find out that he was fairly well-off too. That's what had kept her away from the men she met in Miami Beach—they all seemed to be broke and out after her money. Couldn't he just take a week off for a flying visit?

Lou Manning thought it over. He weighed the possible risks, and found them negligible. He inspected his bankroll. That was negligible, too.

Then he sent the wire and took off for Miami Beach.

Fortunately, the season was over and he was able to get a decent break at a nice hotel. A week there would be all he could possibly afford, but a week might be long enough. It *had* to be long enough.

The minute he got into his room he phoned Mrs. Goodrich at the number she'd given him in her last letter. Some woman answered—sounded like the maid—and said Mrs. Goodrich was out at the real estate office, but she'd left word for him to meet her if he called. She'd be in the dining room of the Savoy, at one. Did he know where the Savoy was, in Miami?

Lou knew where the Savoy was, all right. Less than three blocks away from the hotel where he'd stayed with Bessie.

But what the hell. He couldn't turn chicken. Besides, there wasn't any possible risk. Bessie was dead and buried and forgotten. And Mrs. Goodrich was spending the morning at the real estate office. Did that mean she'd changed her mind and was planning to sell her property and surprise him?

He had to find out.

So Lou Manning put on a blue suit and a red tie and inspected his black mustache in the mirror. Then he rented himself a nice, shiny convertible and drove into Miami. A lot depended on making a good first impression. As he rode along he began to plan his opening remarks. By the time he entered the lobby of the Savoy he was all ready to go to work on Amy Goodrich. He glanced at his watch. One o'clock on the head. She'd be waiting for him in the dining room.

He started across the lobby towards the dining room entrance, but he never got that far. Midway in his progress he bumped into somebody, muttered, "Excuse me," and started to brush past. But a hand on his arm detained him.

Lou turned around and stared at Bert Jackson.

The little baldheaded man blinked up at him and smiled. "Here you are," he said. "I've been trying to locate you for over a month now, but they said you left town. How about that?"

"I—I was sick," Lou told him. "It was the shock and everything. Doctor told me to get away for a rest."

"Which doctor?" Bert Jackson asked. "The house physician?"

Lou stiffened. What did the creep mean, making a crack like that?

But Bert Jackson was smiling, and Lou remembered to relax. Of course her brother would talk to the house physician when he came down here. Naturally, he'd ask for details. There was nothing out of line. Jackson sounded friendly enough.

"How about a drink?" he was saying. "We ought to have a talk."

For a moment Lou was tempted to brush him off, then

thought better of it. He had to find out what Bert Jackson knew and he couldn't afford to make him suspicious by running away. Amy Goodrich would wait. Lucky for him he'd met Bert while he was still alone.

So Lou nodded and they went into the bar and took a booth and talked.

There was no need to ask any leading questions, because the little man went right ahead and told his story. He had been pretty upset when Bessie had run off with Lou that way in Daytona Beach, but when she wrote and assured him of her happiness he got over it. He'd received the letter in Newark, where he was working a few club bookings with the old act. Funny thing, he'd run into one of the Six Brown Brothers—did Lou by any chance happen to remember them?

Lou didn't remember the Six Brown Brothers, and he wasn't interested. He prodded Bert Jackson to continue.

"I was out of town when your wire came," Bert said, "and when I got back I knew the funeral must have been held already. But I called the hotel. You must have known I would—why didn't you stick around?"

"I was too upset," Lou answered. "Like I told you, I had to get away."

"You should have left me a forwarding address."

"I didn't know where I'd be. I meant to write you again when I got settled down. Just arrived in town today." He paused, wondering whether or not to ask the question. But he had to.

"How come you're here?"

Bert Jackson shrugged. "Got myself a booking. Three weeks, maybe four. I've been in town a week already."

That sounded logical. Lou decided it was safe for him to turn on the grief. A nice little act—bereaved husband describes his wife's last hours to her brother.

But Bert was sparing him the trouble. "Naturally, I did a little checking up," he was saying. "I talked to the people at the hotel, and to the doctor you called in for Bessie. But I didn't find out until today that you'd gone to Havana."

Lou took a big gulp of his drink. All at once he felt very cold.

"Nice place to rest up," Bert continued. "And even if you had a shock, there was Bessie's money to cushion it for you."

"Bessie's money? But she didn't have—"

"Eight thousand dollars," Bert Jackson said, nodding. "Oh, I knew all about her bank account, my friend. And so did you. You came down here with Bessie and her eight thousand dollars. Now Bessie is gone, and I suppose the money is gone, too."

"What business is that of yours?"

"I'm not concerned with the money. It's Bessie I'm thinking about." Bert Jackson wasn't smiling now. He leaned forward, one slim white hand tapping the table. "What really happened to my sister? Tell me."

"But you know what happened. She had this attack—"

Bert sighed. "Never mind. I didn't think you'd really level with me, anyway."

"I *am* leveling with you! What do you *want* me to tell you?"

"Just the truth. Did she really have a heart attack, Lou? Or—"

Lou took a deep breath. "Look here, I don't have to sit here and take this kind of stuff from you. You say you talked to the people at the hotel. You talked to her doctor. They'll back me up."

Bert Jackson sighed again. "Yes. They already have. As far as the record goes, you're clean. And being her husband, I suppose you're entitled to the money, too. But I know what you were up to, Lou. Romancing a fat, foolish middle-aged woman, giving her the big rush act—"

Lou Manning knew that the crisis was over. Bert didn't really have a leg to stand on; he'd just admitted as much. So he could relax and go into his pitch again.

"You've got me all wrong, Bert. I loved her, and she loved me. She was happy, but you wouldn't understand that. You're a bachelor—you don't know anything about women—"

Now what in hell had he said wrong? It must have been something, because Bert Jackson wasn't reacting properly.

The little man was laughing.

It wasn't a mirthful laugh, but it was genuine. Bert Jackson's shoulder shook. He stood up and gazed down at Lou, and there was no mistaking the hatred that shone in his eyes. But he laughed.

"All right," he said. "All right, Lou. Have it your way."

Then he was gone.

Lou sat there and finished his drink. He had a lot of thinking to do. The creep suspected him. He'd snooped around and gotten nowhere. That was plain enough, because there'd been no threat of calling in the law. But Bert suspected him and he was an enemy. And why had he laughed? Lou had told him the truth—at least about the way Bessie had felt. She *did* love him, she *was* happy with him, until the end. Why had Bert laughed?

Lou Manning didn't know. All he knew was that he mus' work fast. Sew up Amy Goodrich and get out of town, quickly, before Bert could get hold of him again. Then he'd be safe. That was the ticket—get hold of Mrs. Goodrich right now.

He glanced at his watch. Almost quarter to two. He practically ran out into the lobby and across to the dining room entrance. His eyes scanned the faces of the late diners. Young couples, old couples, three or four singles, male. No solitary middle-aged woman in sight. He asked the head waiter if he'd seen a woman sitting alone, asked if there was anyone who'd left a message for Lou Manning.

The head waiter shook his head.

Lou went outside, got his car, and drove back to Miami Beach and the hotel. He phoned Mrs. Goodrich from his room. This time there was no answer at all.

Something had gone wrong. Damn that little creep! He was lousing up everything.

Lou hadn't eaten lunch, but he wasn't hungry. He was scared. Looking into the mirror he had to admit the truth. He was losing the old grip. He could see Lou Manning's face in the glass, but Luis Manuel showed through. And Luis Manuel, underneath the toupee and the hair-dye, was scared silly.

Ths would have to be different. Maybe meeting Bert Jackson had been a blessing in disguise—a warning. He couldn't handle any more women the way he'd handled Bessie. And maybe there *shouldn't* be any more women. Just this Amy Goodrich.

He took out her picture and stared at it again. Suppose she was only forty-one, like she said. And she had a fair-sized hunk of dough. Wasn't that enough? Couldn't he make an honest try for once, if she turned out to be halfway decent? Why not marry her and really settle down? Life could be quiet and peaceful. No more disguises, no more writing to the Romance Club, no more skulking around and narrow escapes. Yes, and no more crazy flings like that trip to Havana, either. Well, he was willing to call it quits. He might as well face the facts. He wasn't getting any younger. If he could swing it with Amy Goodrich, that would be good enough for him. He'd hit it off with her all right—after all, he knew how to make a woman happy.

Twice more he called her number, and twice more he listened to the unanswered ring. The loneliest sound in the world.

Just sitting around like that gave him the jitters worse than ever, so finally he called Room Service and had the boy bring up a pint of rye. All he needed was one or two drinks to steady his nerves. He had to have steady nerves from now on in. So he could handle this woman right.

But what had happened to her? Where was she? Why hadn't she showed up at lunch? What was going on at the real estate office?

Maybe there'd been an accident. Maybe something crazy had come up. There were all sorts of ways to foul the details in a deal like this. But the deal couldn't get fouled up. He was counting on it. It had to go through. It had to—

The drinks only made him feel worse. All at once Lou noticed the room was getting dark. He'd been sitting here for hours. Maybe he'd better not wait around. Maybe he'd better give up and get out of town while the getting was good—before that little fink of a Bert Jackson got some new ideas.

Lou scowled. Why should he be afraid of a broken-down vaudeville ham? But the little man had laughed at him. Maybe he was off his rocker. Lou knew the feeling. He was getting close to going off his rocker himself.

Well, one more phone call. Just one more. If Amy Goodrich wasn't home by now he might as well kiss her off for good.

He was just getting ready to pick up the telephone when it rang. It made him jump about a foot and his voice wasn't any steadier than his hand when he finally answered.

"Hello?"

"Hello—is this Mr. Manning—Lou? This is Amy Goodrich."

A warm contralto voice, slightly slurred.

"Yes. What happened? We were to meet for lunch."

"I know. I'm sorry about that. I'll explain everything when I see you. So much has happened—"

"Good. Where are you now?"

"Why, I'm right downstairs in the lobby. I thought we might go out for dinner, maybe have a little drink first to celebrate—"

Lou grinned. He recognized the slur in her voice now. Why, the dame was half-crocked! He hesitated another moment, then decided to chance it. "Why not come on up here for your drink?" he asked. "I happen to have the makings."

"Well, I don't know," Amy Goodrich giggled. "You think it would be all right?"

"Of course. You come right up. I'm in five-seventeen."

She hung up and Lou got to work. He switched on the side lamp, straightened the room, fetched clean glasses and scrabbled around in the dregs of the ice-bucket. Then he checked his face in the mirror. By the time he heard the knock on the door everything was ready.

Amy Goodrich stood there, swaying slightly, and blinking in the light.

Lou Manning smiled at her, and his smile was genuine—because she was genuine, too. Small, slender, her wavy brown hair gathered in a pug, and just like her photograph. Her carefully made-up face betrayed no wrinkles, and she couldn't have been any older than she claimed. Lou wasn't exactly the type to fall for the old love-at-first-sight gag, but he liked her at first sight. No doubt about that.

And when she came in, flopped into a chair without

ceremony, accepted a drink with a smile and leaned back he made a sudden decision. He'd play this one straight.

"It all happened so suddenly I don't exactly know how to begin," she was saying. "And then I've had three cocktails and this drink—" She giggled and held out her empty glass. Lou refilled it quickly.

"Anyway, I got the call this morning. From the real estate people. Remember, I told you I hadn't made any plans to sell? Well, I hadn't. But this agency knew about the apartments and they phoned today to say they had a client who was interested in just that kind of property. They wanted me to come down right away. So I went, and left a message for you—"

Lou nodded. "I got it," he said.

"I'm dreadfully sorry I had to break our luncheon engagement," Amy Goodrich said. "But they had the client right there in the office and he insisted on taking me out and talking things over. It went on for quite a long time. Finally, though, I had to say yes."

"Yes to what?" Lou asked.

"Why, to selling the place, of course. You know what he paid me? Sixty thousand dollars. Sixty thousand dollars in cash!"

"You mean you—?"

"Oh, I don't have the money yet. But I will before the week is out. I've got the option payment and all that's left is the title search and making out the final papers." She beamed up at him. "I guess I'm entitled to a little celebration, aren't I?"

Lou took her hand. It was warm and soft. He wasn't at all sure about that love-at-first-sight business being a gag now. Ever since he'd heard about the sixty grand he'd felt a genuine stirring of emotion. Money had always been an aphrodisiac to Lou. Just like liquor is an aphrodisiac to some people. Some women, for instance.

Holding her hand that way, the idea hit him. Why not? He had to work fast, didn't he? And the best way to do that was to cut out all the preliminaries. What he wanted to do was to sew up the deal, sew her up, and get out of town before there was any possibility of trouble with Bert Jackson.

This was a heaven-sent opportunity. Here was Amy Goodrich, already a little bit stiff. Another drink or two, she'd be a pushover. The whole thing would be a pushover. Besides, she wouldn't be hard to take. Lou knew women, and this one was desirable. He thought back, with a shudder, to all the old bats he'd known—fat, repulsive old creatures like Bessie. But Amy Goodrich was something different. She was warm and soft. And she wasn't a prude.

She giggled up at him now and pointed at the empty bottle on the table. "I've got another surprise for you," she said. "Maybe you'll be shocked. But I was hoping you'd ask me up when I called, and I didn't know if you'd have any liquor in your room, and I wanted to celebrate. So I bought this and put it in my purse."

Sure enough, she hauled out a pint of bourbon. The seal had been broken, but it was more than three-quarters full.

Lou grinned at her and accepted the bottle. He poured two stiff ones. He could stand another jolt, and it would just about take care of her.

"I'm glad you thought to bring it," he said. "And don't worry about shocking me. You'll find out I like a drink now and then. You'll find out I like a lot of the good things in life. And might I say that you're definitely one of them?"

He raised his glass. "To our better acquaintance," he said. The bourbon tasted much stronger than the rye—it burned as it went down. But he emptied it at a gulp, hoping she'd follow suit. Then, in a few minutes, he'd make a few passes. She'd never know what hit her until it was too late to resist. Tomorrow they could apply for a license—let's see now, they could be married just about the time the money for the apartment building came through.

He started to move towards her, then noticed that she hadn't taken a drink. As he watched, she set the glass down on the buréau next to the chair.

"But you were talking about getting acquainted," she said. "Tell me something about yourself."

Lou smiled. "What do you want to know?" he began. "You've read my letters. I'm like you are. One of the lonely ones. Looking for companionship, someone I can trust, someone who understands me—"

"What's the matter?" She stood up now, staring at him. Lou bit his lip. How could she tell? He had felt the sudden cramp as he was speaking, but thought he'd concealed it. Now it came on again, worse than before. He knew he had turned pale, knew he was sweating. All at once he had to sit down on the bed. He smiled weakly.

"I'm all right," he said. The pain bored in again, stronger.

She nodded and moved closer. "Then tell me some more," she said. "About understanding. Didn't Bessie understand you?"

"Bessie?" The pain flared up again, but he ignored it. "What do you know about Bessie?"

"Everything. You married her less than two months ago, didn't you? And you took her money—"

Lou fell back on the bed. He was trying to sit up, trying to get up, but the pain pressed him down. It was a huge stone, crushing his stomach. A pointed stone that ripped and tore. And her words were ripping and tearing, worse than the pain.

"You fed her the digitalis in a drink, didn't you? Of course, nobody can prove it. They found it there when they exhumed the body, but there's no way of making certain she didn't take an overdose for herself, because of her heart. Of course, Bessie really didn't have heart trouble, did she? But you spread the word around, and now that she's dead it's just your word against a lot of suspicions. Even if you went to trial, they wouldn't have a chance at a conviction."

The pain was rising in his chest now, rising in his throat. He wanted to vomit it out, just as he was vomiting out the words.

"So Bert told you," he wheezed. "You're a friend of Bert Jackson's. He put you up to this, didn't he? He must have seen Bessie's letters from the Romance Club and figured out I'd write them again. So he hired you as bait for me. Is that it? Go ahead—tell me the rest."

"What's there to tell?" Amy Goodrich was still smiling. "You can probably figure it out. Bert ordered the body exhumed for an autopsy—a brother has the right, you know. And he checked up on you, all the way back. Then he went to the police. But the trouble is, he had no proof. No proof at all. He wasn't even sure you'd blown in the money until he met you today. Then he decided to go ahead with it."

"Go ahead with what?" Everything was blurring, but Lou gritted his teeth and forced himself to sit up. He had to hear the rest. "Go ahead with what?" he gasped.

"Why—this." Amy Goodrich pointed at the bottle of bourbon. "He wasn't going to let you get away with murder. An eye for an eye, you know. So now you've taken the digitalis too, and in a few minutes—"

"Digitalis?"

"Why not? It worked on Bessie. It will work on you.

145

Nobody saw me come up to your room. Nobody knows
about the two of us. Nobody ever will. You were drinking,
you had a little spell, your heart gave out. There's a house
physician in this hotel, too. He'll write out the death
certificate."

"No—"

The pain was blinding. Lou tried to stand up. He tried
three times, then doubled over on the bed, sobbing.

"Don't let me die—I don't want to die—get a doctor—
quick—"

"Too late for that. But I've got an antidote."

"Antidote? Where is it?"

"Right here."

She was fishing in her purse again, and he could see,
dimly, that she was holding a small vial in her hand.

"Give it to me—"

"Not until you confess."

"All right, I confess. I did it. Now, give it to me—"

"That isn't enough. There has to be a witness. I'll call
the police."

"You can't do that."

She shrugged. "All right. Have it your way." She
walked across the room.

Pain came in continuous waves now. He could just
about see her, just about talk. "Where are you going?"

"To turn on the shower. In a little while you'll start
screaming."

"Wait—"

She had to wait, because it hit him so hard then he
couldn't get the words out for a minute.

"All right. Call the cops. I'll tell—"

And she called them, and they came, and he told. He
nearly passed out, twice, and they slapped his face to
bring him around, but he told.

Then at the end he managed to wheeze out the rest. The dirty slut thought she'd fixed his goose, but she'd forgotten that he could pay her back.

"Don't let her get away with anything," he finished. "She's as guilty as I am. Trying to kill me with digitalis. It's in that bottle, over there." Then his voice cracked. "And now, for God's sake, give me the antidote!"

Amy Goodrich looked at the cops and shook her head.

"There is no antidote," she said.

"But there has to be—you promised—"

"There is no digitalis in the whiskey, either. All I slipped you was a Mickey Finn. That's right, the old Mickey. You're going to be sick as hell in another five minutes, and then you'll pass out. But that's all right. They'll take care of you fine when you wake up again. You're going to be right in shape for the trial."

One of the cops helped Lou get to the bathroom. Amy was right; he was very sick indeed. When he got back they were waiting to take him downstairs.

"I'm afraid we'll have to ask you to come along too," the cop said. "We'll need a complete explanation of all this, Mrs. Goodrich."

"Whatever you say," she answered.

Lou stared at her. She was a fine figure of a woman. For a moment he felt a twinge of regret and somehow it was worse than the physical pain. If only she had been content to let things ride! They could have been happy together. He knew that he could have been happy with a woman like her. But she had to turn out to be a dirty double-crosser, a friend of Bert's.

Suddenly she turned to Lou and began to laugh. Sick as he was, he recognized the sound.

"All right," she said, softly. "I'm sorry. But I had to do it this way. A long shot, but I figured it was the only chance.

And it worked." She nodded at Lou soberly. "And I couldn't help laughing when I thought about this noon."

Slowly, Mrs. Goodrich removed the brown wig and revealed the bald head beneath. And the laughter came again. "Telling me you knew all about women and I didn't. Me, Bert Jackson—one of the best female impersonators in the business!"

Why do I like "The Question" most of any of my stories? For one thing, its subject—capital punishment—tends to draw from those favoring it or opposing it fervently self-righteous and simplistic argumentation, and in attempting a story on the theme I had to dig very deep into myself to come up with an insight into my own feelings. That kind of self-discovery is intensely gratifying to me.

For another thing, the large mail response, pro and con, to the story on its publication, indicated that I had certainly touched a nerve here, and touching nerves—which doesn't happen all that often—is what I most hope to achieve in any story.

—Stanley Ellin

THE QUESTION

STANLEY ELLIN

I am an electrocutioner . . . I prefer this word to executioner; I think words make a difference. When I was a boy, people who buried the dead were undertakers, and then somewhere along the way they became morticians and are better off for it.

Take the one who used to be the undertaker in my town. He was a decent, respectable man, very friendly if you'd let him be, but hardly anybody would let him be. Today, his son—who now runs the business—is not an undertaker but a mortician, and is welcome everywhere. As a matter of fact, he's an officer in my Lodge and is one of the most popular members we have. And all it took to do that was changing one word to another. The job's the same but the word is different, and people somehow will always go by words rather than meanings.

So, as I said, I am an electrocutioner—which is the proper professional word for it in my state where the electric chair is the means of execution.

Not that this is my profession. Actually, it's a sideline, as it is for most of us who perform executions. My real business is running an electrical supply and repair shop just as my father did before me. When he died I inherited not only the business from him, but also the position of state's electrocutioner.

150

The Question

We established a tradition, my father and I. He was running the shop profitably even before the turn of the century when electricity was a comparatively new thing, and he was the first man to perform a successful electrocution for the state. It was not the state's first electrocution, however. That one was an experiment and was badly bungled by the engineer who installed the chair in the state prison. My father, who had helped install the chair, was the assistant at the electrocution, and he told me that everything that could go wrong that day did go wrong. The current was eccentric, his boss froze on the switch, and the man in the chair was alive and kicking at the same time he was being burned to a crisp. The next time, my father offered to do the job himself, rewired the chair, and handled the switch so well that he was offered the job of official electrocutioner.

I followed in his footsteps, which is how a tradition is made, but I am afraid this one ends with me. I have a son, and what I said to him and what he said to me is the crux of the matter. He asked me a question—well, in my opinion, it was the kind of question that's at the bottom of most of the world's troubles today. There are some sleeping dogs that should be left to lie; there are some questions that should not be asked.

To understand all this, I think you have to understand me, and nothing could be easier. I'm sixty, just beginning to look my age, a little overweight, suffer sometimes from arthritis when the weather is damp. I'm a good citizen, complain about my taxes but pay them on schedule, vote for the right party, and run my business well enough to make a comfortable living from it.

I've been married thirty-five years and never looked at another woman in all that time. Well, looked maybe, but no more than that. I have a married daughter and a

151

granddaughter almost a year old, and the prettiest, smilingest baby in town. I spoil her and don't apologize for it, because in my opinion that is what grandfathers were made for—to spoil their grandchildren. Let mama and papa attend to the business; grandpa is there for the fun.

And beyond all that I have a son who asks questions. The kind that shouldn't be asked.

Put the picture together, and what you get is someone like yourself. I might be your next-door neighbor, I might be your old friend, I might be the uncle you meet whenever the family gets together at a wedding or a funeral. I'm like you.

Naturally, we all look different on the outside but we can still recognize each other on sight as the same kind of people. Deep down inside where it matters we have the same feelings, and we know that without any questions being asked about them.

"But," you might say, "there is a difference between us. You're the one who performs the executions, and I'm the one who reads about them in the papers, and that's a big difference, no matter how you look at it."

Is it? Well, look at it without prejudice, look at it with absolute honesty, and you'll have to admit that you're being unfair.

Let's face the facts, we're all in this together. If an old friend of yours happens to serve on a jury that finds a murderer guilty, you don't lock the door against him, do you? More than that: if you could get an introduction to the judge who sentences that murderer to the electric chair, you'd be proud of it, wouldn't you? You'd be honored to have him sit at your table, and you'd be quick enough to let the world know about it.

And since you're so willing to be friendly with the jury that convicts and the judge that sentences, what about the man who has to pull the switch? He's finished the job you wanted done, he's made the world a better place for it. Why must he go hide away in a dark corner until the next time he's needed?

There's no use denying that nearly everybody feels he should, and there's less use denying that it's a cruel thing for anyone in my position to face. If you don't mind some strong language, it's a damned outrage to hire a man for an unpleasant job, and then despise him for it. Sometimes it's hard to abide such righteousness.

How do I get along in the face of it? The only way possible—by keeping my secret locked up tight and never being tempted to give it away. I don't like it that way, but I'm no fool about it.

The trouble is that I'm naturally easygoing and friendly. I'm the sociable kind. I like people, and I want them to like me. At Lodge meetings or in the clubhouse down at the golf course I'm always the center of the crowd. And I know what would happen if at any such time I ever opened my mouth and let that secret out. A five-minute sensation, and after that the slow chill setting in. It would mean the end of my whole life then and there, the kind of life I want to live, and no man in his right mind throws away sixty years of his life for a five-minute sensation.

You can see I've given the matter a lot of thought. More than that, it hasn't been idle thought. I don't pretend to be an educated man, but I'm willing to read books on any subject that interests me, and execution has been one of my main interests ever since I got into the line. I have the books sent to the shop where nobody takes notice of another piece of mail, and I keep them locked in a bin in my office so that I can read them in private.

There's a nasty smell about having to do it this way—at my age you hate to feel like a kid hiding himself away to read a dirty magazine—but I have no choice. There isn't a soul on earth outside of the warden at state's prison and a couple of picked guards there who know I'm the one pulling the switch at an execution, and I intend it to remain that way.

Oh, yes, my son knows now. Well, he's difficult in some ways, but he's no fool. If I wasn't sure he would keep his mouth shut about what I told him, I wouldn't have told it to him in the first place.

Have I learned anything from those books? At least enough to take a pride in what I'm doing for the state and the way I do it. As far back in history as you want to go there have always been executioners. The day that men first made laws to help keep peace among themselves was the day the first executioner was born. There have always been lawbreakers; there must always be a way of punishing them. It's a simple as that.

The trouble is that nowadays there are too many people who don't want it to be as simple as that. I'm no hypocrite, I'm not one of those narrow-minded fools who thinks that every time a man comes up with a generous impulse he's some kind of crackpot. But he can be mistaken. I'd put most of the people who are against capital punishment in that class. They are fine, high-minded citizens who've never in their lives been close enough to a murderer or rapist to smell the evil in him. In fact, they're so fine and high-minded that they can't imagine anyone in the world not being like themselves. In that case, they say anybody who commits murder or rape is just a plain, ordinary human being who's had a bad spell. He's no criminal, they say, he's just sick. He doesn't need the electric chair; all he needs is a kindly old doctor to examine his head and straighten out the kinks in his brain.

In fact, they say there is no such thing as a criminal at

all. There are only well people and sick people, and the ones who deserve all your worry and consideration are the sick ones. If they happen to murder or rape a few of the well ones now and then, why, just run for the doctor.

This is the argument from beginning to end, and I'd be the last one to deny that it's built on honest charity and good intentions. But it's a mistaken argument. It omits the one fact that matters. When anyone commits murder or rape he is no longer in the human race. A man has a human brain and a God-given soul to control his animal nature. When the animal in him takes control he's not a human being any more. Then he has to be exterminated the way any animal must be if it goes wild in the middle of helpless people. And my duty is to be the exterminator.

It could be that people just don't understand the meaning of the word *duty* any more. I don't want to sound old-fashioned, God forbid, but when I was a boy things were more straightforward and clear-cut. You learned to tell right from wrong, you learned to do what had to be done, and you didn't ask question every step of the way. Or if you had to ask any questions, the ones that mattered were *how* and *when*.

Then along came psychology, along came the professors, and the main question was always *why*. Ask yourself *why, why, why* about everything you do, and you'll end up doing nothing. Let a couple of generations go along that way, and you'll finally have a breed of people who sit around in trees like monkeys, scratching their heads.

Does this sound far-fetched? Well, it isn't. Life is a complicated thing to live. All his life a man finds himself facing one situation after another, and the way to handle them is to live by the rules. Ask yourself *why* once too often, and you can find yourself so tangled up that you go under. The show must go on. Why? Women and children

155

first. Why? My country, right or wrong. Why? Never mind your duty. Just keep asking *why* until it's too late to do anything about it.

Around the time I first started going to school my father gave me a dog, a collie pup named Rex. A few years after, Rex suddenly became unfriendly, the way a dog will sometimes, and then vicious, and then one day he bit my mother when she reached down to pat him.

The day after that I saw my father leaving the house with his hunting rifle under his arm and with Rex on a leash. It wasn't the hunting season, so I knew what was going to happen to Rex and I knew why. But it's forgivable in a boy to ask things that a man should be smart enough not to ask.

"Where are you taking Rex?" I asked my father. "What are you going to do with him?"

"I'm taking him out back of town," my father said. "I'm going to shoot him."

"But why?" I said, and that was when my father let me see that there is only one answer to such a question.

"Because it has to be done," he said.

I never forgot that lesson. It came hard; for a while I hated my father for it, but as I grew up I came to see how right he was. We both knew why the dog had to be killed. Beyond that, all questions would lead nowhere. Why the dog had become vicious, why God had put a dog on earth to be killed this way—these are the questions that you can talk out to the end of time, and while you're talking about them you still have a vicious dog on your hands.

It is strange to look back and realize now that when the business of the dog happened, and long before it and long after it, my father was an electrocutioner, and I never knew it. Nobody knew it, not even my mother. A few times a year my father would pack his bag and a few tools and go away for a couple of days, but that was all any of us knew. If you asked him where he was going he would simply say he had a job to do out of town. He was not a man you'd ever suspect of philandering or going off on a solitary drunk, so nobody gave it a second thought.

It worked the same way in my case. I found out how well it worked when I finally told my son what I had been doing on those jobs out of town, and that I had gotten the warden's permission to take him on as an assistant and train him to handle the chair himself when I retired. I could tell from the way he took it that he was as thunderstruck at this as I had been thirty years before when my father had taken me into his confidence.

"Electrocutioner?" said my son. *"An electrocutioner?"*

"Well, there's no disgrace to it," I said. "And since it's got to be done, and somebody has to do it, why not keep it in the family? If you knew anything about it, you'd know it's a profession that's often passed down in a family from generation to generation. What's wrong with a good, sound tradition? If more people believed in tradition you wouldn't have so many troubles in the world today."

It was the kind of argument that would have been more than enough to convince me when I was his age. What I hadn't taken into account was that my son wasn't like me, much as I wanted him to be. He was a grown man in his own right, but a grown man who had never settled down to his responsibilities. I had always kept closing my eyes to that, I had always seen him the way I wanted to and not the way he was.

When he left college after a year, I said, all right, there are some people who aren't made for college, I never went there, so what difference does it make. When he went out with one girl after another and could never make up his mind to marrying any of them. I said, well, he's young, he's sowing his wild oats, the time will come soon enough when he's ready to take care of a home and family. When he sat daydreaming in the shop instead of tending to business I never made a fuss about it. I knew when he put his mind to it he was as good an electrician as you could ask for and in these soft times people are allowed to do a lot more dreaming and a lot less working than they used to.

The truth was that the only thing that mattered to me was being his friend. For all his faults he was a fine-looking boy with a good mind. He wasn't much for mixing with people, but if he wanted to he could win anyone over. And in the back of my mind all the while he was growing up was the thought that he was the only one who would learn my secret some day, and would share it with me, and make it easier to bear. I'm not secretive by nature. A man like me needs a thought like that to sustain him.

So when the time came to tell him he shook his head and said no. I felt that my legs had been kicked out from under me. I argued with him and he still said no, and I lost my temper.

"Are you against capital punishment?" I asked him. "You don't have to apologize if you are. I'd think all the more of you, if that's your only reason."

"I don't know if it is," he said.

"Well, you ought to make up your mind one way or the other," I told him. "I'd hate to think you were like every other hypocrite around who says it's all right to condemn a man to the electric chair and all wrong to pull the switch."

"Do I have to be the one to pull it?" he said. "Do you?"

"Somebody has to do it. Somebody always has to do the dirty work for the rest of us. It's not like the Old Testament days when everybody did it for himself. Do you know how they executed a man in those days? They laid him on the ground tied hand and foot, and everybody around had to heave rocks on him until he was crushed to death. They didn't invite anybody to stand around and watch. You wouldn't have had much choice then, would you?"

"I don't know," he said. And then because he was as smart as they come and knew how to turn your words against you, he said, "After all, I'm not without sin."

"Don't talk like a child," I said. "You're without the sin of murder on you or any kind of sin that calls for execution. And if you're so sure the Bible has all the answers, you might remember that you're supposed to render unto Caesar the things that are Caesar's."

"Well," he said, "in this case I'll let you do the rendering."

I knew then and there from the way he said it and the way he looked at me that it was no use trying to argue with him. The worst of it was knowing that we had somehow moved far apart from each other and would never really be close again. I should have had sense enough to let it go at that. I should have just told him to forget the whole thing and keep his mouth shut about it.

Maybe if I had ever considered the possibility of his saying no, I would have done it. But because I hadn't considered any such possibility I was caught off balance, I was too much upset to think straight. I will admit it now. It was my own fault that I made an issue of things and led him to ask the one question he should never have asked.

"I see," I told him. "It's the same old story, isn't it? Let somebody else do it. But if they pull your number out of a hat and you have to serve on a jury and send a man to the chair, that's all right with you. At least, it's all right as long as there's somebody else to do the job that you and the judge and every decent citizen wants done. Let's face the facts, boy, you don't have the guts. I'd hate to think of you even walking by the death house. The shop is where you belong. You can be nice and cozy there, wiring up fixtures and ringing the cash register. I can handle my duties without your help."

It hurt me to say it, I had never talked like that to him before, and it hurt. The strange thing was that he didn't seem angry about it; he only looked at me puzzled.

"Is that all it is to you?" he said. "A duty?"

"Yes."

"But you get paid for it, don't you?"

"I get paid little enough for it."

He kept looking at me that way. "Only a duty?" he said, and never took his eyes off me. "But you enjoy it, don't you?"

That was the question he asked.

You enjoy it, don't you? You stand there looking through a peephole in the wall at the chair. In thirty years I have stood there more than a hundred times looking at that chair. The guards bring somebody in. Usually he is in a daze; sometimes he screams, throws himself around and fights. Sometimes it is a woman, and a woman can be as hard to handle as a man when she is led to the chair. Sooner or later, whoever it is is strapped down and the black hood is dropped over his head. Now your hand is on the switch.

The warden signals, and you pull the switch. The current hits the body like a tremendous rush of air suddenly filling it. The body leaps out of the chair with only the straps holding it back. The head jerks, and a curl of smoke comes from it. You release the switch and the body falls back again.

You do it once more, do it a third time to make sure. And whenever your hand presses the switch you can see in your mind what the current is doing to that body and what the face under the hood must look like.

Enjoy it?

That was the question my son asked me. That was what he said to me, as if I didn't have the same feelings deep down in me that we all have.

Enjoy it?

But, my God, how could anyone *not* enjoy it!

As a novelist, I think in terms of long, complex plots, rather than the short, snappy ones that make short stories. A few years ago I edited an MWA anthology, and the required reading and evaluating gave me an insight as to how short stories are written. Taking my brand new knowledge in hand, I stalled on my novel-writing long enough to create two short stories of my own. This selection is the second of those two.

—HILLARY WAUGH

GALTON AND THE YELLING BOYS

HILLARY WAUGH

"Human nature," said Mike Galton, the captain of detectives, "is the key to man's universe. And," the old man went on, "if you want my opinion, a good, experienced cop knows more about human nature than a good, experienced psychiatrist."

Detective Bill Dennis, his young sidekick, said, "Oh, come on, Cap. That's stretching it a little."

They were having coffee with the desk sergeant and it was a mild May night with a full moon up. "I think he's right, Bill," the sergeant said.

"Given equal mentalities, of course," the old man cautioned. "but the reason I say that is because the opportunities are so great. We routinely encounter examples of human behavior the average man couldn't imagine, and psychiatrists have only read about."

The others couldn't gainsay that and were silent a moment, reflecting on personal experiences. Galton lighted his pipe and sat back enjoying the night. It had been a quiet one, with the citizens, for the most part, behaving themselves. There'd been a complaint of a fight over in the east end of town, but it was a husband and wife, and the appearance of a patrolman stopped it. There'd been a complaint south of City Park about a car full of boys helling it up, yelling and honking, but they were gone by the time the radio car went by. Even the missing child, reported by a frantic mother at six o'clock, had turned up fifteen minutes later. Violence had not gone abroad that night. The natives weren't restless and the police on duty could relax over their coffee, talk about non-cop things, and let the softness of the night steal through the open doors.

Then there was a screech of brakes, the slamming of a car door, and the clatter of racing feet on the outside steps. Galton sighed with regret, for the sounds told him peace was at an end even before the youth burst through the doorway and rushed up to the desk.

He was about nineteen, tall, with curly hair and good quality clothes. The clothes, however, were a mess, and so was his face. He was panting, and he looked in shock.

"Help me," he said, looking first at the detectives, then to the uniformed sergeant behind the big desk. "You gotta help me."

"That's what we're here for," the sergeant said easily. "What's the problem?"

"Three men!" the boy panted. "They kidnapped my girl."

"Whereabouts?"

"City Park. Hurry, hurry."

"We will," the sergeant said. "Relax, young fella. Calm down and tell us your name."

"But she's in trouble."

"And when we hear your story we'll know what to do about it. What's your name?"

The boy said impatiently, "Lawrence Wainwright."

"Where do you live?"

"Is that important? My girl—"

"You're wasting time, fella. What's your address?"

The boy told him, giving an address in one of the best sections of town.

"Now tell us what happened," the sergeant went on, writing in the blotter, keeping his manner calm.

"We were parked in the park, minding our own business, when all of a sudden three men appeared and dragged us out of the car. I tried to fight them, but they ganged up and knocked me out. And when I came to, they were gone and she was gone."

"When did this take place?"

"About twenty minutes ago. About quarter of eleven."

"What's the girl's name and address?"

"What does it matter?" the boy cried. "We've got to save her."

"We'll save her just as soon as we know she needs saving. What's her name and where does she live?"

"Her name is Helen MacKenzie and she lives over on Wells Street. Thirty-one Wells."

Galton moved behind the desk and thumbed through the phone book as the sergeant recorded the information and asked where the youth had seen the girl last.

"In City Park. I told you."

"It's a big park, Mr. Wainwright. Just where in City Park?"

"Near the pond."

"That doesn't help much. It's a big pond.

"I've got my car outside. I'll show you."

Galton dialed a number and while he waited, said, "Did you know any of the men, Mr. Wainwright?"

"No. Of course not. Please, we're wasting time. Can't we go now?"

Galton said into the phone, "Mrs. MacKenzie? This is Captain Galton of the police department. I'm sorry to disturb you at this hour. Is your daughter Helen there, please?" He listened briefly, his face becoming still more sober. "What's the name of the boy she's out with?" he asked, and then, "Do you know where they went?" He listened for a bit and said, "When she comes in, would you have her call the police department? The moment she comes in. It doesn't matter what time." When he spoke again, it was to say, reassuringly, "No, she's not in trouble with the police, Mrs. MacKenzie. She hasn't done anything wrong. We just want to get in touch with her."

He put down the phone and said to Dennis and the sergeant, "It checks out and she's not home yet." To the boy, he said, "These men. What did they look like?"

"Two were dark and one was blond. They were my height but heavier."

"How old?"

"Maybe twenty."

"What were they wearing?"

"Sport clothes. Dark sport clothes. No jackets."

Galton's manner was brisk now. He took out a notebook. "Tell us exactly what happened."

The boy touched the blood on his cheek and absently wiped it on his shirt. "We were parked in the park doing a little—you know—smooching. All of a sudden I looked up and two men were staring at us through her window. Then, before I could do anything, they opened her door and at the same time the third man opened my door. He grabbed me and the others grabbed Helen. I fought with the one who grabbed me, but one of the others came and hit me and they both jumped on me and knocked me down and kicked me unconscious."

"What did Helen do? She scream?"

"No. I think they had a hand over her mouth. I heard her say, 'Stop it! Don't!' but that's all."

"You know if they had a car?"

"I think they did. I think they're the same men we saw when we went into the park."

The old man arched an eyebrow. "Tell us about that."

"Just when we were driving in, this cream-colored convertible went racing past us with three boys in it yelling and screaming. I think they were the same ones."

The desk sergeant said, "Say, that's the car we got a call on, Captain."

Galton turned. "When? What about?"

"We got a complaint." The sergeant looked back on the blotter. "Nine forty-two. Call from a Mrs. Stanley Turner on Westlake Avenue about a light-colored convertible with three boys in it driving around her neighborhood yelling and honking and raising hell. I sent Charlie car to respond, but they were gone."

Galton nodded. "Better alert all units." He said to the boy, "You didn't make out the license plate, did you? Or notice what make of car?"

"No, sir. I just saw the three boys in it. Two dark and one blond."

Galton took a last swallow from his cup. "All right, we'll go out and take a look around. You feel up to it, son? Would you like some coffee?" he asked the boy solicitiously.

"No, thanks. I'm all right."

"You'd better have a doctor look at your face."

"Later. Right now I want to find my girl."

Dennis finished his own coffee and tucked away his notebook. He and Galton led the way outside. A shiny new hardtop was against the curb with the lights on and the boy started toward it, but Galton stopped him. "We'll go in ours. It's got a radio."

They climbed into a black, unmarked cruiser, the detectives in front, the boy in back. They headed for the park, watching for convertibles. Dennis, driving, said, "What were you and the girl doing in the car?"

Wainwright hesitated and said, "A little necking."

"How were you making out with her?"

"Believe me, it's not what you think."

Galton said, "What was it?"

"We were kissing. That's all."

The detectives slid knowing looks at each other. Galton said, "You pick her up and take her out in the park and all you do is kiss?"

Wainwright swallowed. "No," he said. "We also talk. We sit and we talk and sometimes we kiss. When those men looked in the window, we were kissing."

"What kind of a girl is she?"

"A nice girl."

"What makes you so sure?"

"Well—what do you mean? I date her."

"What I mean is, she comes from another part of town. She comes from a different social station that you do. I'm not saying it's this way in your case, but usually when men date girls below their social class, it's for only one reason."

Wainwright said heatedly, "I'm not a snob. We happen to like each other. We've talked about marriage, if you really want to know. I mean, we aren't formally engaged and we haven't said anything to our folks, but we're serious."

Galton didn't push it. "Any chance she knew the boys? She call any of them by name?"

Wainwright said no, nor had her abductors used names. They hadn't said a word.

Dennis turned into the park and followed its winding roads. He looked at the moon and said, "If a bunch of boys want to raid neckers, Cap, this is the night to find them."

When they drove past the pond, Wainwright pointed to a stand of trees, black against the moonlit sky. "That's where we were," he said.

Dennis pulled off the road and crossed the fields some fifty yards to the trees. They got out and the detectives looked around by flashlight. Some grass had been flattened by wheels, but that was all.

Galton said, "You didn't see or hear anything before you saw them at the window? No car headlights? No motor?"

Wainwright shook his head. Dennis said, "They must have seen a girl in the car and doubled back with their lights off."

Galton agreed. He said, "In what direction did they drag her?"

Wainwright pointed toward black woods a hundred yards distant, "That way. At least, the last I saw."

"You see or hear a car any time after they slugged you?"

"No, sir."

Dennis said to the old man, "You think they might still be around?"

"It doesn't look like it. They probably took off after he did." Galton got back into the cruiser and picked up the microphone.

"Headquarters from Galton. The girl been heard from yet?"

The sergeant came on. "Negative."

"Anything on that convertible?"

"No, sir."

Galton depressed the mike button again and said, "Send all available units and all available men to City Park, the field opposite the pond. I want search parties prepared to go through the woods."

"Affirmative, Captain. All units. Calling all units—" in a monotone.

When Galton got out of the car, the youth said, "You think she's in the woods?"

Galton's tone was heavier, his voice distracted. "I don't know where she is, son, but you say that's where she was dragged, so that's the first place to look."

The two detectives and the boy reconnoitered the nearby areas while waiting and then, shortly after midnight, the squad cars began arriving and men poured out. By quarter past twelve, thirty policemen were on hand with flashlights and hand lamps, and the headlights of the cars gave a daylight look to the fields.

The men spread out and broke into the woods in a row, tramping through, throwing the beams of the lights in all the shadowy areas, calling the girl's name at intervals, looking for signs of her passing. The youth hunted with Galton and Dennis, but they made him stay in back of them lest his inexperienced bumbling destroy a clue.

They pushed through briars and bushes and trees for a long five minutes and then, from far on the left, there came a shout. Galton, Dennis and the boy started in that direction following the others.

When they reached the spot, the other men were clustered and mumbling, heads and shoulders bowed. The air was black and electric.

"You find her?" the old man said, pushing through.

"We found her."

They stepped aside so Galton, Dennis and the youth could see.

It was a sad and ugly sight. The young girl lay dead and cold under a tree. Her pants were down, her skirt was up and her blouse and bra were off. Her once-pretty head was bloody and broken, and a redstained rock, wrenched from the nearby earth, lay beside her.

The boy said, "No! Oh, God, no!" and turned away,

moaning. Dennis muttered a prayer under his breath; the captain shook his head and sighed.

"I was afraid of that," the old man muttered. "When she still wasn't home, I was afraid." He turned away and, with head down, started back. Dennis, the distraught youth and the searchers followed.

At the car they gathered around as Galton radioed in. The girl was dead, he reported heavily. The medical examiner was to be notified, the photo lab and the morgue. He got out of the car again, closed the door and leaned an elbow on the roof. He shook his head once, straightened a little and took a breath. "All right," he said wearily to the boy, "tell us what happened."

The boy said, "I did tell you."

The old mouth tightened and the tone grew firmer. "Tell it again, son. But this time tell it right."

The youth, glancing nervously at the large group of encircling men, said querulously, "What do you mean by right?"

"Tell it the way it really happened."

"I don't get you."

"You know, like this. You brought the girl into the park and a car with three yelling boys went by. You pulled off and parked under these trees. You took the girl down into the woods and started to pitch woo. Only she didn't want to go as far as you did and she tried to fight you off. But you were determined and you hit her with a rock to quiet her down, only, when it was all over, you found out you'd hit her too hard and she was dead. So you remembered the car full of boys and then you came in and told us the boys had kidnapped her." The old man turned his light on the youth's face. "That's pretty close to what happened, isn't it?"

The stunned boy blinked in the glare. "No," he whispered, his face white. "It's like I told you. They grabbed her. They hit me . . ." He looked around desperately, but all the faces were cold and disbelieving.

The old man shook his head impatiently. "Do you think you're the first person who's ever tried to sell the police a phony story? Do you think we con that easy? We get it all the time. All of us. I've heard so many phonies I could smell this one the moment you came in tonight. I hoped like hell you were telling the truth, but when she wasn't in by midnight, I was afraid you weren't."

The boy said heatedly, "You're crazy. I am telling the truth! I don't know what you've heard before, but this time you're wrong."

The old man snorted. "Are you kidding? All I have to do is look at her and look at you and I know the story's a lie. We all do."

"I defy you. What's not true about it? Show me what's not true!"

"The fact that you're alive and she's dead makes it not true."

He stopped and blinked in astonishment. "What's that got to do with it?"

Galton glanced helplessly at his grim-faced crew. "That's got everything to do with it," he explained to the boy. "Three guys, right? That's your story. There were three guys?"

"Yes."

"So what did they want? Did they want to kill people? Then why didn't they kill you both? That answer won't do. Did they just want to rape a girl? Then they'd mess you up to keep you from interfering. That's all right. But then they wouldn't kill the girl. They wouldn't do anything to her at all—outside of the rape, that is. She'd have gotten home alive."

"But she resisted! They hit her with the rock to subdue her!"

"Uh uh." Mike Galton shook his head. "One man, maybe. You, alone, might have to use a rock to have your way with her. But three men? What would they need rocks for? Two could hold her for the third so tight she couldn't move a muscle." The old man, studying the boy's face in the light, dropped the bitterness and said quietly, "Forget the fancy tales, son. That girl's body is going to be examined very, very carefully for physical evidence."

The boy's face crinkled suddenly and he started to sob.

My favorite story of my own making? Of course MWA shall have it! Let me think . . .

You shall have one of my tales of Dr. Sam: Johnson, detector, as told by his friend and biographer, James Boswell—inevitably, since all my short stories of detection involve that engaging pair of real-life 18th-century personalities.

My favorite is always the last one I wrote; but that one is just off the typewriter, and not yet ripe for anthologizing.

So which recent story shall it be? A locked room, a blackamoor trepanned, a lost heir, a bamboozle in Bedlam, a scandalous duchess . . .

Scandal in high life? By all means, let us have the duchess!

So here I present "Milady Bigamy." Milady is modeled on a real person, the notorious "Maid" of Honor, Elizabeth Chudleigh, Duchess of Kingston—or was she rather Mrs. Augustus Hervey, Countess of Bristol? It took a trial in the House of Lords to decide. Add Boswell for the defense, masterminded by Dr. Johnson, and what possibilities ensue!

I value this story especially, because I had fun writing it, and because I have a sneaking fondness for both the naughty duchess and her bold partner. So here she is, scandalous but appealing, Milady Bigamy!

LILLIAN DE LA TORRE

MILADY BIGAMY

(as told by James Boswell, Spring, 1778)

LILLIAN DE LA TORRE

"I have often thought," remarked Dr. Sam: Johnson, one Spring morning in the year 1778, "that if I kept a seraglio—"

He had often thought!—Dr. Sam: Johnson, moral philosopher, defender of right and justice, *detector* of crime and chicane, had often thought of keeping a seraglio! I looked at his square bulk, clad in his old-fashioned full-skirted coat of plain mulberry broadcloth, his strong rugged countenance with his little brown scratch-wig clapped on askew above it, and suppressed a smile.

"I say, sir, if I kept a seraglio, the houris should be clad in cotton and linen, and not at all in wool and silk, for the animal fibres are nasty, but the vegetable fibres are cleanly."

"Why sir," I replied seriously, "I too have long meditated on keeping a seraglio, and wondered whether it may not be lawful to a man to have plurality of wives, say one for comfort and another for shew."

"What, sir, you talk like a heathen Turk!" growled the great Cham, rounding on me. "If this cozy arrangement be permitted a man, what is to hinder the ladies from a like indulgence?—one husband, say, for support, and 'tother for sport? 'Twill be a wise father then that knows

175

his own heir. You are a lawyer, sir, you know the problems of filiation. Would you multiply them? No, sir: bigamy is a crime, and there's an end on't!"

At this I hastily turned the topick, and of bigamy we spoke no more. Little did we then guess that a question of bigamy was soon to engage my friend's attention, in the affair of the Duchess of Kingsford—if Duchess in truth she was.

I had first beheld this lady some seven years before, when she was Miss Bellona Chamleigh, the notorious Maid of Honour. At Mrs. Cornelys's Venetian ridotto she flashed upon my sight, and took my breath away.

Rumour had not exaggerated her flawless beauty. She had a complection like strawberries and cream, a swelling rosy lip, a nose and firmset chin sculptured in marble. Even the small-pox had spared her, for the one mark it had left her touched the edge of her pouting mouth like a tiny dimple. In stature she was low, a pocket Venus, with a bosom of snow tipped with fire. A single beauty-spot shaped like a new moon adorned her perfect navel—

I go too far. Suffice it to say that for costume she wore a girdle of silken fig-leaves, and personated Eve—Eve after the fall, from the glances she was giving her gallants. One at either rosy elbow, they pressed her close, and she smiled upon them impartially. I recognised them both.

The tall, thin, swarthy, cadaverous apparition in a dark domino was Philip Piercy, Duke of Kingsford, once the handsomest Peer in the Kingdom, but now honed to an edge by a long life of dissipation. If he was no longer the handsomest, he was still the richest. Rumour had it that he was quite far gone in infatuation, and would lay those riches, with his hand and heart, at Miss Bellona's feet.

Would she accept of them? Only one obstacle intervened. That obstacle stood at her other elbow: Captain

Aurelius Hart, of H.M.S. *Dangerous*, a third-rate of fifty guns, which now lay fitting at Portsmouth, leaving the gallant Captain free to press his suit.

In person, the Captain was the lady's match, not tall, but broad of shoulder, and justly proportioned in every limb. He had farseeing light blue eyes in a sun-burned face, and his expression was cool, with a look of incipient mirth. The patches of Harlequin set off his muscular masculinity.

With his name too Dame Rumour had been busy. He had won the lady's heart, it was averred; but he was not likely to win her hand, being an impecunious younger son, tho' of an Earl.

So she passed on in her nakedness, giving no sign of which lover—if either—should possess her.

A black-avised young fellow garbed like the Devil watched them go. He scowled upon them with a look so lowering I looked again, and recognised him for Mr. Eadwin Maynton, Kingsford's nephew, heir-presumptive to his pelf (tho' not his Dukedom), being the son of the Duke's sister. If Bellona married his Uncle, it would cost Mr. Eadwin dear.

The audacity of the Maid of Honour at the masquerade had been too blatant. She was forthwith banished from the Court. Unrepentant, she had rusticated herself. Accompanied only by her confidential woman, one Ann Crannock, she slipped off to her Aunt Hammer's country house at Linton, near Portsmouth.

Near Portsmouth! Where lay the Captain's ship! No more was needed to inflate the tale.

"The Captain calls daily to press his suit."

"The Captain has taken her into keeping."

"There you are out, the Captain has wedded her secretly."

"You are all misled. The *Dangerous* has gone to sea—the Captain has deserted her."

"And serve her right, the hussy!"

The hussy Maid of Honour was not one to be rusticated for long. Soon she was under their noses again, on the arm of the still infatuated Duke of Kingsford. Mr. Eadwin Maynton moved Heaven and earth to forestall a marriage, but only succeeded in mortally offending his wealthy Uncle. Within a year of that scandalous masquerade, Miss Bellona Chamleigh was Duchess of Kingsford.

Appearing at Court on the occasion, she flaunted herself in white sattin encrusted with Brussels point and embroidered with a Duke's ransom in pearls. She would give the world something to talk about!

They talked with a will. They talked of Captain Hart, jilted on the Jamaica station. They talked of Mr. Eadwin Maynton, sulking at home. They were still talking several years later when the old Duke suddenly died—of his Duchess's obstreperous behaviour, said some with a frown, of her amorous charms, said others with a snigger.

It was at this juncture that one morning in the year '78 a crested coach drew rein in Bolt Court and a lady descended. From an upper window I looked down on her modish tall powdered head and her furbelowed polonaise of royal purple brocade.

I turned from the window with a smile. "What, sir, you have an assignation with a fine lady? Am I *de trop*?"

"You are never *de trop*, Bozzy. Pray remain, and let us see what this visitation portends."

The Duchess of Kingsford swept in without ceremony.

"Pray forgive me, Dr. Johnson, my errand is to Mr. Boswell. I was directed hither to find him—I *must* have Mr. Boswell!"

"And you *shall* have Mr. Boswell," I cried warmly, "tho' it were for wager of battle!"

"You have hit it, sir! For my honour, perhaps my life, is at stake! You shall defend me, sir, in my need—and Dr. Johnson," she added with a sudden flashing smile, "shall be our counsellor."

"If I am to counsel you, Madam, you must tell me clearly what is the matter."

"Know then, gentlemen, that in the winter last past, my dear husband the Duke of Kingsford died, and left me inconsolable—inconsolable, yet not bare, for in token of our undying devotion, he left me all that was his. In so doing, he cut off his nephew Eadwin with a few guineas, and therein lies the difficulty. For Mr. Eadwin is no friend to me. He has never spared to vilify me for a scheaming adventuress. And now he has hit upon a plan—he thinks—in one motion to disgrace me and deprive me of my inheritance. He goes about to nullify my marriage to the Duke."

"How can this be done, your Grace?"

"He has resurrected the old gossip about Captain Hart, that we were secretly married at Linton long ago. The whole town buzzes with the tale, and the comedians lampoon me on the stage as Milady Bigamy."

"What the comedians play," observed Dr. Johnson drily, "is not evidence. Gossip cannot harm you, your Grace—unless it is true."

"It is false. There was no such marriage. There might have been, it is true (looking pensive) had he not abandoned me, as Aeneas abandoned Dido, and put to sea in the *Dangerous*—leaving me," she added frankly, "to make a better match."

"Then where is the difficulty?"

"False testimony is the difficulty. Aunt Hammer is

dead, and the clergyman is dead. But his widow is alive, and Eadwin has bought her. Worst of all, he has suborned Ann Crannock, my confidential woman that was, and she will swear to the wedding."

"Are there marriage lines?"

"Of course not. No marriage, no marriage lines."

"And the Captain? Where is he?"

"At sea. He now commands a first-rate, the *Challenger*, and wins great fame, and much prize money, against the French. I am well assured I am safe in that quarter."

"Then," said I, "this accusation of bigamy is soon answered. But I am not accustomed to appear at the Old Bailey."

"The Old Bailey!" cried she with scorn. "Who speaks of the Old Bailey? Shall a Duchess be tried like a greasy bawd at the Old Bailey? I am the Duchess of Kingsford! I shall be tried by my Peers!"

"If you are Mrs. Aurelius Hart?"

"I am not Mrs. Aurelius Hart! But if I were—Aurelius's brothers are dead in the American war, his father the Earl is no more, and Aurelius is Earl of Westerfell. As Duchess or as Countess, I shall be tried by my Peers!"

Flushed and with flashing eyes, the ci-devant Maid of Honour looked every inch a Peeress as she uttered these words.

" 'Tis for this I must have Mr. Boswell. From the gallery in the House of Lords I recently heard him plead the cause of the heir of Douglas: in such terms of melting eloquence did he defend the good name of Lady Jane Douglas, I will have no other to defend mine!"

My new role as the Duchess's champion entailed many duties that I had hardly expected. There were of course long consults with herself and her solicitor, a dry, prosy old solicitor named Pettigree. But I had not counted on attending her strolls in the park, or carrying her bandboxes from the milliner's.

"And to-morrow, Mr. Boswell, you shall squire me to the ridotto."

"The masquerade! Your Grace jests!"

"Far from it, sir. Edwin Maynton seeks to drive me under ground, but he shall not succeed. No, sir; my heart is set on it, and to the ridotto I will go!"

To the ridotto we went. The Duchess was regal in a domino of Roman purple over a gown of lavender lutestring, and wore a half-mask with a valance of provocative black lace to the chin. I personated a wizard, with my black gown strewn with cabbalistick symbols, and a conical hat to make me tall.

It was a ridotto *al fresco*, in the groves of Vauxhall. In the soft May evening, we listened to the band of musick in the pavilion; we took a syllabub; we walked in the allées to hear the nightingale sing. It was pleasant strolling beneath the young green of the trees by the light of a thousand lamps, watching the masquers pass: a Boadicea in armour, a Hamlet all in black, an Indian Sultana, a muscular Harlequin with a long-nosed Venetian mask, a cowled monk—

"So, Milady Bigamy!" The voice was loud and harsh. "You hide your face, as is fit; but we know you for what you are!"

Passing masquers paused to listen. Pulling the mask from her face, the Duchess whirled on the speaker. A thin swarthy countenance glowered at her under the monk's cowl.

"Eadwin Maynton!" she said quietly. "Why do you pursue me? How have I harmed you? 'Twas your own folly that alienated your kind Uncle."

" 'Twas your machinations!" He was perhaps inebriated, and intent on making a scene. More listeners arrived to enjoy it.

"I have irrefutable evidences of your double dealing," he bawled, "and when it comes to the proof, I'll unduchess you, Milady Bigamy!"

"This fellow is drunk. Come, Mr. Boswell."

The Duchess turned away contemptuously. Mr. Eadwin seized her arm and swung her back. The next minute he was flat on the ground, and a menacing figure in Harlequin's patches stood over him.

"What is your pleasure, Madam?" asked the Harlequin calmly. "Shall he beg pardon?"

"Let him lie," said the Duchess. "He's a liar, let him lie."

"Then be off!"

Maynton made off, muttering.

"And you, ladies and gentlemen, the comedy is over."

Behind the beak-nosed mask, light eyes of ice-blue raked the gapers, and they began to melt away.

"I thank you, my friend. And now, as you say, the comedy is over," smiled the Duchess.

"There is yet a farce to play," said the Harlequin. *"The Fatal Marriage."* He lifted his mask by its snout, and smiled at her. "Who, unless a husband, shall protect his lady wife?"

The Duchess's face stiffened.

"I do not know you."

"What, forgot so soon?" His glance laughed at her. "Such is the fate of the sailor!"

"Do not mock me, Aurelius. You know we are nothing to one another."

"Speak for yourself, Bellona."

"I will speak one word, then: Good-bye."

She reached me her hand, and I led her away. Captain

Hart watched us go, his light eyes intent, and a small half-smile upon his lips.

That was the end of Milady Duchess's ridotto. What would come of it?

Nothing good, I feared. My fears were soon doubled. Returning from the river one day in the Duchess's carriage, we found ourselves passing by Mr. Eadwin Maynton's lodging. As we approached, a man issued from the door, an erect figure in nautical blue, whose ruddy countenance wore a satisfied smile. He turned away without a glance in our direction.

"Aurelius calling upon Eadwin!" cried the Duchess, staring after him. "What are they plotting against me?"

To this I had no answer.

Time was running out. The trial was looming close. In Westminster Hall, carpenters were knocking together scaffolding to prepare for the shew. At Kingsford House, Dr. Johnson was quoting Livy, I was polishing my oration, and old Pettigree was digging up learned instances.

"Keep up your heart, your Grace," said the solicitor earnestly in his rusty voice, "for should the worst befall, I have instances to shew that the penalty is no longer death at the stake—"

"At the stake!" gasped the Duchess.

"No, your Grace, certainly not, not death by burning. I shall prove it, but meerly branding on the hand—"

"Branding!" shrieked the Duchess. Her white fingers clutched mine.

"No *alibi*," fretted old Pettigree, "no testimony from Linton on your behalf, Captain Hart in the adverse camp—no, no, your Grace must put your hope in me!"

At such Job's comfort Dr. Johnson could scarce repress a smile.

"Hope rather," he suggested, "in Mr. Boswell, for if

these women lie, it must be made manifest in cross-examination. I shall be on hand to note what they say, as I once noted the Parliamentary debates from the gallery; and it will go hard but we shall catch them out in their lies."

Bellona Chamleigh lifted her head in a characteristick wilful gesture.

"I trust in Mr. Boswell, and I am not afraid."

Rising early on the morning of the fateful day, I donned my voluminous black advocate's gown, and a lawyer's powdered wig that I had rented from Tibbs the perruquier for a guinea. I thought that the latter well set off my dark countenance, with its long nose and attentive look. Thus attired, I posted myself betimes outside Westminster Hall to see the procession pass.

At ten o'clock it began. First came the factotums and the functionaries, the yeoman-usher robed, heralds in tabards, serjeants-at-arms with maces in their hands. Then the Peers paced into view, walking two and two, splendid in their crimson velvet mantles and snowy capes of ermine powdered with black tail-tips. Last came the Lord High Steward, his long crimson train borne up behind him, and so they passed into Westminster Hall.

When I entered at last, in my turn as a lowly lawyer, the sight struck me with something like awe. The noble hall, with its soaring roof, was packed to the vault with persons of quality seated upon tier after tier of scaffolding. Silks rustled, laces fluttered, brocades glowed, high powdered foretops rose over all. Around three sides of the level floor gathered the Peers in their splendid robes.

All stood uncovered as the King's Commission was read aloud and the white staff of office was ceremoniously handed up to the Lord High Steward where he sat under a crimson canopy. With a sibilant rustle, the packed hall sat, and the trial began.

"Oyez, oyez, oyez! Bellona, duchess-dowager of Kingsford, come into court!"

She came in a little procession of her own, her ladies of honour, her chaplain, her physician and her apothecary attending; but every staring eye saw her only. Old Pettigree had argued in vain that deep mourning was the only wear; she would have none of it. She walked in proudly in white sattin embroidered with pearls, that very courtdress she had flaunted as old Kingsford's bride: "In token of my innocence," she told old Pettigree.

With a deep triple reverence she took her place on the elevated platform that served for a dock, and stood with lifted head to listen to the indictment.

"Bellona, duchess-dowager of Kingsford, you stand indicted by the name of Bellona, wife of Aurelius Hart, now Earl of Westerfell, for that you, in the eleventh year of our sovereign lord King George the Third, being then married and the wife of the said Aurelius Hart, did marry and take to husband Philip Piercy, Duke of Kingsford, feloniously and with force and arms—"

Though it was the usual legal verbiage to recite that every felony was committed "with force and arms," the picture conjured up of little Bellona, like a highwayman, clapping a pistol to the old Duke's head and marching him to the altar, was too much for the Lords. Laughter swept the benches, and the lady at the bar frankly joined in.

"How say you? Are you guilty of the felony whereof you stand indicted, or not guilty?"

Silence fell. Bellona sobered, lifted her head, and pronounced in her rich voice: "Not guilty!"

"Culprit, how will you be tried?"

"By God and my Peers."

"Oyez, oyez, oyez! All manner of persons that will give evidence on behalf of our sovereign lord the King, against Bellona, duchess-dowager of Kingsford, let them come forth, and they shall be heard, for now she stands at the bar upon her deliverance."

Thereupon Edward Thurlow, Attorney General, came forth, formidable with his bristling hairy eyebrows and his growling voice like distant thunder.

He began with an eloquent denunciation of the crime of bigamy, its malignant complection, its pernitious example, *et caetera, et caetera.* That duty performed, he drily recited the story of the alleged marriage at Linton as, he said, his witnesses would prove it.

"And now, my Lords, we will proceed to call our witnesses. Call Margery Amys."

Mrs. Amys, the clergyman's widow, was a tall stick of a woman well on in years, wearing rusty bombazine and an old-fashioned lawn cap tied under her nutcracker chin. She put a gnarled hand on the Bible the clerk held out to her.

"Hearken to your oath. The evidence you shall give on behalf of our sovereign lord the King's majesty, against Bellona duchess-dowager of Kingsford, shall be the truth, the whole truth, and nothing but the truth, so help you God."

The old dame mumbled something, and kissed the book. But when the questions began, she spoke up in a rusty screech, and graphically portrayed a clandestine marriage at Linton church in the year '71.

"They came by night, nigh upon midnight, to the church at Linton, and desired of the late Mr. Amys that he should join them two in matrimony."

Q. Which two?

A. Them two, Captain Hart and Miss Bellona Chamleigh.

Q. And did he so unite them?

A. He did so, and I stood by and saw it done.

Q. Who was the bride?

A. Miss Bellona Chamleigh.

Q. Say if you see her now present?

A. (pointing) That's her, her in white.

The Duchess stared her down contemptuously.

As I rose to cross-examine, I sent a glance to the upper tier, where sat Dr. Johnson. He was writing, and frowning as he wrote; but no guidance came my way. Making up with a portentous scowl for what I lacked in matter, I began:

Q. It was dark at midnight?

A. Yes, sir, mirk dark.

Q. Then, Mrs. Amys, how did you see the bride to know her again?

A. Captain Hart lighted a wax taper, and put it in his hat, and by that light they were married, and so I know her again.

Q. (probing) You know a great deal, Madam. What has Mr. Eadwin Maynton given you to appear on his behalf?

A. Nothing, sir.

Q. What has he promised you?

A. Nothing neither.

Q. Then why are you here?

A. (piously) I come for the sake of truth and justice, sir.

And on that sanctimonious note, I had to let her go.

"Call Ann Crannock!"

Ann Crannock approached in a flurry of curtseys, scattering smiles like sweetmeats. The erstwhile confidential woman was a plump, round, rosy little thing, of a certain age, but still pleasing, carefully got up like a stage milkmaid in snowy kerchief and pinner. She mounted the platform with a bounce, and favoured the Attorney General with a beaming smile.

The Duchess hissed something between her teeth. It sounded like "Judas!"

The clerk with his Bible hastily stepped between. Ann Crannock took the oath, smiling broadly, and Thurlow commenced his interrogation:

Q. You were the prisoner's woman?

A. Yes, sir, and I loved her like my own child.

Q. You saw her married to Captain Hart?

A. Yes, sir, the pretty dears, they could not wait for very lovesickness.

Q. That was at Linton in July of the year 1771?

A. Yes, sir, the third of July, for the Captain sailed with the Jamaica squadron on the fourth. Ah, the sweet poppets, they were loath to part!

Q. Who married them?

A. Mr. Amys, sir, the vicar of Linton. We walked to the church together, the lady's Aunt Mrs. Hammer, and I myself, and the sweet lovebirds. The clock was going towards midnight, that the servants might not know.

Q. Why must not the servants know?

A. Sir, nobody was to know, lest the Captain's father the Earl cut him off for marrying a lady without any fortune.

Q. Well, and they were married by Mr. Amys. Did he give a certificate of the marriage?

A. Yes, sir, he did, he wrote it out with his own hand, and I signed for a witness. I was happy for my lady from my heart.

Q. You say the vicar gave a certificate. (Thurlow sharply raised his voice as he whipped out a paper.) Is this it?

A. (clasping her hands and beaming with pleasure) O sir, that is it. See, there is my handwriting. Well I mind how the Captain kissed it and put it in his bosom to keep!

"'Tis false!"

The Duchess was on her feet in a rage. For a breath she stood so in her white sattin and pearls; then she sank down in a swoon. Her attendants instantly raised her and bore her out among them. I saw the little apothecary hopping like a grasshopper on the fringes, flourishing his hartshorn bottle.

The Peers were glad enough of an excuse for a recess, and so was I. I pushed my way to the lobby in search of Dr. Johnson. I was furious. "The jade has lied to us!" I cried as I beheld him. "I'll throw up my brief!"

"You will do well to do so," murmured the Attorney General at my elbow. He still held the fatal marriage lines.

"Pray, Mr. Thurlow, give me a sight of that paper," requested Dr. Johnson.

"Dr. Johnson's wish is my command," said Thurlow with a bow: he had a particular regard for the burly philosopher.

Dr. Johnson held the paper to the light, peering so close with his near-sighted eyes that his lashes almost brushed the surface.

"Aye, sir, look close," smiled Thurlow. "'Tis authentick, I assure you. I have particular reason to know."

"Then there's no more to be said."

Thurlow took the paper, bowed, and withdrew.

All along I had been conscious of another legal figure hovering near. Now I looked at him directly. He was hunched into a voluminous advocate's gown, and topped by one of Mr. Tibbs's largest wigs; but there was no missing those ice-blue eyes.

"Captain Hart! You here?"

"I had a mind to see the last of my widow," he said sardonically. "I see she is in good hands."

"But to come here! Will you not be recognised, and detained, and put on the stand?"

"What, Peers detain a Peer? No, sir. While the House sits, I cannot be summoned: and when it rises, all is over. Bellona may be easy; I shan't peach. Adieu."

"Stay, sir—" But he was gone.

After an hour, the Duchess of Kingsford returned to the hall with her head held high, and inquiry resumed. There was not much more harm Mistress Crannock could do. She was led once more to repeat: she saw them wedded, the sweet dears, and she signed the marriage lines, and that was the very paper now in Mr. Thurlow's hand.

"You say this is the paper? That is conclusive, I think. (smiling) You may cross-examine, Mr. Boswell."

Ann Crannock smiled at me, and I smiled back, as I began:

Q. You say, Mistress Crannock, that you witnessed this marriage?

A. Yes, sir.

Q. And then and there you signed the marriage lines?

A. Yes, sir.

Q. On July 3, 1771?

A. Yes, sir.

Q. Think well, did you not set your hand to it at some subsequent date?

A. No, sir.

Q. Perhaps to oblige Mr. Eadwin Maynton?

A. No, sir, certainly not. I saw them wedded, and signed forthwith.

Q. Then I put it to you: *How did you on July 3, 1771, set your hand to a piece of paper that was not made at the manufactory until the year 1774?*

Ann Crannock turned red, then pale, opened her mouth, but no sound came. "Can you make that good, Mr. Boswell?" demanded Thurlow.

"Yes, sir if I may call a witness, tho' out of order."

"Aye, call him—let's hear him—" the answer swept the Peers' benches. Their Lordships cared nothing for order.

"I call Dr. Samuel Johnson."

Dr. Johnson advanced and executed one of his stately obeisances.

"You must know, my Lords and gentlemen," he began, "that I have dealt with paper for half a century, and I have friends among the paper-makers. Paper, my Lords, is made by grinding up rag, and wetting it, and laying it to dry upon a grid of wires. Now he who has a mind to sign his work, twists his mark in wire and lays it in, for every wire leaves its impression, which is called a watermark. With such a mark, in the shape of an S, did my friend Sully the paper-maker sign the papers he made before the year '74.

"But in that year, my Lords, he took his son into partnership, and from thenceforth marked his paper with a double S. I took occasion this afternoon to confirm the date, 1774, from his own mouth. Now, my Lords, if you take this supposed document of 1771 (taking it in hand) and hold it thus to the light, you may see in it the double S watermark: which, my Lords, proves this so-called conclusive evidence to be a forgery, and Ann Crannock a liar!"

The paper passed from hand to hand, and the Lords began to seethe.

"The Question! The Question!" was the cry. The clamour persisted, and did not cease until perforce the Lord High Steward arose, bared his head, and put the question:

"Is the prisoner guilty of the felony whereof she stands indicted, or not guilty?"

In a breathless hush, the first of the barons rose in his ermine. Bellona lifted her chin. The young nobleman put his right hand upon his heart and pronounced clearly:

"Not guilty, upon my honour!"

191

So said each and every Peer:
"Not guilty, upon my honour!"
My client was acquitted!

At her Grace's desire, I had provided means whereby, at the trial's end, come good fortune or ill, the Duchess might escape the press of the populace. A plain coach waited at a postern door, and thither, her white sattin and pearls muffled in a capuchin, my friend and I hurried her.

Quickly she mounted the step and slipped inside. Suddenly she screamed. Inside the coach a man awaited us. Captain Aurelius Hart in his blue coat lounged there at his ease.

"Nay, sweet wife, my wife no more," he murmured softly, "do not shun me, for now that you are decreed to be another man's widow, I mean to woo you anew. I have prepared a small victory feast at my lodgings, and I hope your friends will do us the honour of partaking of it with us."

"Victory!" breathed Bellona as the coach moved us off. "How could you be so sure of victory?"

"Because," said Dr. Johnson, "he brought it about. Am I not right, sir?"

"Why, sir, as to that—"

"As to that, sir, there is no need to prevaricate. I learned this afternoon from Sully the paper-maker that a seafaring man resembling Captain Hart had been at him last week to learn about papers, and had carried away a sheet of the double S kind. It is clear that it was you, sir, who foisted upon Eadwin Maynton the forgery that, being exposed, defeated him."

All this while the coach was carrying us onward. In the shadowy interior, Captain Hart frankly grinned.

" 'Twas easy, sir. Mr. Eadwin was eager, and quite

without scruple, and why should he doubt a paper that came from the hands of the wronged husband? How could he guess that I had carefully contrived it to ruin his cause?"

"It was a bad cause," said Dr. Johnson, "and he is well paid for his lack of scruple."

"But, Captain Hart," I put in, "how could you be sure that we would detect the forgery and proclaim it?"

"To make sure, I muffled up and ventured into the lobby. I was prepared to slip a billet into Mr. Boswell's pocket; but when I saw Dr. Johnson studying the water-mark, I knew that I need not interfere further."

We were at the door. Captain Hart lifted down the lady, and with his arm around her guided her up the stair. She yielded mutely, as in a daze.

In the withdrawing room a pleasing cold regale awaited us, but Dr. Johnson was in no hurry to go to table. There was still something on his mind.

"Then, sir, before we break bread, satisfy me of one more thing. How came Ann Crannock to say the hand-writing was hers?"

"Because, sir," said Captain Hart, with a self-satisfied look, "it was so like her own. I find I have a pretty turn for forgery."

"That I can believe, sir. But where did you find an exemplar to fashion your forgery after?"

"Why, sir, I—" The Captain darted a glance from face to face. "You are keen, sir. There could only be one docu-ment to forge after—and here it is (producing a folded paper from his pocket). Behold the true charter of my happiness!"

I regarded it thunderstruck. A little faded as to ink, a little frayed at the edges, there lay before us a marriage certificate in due form, between Miss Bellona Chamleigh, spinster, and Captain Aurelius Hart, bachelor, drawn up in the Reverend Mr. Amys's wavering hand, and attested by Sophie Hammer and Ann Crannock, July 3, 1771!

"So, Madam," growled Dr. Johnson, "you were guilty after all!"

"Oh, no, sir! 'Twas no marriage, for the Captain was recalled to his ship, and sailed for the Jamaica station, without—without—"

"Without making you in deed and in truth my own," smiled Captain Hart.

At this specimen of legal reasoning, Dr. Johnson shook his head in bafflement, the bigamous Duchess looked as innocent as possible, and Captain Hart laughed aloud.

" 'Twas an unfortunate omission," he said, "whence flow all our uneasinesses, and I shall rectify it this night, my Countess consenting. What do you say, my dear?"

For the first time the Duchess looked directly at him. In spite of herself she blushed, and the tiny pox mark beside her lip deepened in a smile.

"Why, Aurelius, since you have saved me from branding or worse, what can I say but yes?"

"Then at last," cried the Captain, embracing her, "you shall be well and truly bedded, and so farewell to the Duchess of Kingsford!"

It seemed the moment to withdraw. As we descended, we heard them laughing together.

"Never look so put about, Bozzy," murmured Dr. Johnson on the stair. "You have won your case; justice, tho' irregularly, is done; the malignancy of Eadwin Maynton has been defeated; and as to the two above—they deserve each other."

One spring afternoon in 1979 on the island of Maui, four of us had chartered a boat to go out into the Molokai Channel and play with the whales. Waiting for the boat, we strolled along the waterfront in Lahaina, stopped at a curio shop and bought a few trinkets to sent to friends. Curious about some of the ivory carvings in the display cabinets, I asked the shopkeeper to tell me about the art of scrimshaw. You will find out most of what he told me in the course of reading this story.

When we left the shop and went down to the dock, I saw a young woman in extraordinarily ragged clothes picking through one of the mesh trash baskets along the walkway. By the time we reached the boat she had disappeared from view. I never saw her again. But the curious juxtaposition in time and space of the young derelict with the idea of scrimshaw stayed in my mind. A few days later, on the beach at Kapalua Bay, I took out a notebook and scribbled the first draft of this story.

In 1980 an adaptation of the story was filmed as a half-hour episode of the syndicated television series "Tales of the Unexpected," introduced by John Houseman. The film's star, the late Joan Hackett, captured Brenda exactly as I had seen her.

It's a truism that all a writer's stories are his children and that it is impossible to pick one's favorite child. But if pressed as I am now, I'm forced to admit that this one, of the short stories I've written thus far, pleases me most, perhaps because it was realized so exquisitely by the actress who brought the main character stunningly to life. So I am pleased to have Joan Hackett to thank for the inclusion of "Scrimshaw" in this anthology, and am dedicating it to her memory.

—BRIAN GARFIELD

SCRIMSHAW

BRIAN GARFIELD

She suggested liquid undulation: a lei-draped girl in a grass skirt under a windblown palm tree, her hands and hips expressive of the flow of the hula. Behind her, beyond the surf, a whaling ship was poised to approach the shore, its square-rigged sails bold against a polished white sky.

The scene was depicted meticulously upon ivory: a white fragment of tusk the size of a dollar bill. The etched detail was exquisite: the scrimshaw engraving was carved of thousands of thread-like lines and the artist's knife hadn't slipped once.

The price tag may have been designed to persuade tourists of the seriousness of the art form: it was in four figures. But Brenda was unimpressed. She put the piece back on the display cabinet and left the shop.

The hot Lahaina sun beat against her face and she went across Front Street to the Sea Wall, thrust her hands into the pockets of her dress and brooded upon the anchorage.

Boats were moored around the harbor—catamarans, glass-bottom tourist boats, marlin fishermen, pleasure sailboats, outrigger canoes, yachts. Playthings. It's the wrong place for me, she thought.

Beyond the wide channel the islands of Lanai and

Kahoolawe made lovely horizons under their umbrellas of delicate cloud, but Brenda had lost her eye for that sort of thing; she noticed the stagnant heat, the shabbiness of the town and the offensiveness of the tourists who trudged from shop to shop in their silly hats, their sunburnt flab, their hapless T-shirts emblazoned with local graffiti: "Here Today, Gone to Maui."

A leggy young girl went by, drawing Brenda's brief attention: one of those taut tan sunbleached creatures of the surfboards—gorgeous and luscious and vacuous. Filled with youth and hedonism, equipped with all the optional accessories of pleasure. Brenda watched gloomily, her eyes following the girl as far as the end of the Sea Wall, where the girl turned to cross the street. Brenda then noticed two men in conversation there.

One of them was the wino who always seemed to be there: a stringy unshaven tattered character who spent the days huddling in the shade sucking from a bottle in a brown bag and begging coins from tourists. At night he seemed to prowl the alleys behind the seafood restaurants, living off scraps like a stray dog: she had seen him once, from the window of her flyspecked room, scrounging in the can behind the hotel's kitchen; and then two nights ago near a garbage bin—she had taken a short cut home after a dissatisfying lonely dinner and she'd nearly tripped over him.

The man talking with the wino seemed familiar and yet she could not place him. He had the lean bearded look of one who had gone native; but not really, for he was set apart by his fastidiousness. He wore sandals, yet his feet seemed clean, the toenails glimmering; he wore a sandy beard but it was neatly trimmed and his hair was expensively cut, not at all shaggy; he wore a blue denim short-sleeved shirt, fashionably faded but it had sleeve pockets and epaulets and had come from a designer shop; and his white sailor's trousers fit perfectly.

I know him, Brenda thought, but she couldn't summon the energy to stir from her spot when the bearded man and the wino walked away into the town. Vaguely and without real interest she wondered idly what those two could possibly have to talk about together.

She found shade on the harborfront. Inertia held her there for hours while she recounted the litany of her misfortunes. Finally hunger bestirred her and she slouched back to her miserable little third-class hotel.

The next day, half drunk in the afternoon and wilting in the heat, Brenda noticed vaguely that the wino was no longer in his usual place. In fact she hadn't seen the wino at all, not last night and not today.

The headache was painful and she boarded the jitney bus to go up-island a few miles. She got off near the Kapalua headland and trudged down to the public beach. It was cooler here because the northwest end of the island was open to the fresh trade winds; she settled under a palm tree, pulled off her ragged sneakers and dug her toes into the cool sand. The toes weren't very clean. She was going too long between baths these days. The bathroom in the hotel was at the end of the corridor and she went there as infrequently as possible because she couldn't be sure who she might encounter and anyhow the tub was filthy and there was no shower.

Across the channel loomed the craggy mountains of Molokai, infamous island, leper colony, its dark volcanic mass shadowed by perpetual sinister rain clouds, and Brenda lost herself in gruesome speculations about exile, isolation, loneliness and wretched despair, none of which seemed at all foreign to her.

198

The sun moved and took the shade with it and she moved round to the other side of the palm tree, tucking the fabric of the cheap dress under her when she sat down. The dress was about gone—frayed, faded, the material ready to disintegrate. She only had two others left. Then it would be jeans and the boatneck. It didn't matter, really. There was no one to dress up for.

It wasn't that she was altogether ugly; she wasn't ugly; she wasn't even plain, really; she had studied photographs of herself over the years and she had gazed in the mirror and tried to understand, but it had eluded her. All right, perhaps she was too bony, her shoulders too big, flat in front, not enough flesh on her—but there were men who liked their women bony; that didn't explain it. She had the proper features in the proper places and, after all, Modigliani hadn't found that sort of face abominable to behold, had he?

But ever since puberty there'd been something about her gangly gracelessness that had isolated her. Invitations to go out had been infrequent. At parties no one ever initiated conversations with her. No one, in any case, until Briggs had appeared in her life.

. . . She noticed the man again: the well-dressed one with the neatly trimmed beard. A droopy brown Hawaiian youth was picking up litter on the beach and depositing it in a burlap sack he dragged along; the bearded man ambled beside the youth, talking to him. The Hawaiian said something; the bearded man nodded with evident disappointment and turned to leave the beach. His path brought him close by Brenda's palm tree and Brenda sat up abruptly. "Eric?"

The bearded man squinted into the shade, trying to recognize her. Brenda removed her sunglasses. She said, "Eric? Eric Morelius?"

"Brenda?" The man came closer and she contrived a wan smile. "Brenda Briggs? What the devil are you doing here? You look like a beachcomber gone to seed."

Over a drink in Kimo's she tried to put on a front. "Well, I thought I'd come out here on a sabbatical and, you know, loaf around the islands, recharge my batteries, take stock."

She saw that Eric wasn't buying it. She tried to smile. "And what about you?"

"Well, I live here, you know. Came out to Hawaii nine years ago on vacation and never went back." Eric had an easy relaxed attitude of confident assurance. "Come off it, duckie, you look like hell. What's happened to you?"

She contrived a shrug of indifference. "The world fell down around my ankles. Happens to most everybody sometimes, I suppose. It doesn't matter."

"Just like that? It must have been something terrible. You had more promise than anyone in the department."

"Well, we were kids then, weren't we. We were all promising young scholars. But what happens after you've broken all the promises?"

"Good Lord. The last I saw of you, you and Briggs were off to revitalize the University of what, New Mexico?"

"Arizona." She tipped her head back with the glass to her mouth; ice clicked against her teeth. "And after that a state college in Minnesota. And then a dinky jerkwater diploma mill in California. The world," she said in a quiet voice, "has little further need of second-rate Greek and Roman literature scholars—or for any sort of non-tenured Ph.D.'s in the humanities. I spent last year waiting on tables in Modesto."

"Duckie," Eric said, "there's one thing you haven't mentioned. Where's Briggs?"

She hesitated. Then—what did it matter?—she told him: "He left me. Four years ago. Divorced me and married a buxom life-of-the-party girl fifteen years younger than me. She was writing advertising copy for defective radial tires or carcinogenic deodorants or something like that. We had a kid, you know. Cute little guy, we named him Geoff, with a G—you know how Briggs used to love reading Chaucer. In the original. In retrospect, you know, Briggs was a prig and a snob."

"Where's the kid, then?"

"I managed to get custody and then six months ago he went to visit his father for the weekend and all three of them, Briggs and the copy-writer and my kid Geoff well, there was a six-car pileup on the Santa Monica Freeway and I had to pay for the funerals and it wiped me out."

Eric brought another pair of drinks and there was a properly responsive sympathy in his eyes and it had been so long since she'd talked about it that she covered her face with the table napkin and sobbed. "God help me, Eric. Briggs was the only man who ever gave me a second look."

He walked her along the Sea Wall. "You'll get over it, duckie. Takes time."

"Sure," she said listlessly. "I know."

"Sure, it can be tough. Especially when you haven't got anybody. You don't have any family left, do you?"

"No. Only child. My parents died young. Why not? The old man was on the assembly line in Dearborn. We're all on the assembly line in Dearborn. What have we got to aim for? A condominium in some ant-hill and a bag full of golf clubs? Let's change the subject, all right? What about you, then? You look prosperous enough. Did you drop out or were you pushed too?"

"Dropped out. Saw the light and made it to the end of the tunnel. I'm a free man, duckie."

"What do you do?"

"I'm a scrimshander."

"A what?"

"A bone-ivory artist. I do scrimshaw engravings. You've probably seen my work in the shop windows around town."

Eric's studio, high under the eaves in the vintage whaler's house that looked more New Englandish than tropical, revealed its owner's compulsion for orderly neatness.

She had never liked him much. He and Briggs had got along all right but she'd always found Eric an unpleasant sort. It wasn't that he was boorish; hardly anything like that. But she thought him pretentious and totally insincere. He'd always had that air of arrogant self-assurance. And the polish was all on the surface; he had the right manners but once you got to know him a little you realized he had no real understanding of courtesy or compassion. Those qualities were meaningless to people like Eric. She'd always thought him self-absorbed and egotistical to the point of solipsism; she'd felt he had cultivated Briggs's friendship simply because Eric felt Briggs could help him advance in the department.

Eric had been good at toadying up to anyone who could help him learn the arts of politics and ambition. Eric had always been very actorish: he wasn't real—everything was a role, a part, a performance; everything Eric did was done with his audience in mind. If you couldn't be any help to him he could, without a second thought, cut you dead.

He wasn't really handsome. He had a small round head and ordinary features. But he'd always kept himself trim and he'd always been a natty dresser. And the beard sharpened his face, made it longer, added polish to his appearance. Back on the mainland, she remembered, he'd tended to favor three-piece suits.

Eric's studio was spartan, dominated by a scrubbed-clean work-bench under the dormer window's north light. An array of carving tools filled a wooden rack, each tool seated in its proper niche, and there were four tidy wooden bins containing pieces of white bone of graduated sizes. Antique inkwells and jars were arranged beside a tray of paintbrushes and other slender implements. In three glass display cases, each overhung by a museum light, lay examples of Eric's art. One piece, especially striking, was a large ivory cribbage board in the shape of a Polynesian outrigger canoe with intricate black-and-white scenes engraved upon its faceted surfaces.

"That's a sort of frieze," Eric explained. "If you follow those little scenes around the board, they illustrate the whole mythology of the Polynesian emigration that led to the original settlement of Hawaii a thousand years ago. I'm negotiating to sell it to the museum over in Honolulu."

"It must be pretty lucrative, this stuff."

"It can be. Do you know anything about scrimshaw?"

"No," she said, and she didn't particularly care to; but Eric had paid for the bottle and was pouring a drink for her, and she was desperate for company—anyone's, even Eric's—and so she stayed and pretended interest.

"It's a genuine American folk art. It was originated in the early 1800s by the Yankee whalers who came out to the Pacific with endless time on their hands on shipboard. They got into the habit of scrimshanding to pass the time. The early stuff was crude, of course, but pretty quickly some of them started doing quite sophisticated workmanship. They used sail needles to carve the fine lines of the engraving and then they'd trace India ink or lampblack into the carvings for contrast. About the only materials they had were whalebone and whales' teeth, so that's what they carved at first.

"The art became very popular for a while, about a

century ago, and there was a period when scrimshanding became a profession in its own right. That was when they ran short of whalebone and teeth and started illustrating elephant ivory and other white bone materials. Then it all went out of fashion. But it's been coming back into favor the past few years. We've got several scrimshanders here now. The main problem today, of course, is the scarcity of ivory."

At intervals Brenda sipped his whiskey and vocalized sounds indicative of her attentiveness to his monologue. Mainly she was thinking morosely of the pointlessness of it all. Was Eric going to ask her to stay the night? If he did, would she accept? In either case, did it matter?

Watching her with bemused eyes, Eric went on, "The Endangered Species laws have made it impossible for us to obtain whalebone or elephant ivory in any quantities any more. It's a real problem."

"You seem to have a fair supply in those bins there."

"Well, some of us have been buying mastodon ivory and other fossilized bones from the Eskimos—they dig for it in the tundra up in Alaska. But that stuff's in short supply too, and the price has gone through the ceiling."

Eric took her glass and filled it from the bottle, extracting ice cubes from the half-size fridge under the workbench. She rolled the cold glass against her forehead and returned to the wicker chair, balancing herself with care. Eric smiled with the appearance of sympathy and pushed a little box across the bench. It was the size of a matchbox. The lid fit snugly. Etched into its ivory surface was a drawing of a humpback whale.

"Like it?"

"It's lovely." She tried to summon enthusiasm in her voice.

"It's nearly the real thing," he said. "Not real ivory, of

course, but real bone at least. We've been experimenting with chemical processes to bleach and harden it."

She studied the tiny box and suddenly looked away. Something about it had put her in mind of little Geoff's casket.

"The bones of most animals are too rough and porous," Eric was saying. "They tend to decompose, of course, being organic. But we've had some success with chemical hardening agents. Still, there aren't many types of bone that are suitable. Of course there are some people who're willing to make do with vegetable ivory or hard plastics, but those really aren't acceptable if you care about the artistry of the thing. The phony stuff has no grain, and anybody with a good eye can always tell."

She was thinking she really had to pull herself together. You couldn't get by indefinitely on self-pity and the liquid largesse of old acquaintances, met by chance, whom you didn't even like. She'd reached a point-of-no-return: the end of this week her room rent would be due again and she had no money to cover it; the time to make up her mind was now, right now, because either she got a job or she'd end up like that whiskered wino begging for pennies and eating out of refuse bins.

Eric went on prattling about his silly hobby or whatever it was: something about the larger bones of primates— thigh bone, collarbone. "Young enough to be in good health of course—bone grows uselessly brittle as we get older . . ." But she wasn't really listening; she stood beside the workbench looking out through the dormer window at the dozens of boats in the anchorage, wondering if she could face walking into one of the tourist dives and begging for a job waiting on tables.

The drink had made her unsteady. She returned to the chair, resolving to explore the town first thing in the morning in search of employment. She *had* to snap out of it. It was time to come back to life and perhaps these beautiful islands were the place to do it: the proper setting for the resurrection of a jaded soul.

Eric's voice paused interrogatively and it made her look up. "What? Sorry."

"These two here," Eric said. She looked down at the two etched pendants. He said, "Can you tell the difference?"

"They look pretty much the same to me."

"There, see that? That one, on the left, that's a piece of whale's tooth. This other one's ordinary bone, chemically hardened and bleached to the consistency and color of true ivory. It's got the proper grain, everything."

"Fine." She set the glass down and endeavored to smile pleasantly. "That's fine, Eric. Thank you so much for the drinks. I'd better go now—" She aimed herself woozily toward the door.

"No need to rush off, is there? Here, have one more and then we'll get a bite to eat. There's a terrific little place back on the inland side of town."

"Thanks, really, but—"

"I won't take no for an answer, duckie. How often do we see each other, after all? Come on—look, I'm sorry, I've been boring you to tears with all this talk about scrimshaw and dead bones, and we haven't said a word yet about the really important things."

"What important things?"

"Well, what are we going to do about you, duckie? You seem to have a crucial problem with your life right now and I think if you let me maybe I can help sort it out. Sometimes all it takes is the counsel of a sympathetic old friend, you know."

By then the drink had been poured and she saw no plausible reason to refuse it. She settled back in the cane

206

chair. Eric's smile was avuncular. "What are friends for, after all? Relax a while, duckie. You know, when I first came out here I felt a lot the way you're feeling. I guess in a way I was lucky not to've been as good a scholar as you and Briggs were. I got through the Ph.D. program by the skin of my teeth but it wasn't enough. I applied for teaching jobs all over the country, you know. Not one nibble."

Then the quick smile flashed behind the neat beard. "I ran away, you see—as far as I could get without a passport. These islands are full of losers like you and me, you know. Scratch any charter-boat skipper in that marina and you'll find a bankrupt or a failed writer who couldn't get his epic novel published."

Then he lifted his glass in a gesture of toast. "But it's possible to find an antidote for our failure, you see. Sometimes it may take a certain ruthlessness, of course—a willingness to suspend the stupid values we were brought up on. So-called civilized principles are the enemies of any true individualist—you have to learn that or you're doomed to be a loser for all time. The kings and robber barons we've honored throughout history—none of them was the kind to let himself be pushed around by the imbecilic bureaucratic whims of college deans or tenure systems.

"Establishments and institutions and laws are designed by winners to keep losers in their place, that's all. You're only free when you learn there's no reason to play the game by their rules. Hell, duckie, the fun of life only comes when you discover how to make your own rules and laugh at the fools around you. Look—consider your own situation. Is there any single living soul right now who truly gives a damn whether you, Brenda Briggs, are alive or dead?"

Put that starkly it made her gape. Eric leaned forward,

brandishing his glass as if it were a searchlight aimed at her face. "Well?"

"No. Nobody," she murmured reluctantly.

"There you are, then." He seemed to relax; he leaned back. "There's not a soul you need to please or impress or support, right? If you went right up Front Street here and walked into the Bank of Hawaii and robbed the place of a fortune and got killed making your escape, you'd be hurting no one but yourself. Am I right, duckie?"

"I suppose so."

"Then why not give it a try?"

"Give what a try?"

"Robbing a bank. Kidnaping a rich infant. Hijacking a yacht. Stealing a million in diamonds. Whatever you feel like, duckie—whatever appeals to you. Why not? What have you got to lose?"

She twisted her mouth into an uneven smile. "You remind me of the sophomoric sophistry we used to spout when we were undergraduates. Existentialism and nihilism galore." She put her glass down. "Well I guess not, Eric. I don't think I'll start robbing banks just yet."

"And why not?"

"Maybe I'm just not gaited that way."

"Morality? Is that it? What's morality ever done for *you?*"

She steadied herself with a hand against the workbench, set her feet with care, and turned toward the door. "It's a drink too late for morbid philosophical dialectics. Thanks for the booze, though. I'll see you . . ."

"You'd better sit down, duckie. You're a little unsteady there."

"No, I—"

"Sit down." The words came out in a harsher voice. "The door's locked anyway, duckie—you're not going anywhere."

She scowled, befuddled. "What?"

He showed her the key; then he put it away in his pocket. She looked blankly at the door, the keyhole, and— again—his face. It had gone hard; the polite mask was gone.

"I wish you'd taken the bait," he said. "Around here all they ever talk about is sunsets and surfing and the size of the marlin some fool caught. At least you've got a bigger vocabulary than that. I really wish you'd jumped at it, duckie. It would have made things easier. But you didn't, so that's that."

"What on earth are you talking about?"

She stumbled to the door then—and heard Eric's quiet laughter when she tried the knob.

She put her back to the door. Her head swam. "I don't understand . . ."

"It's the ivory, duckie. The best material is fresh human bone. The consistency, the hardness—it takes a fine polish if it's young and healthy enough . . ."

She stared at him and the understanding seeped into her slowly and she said, "That's where the wino went."

"Well, I have to pick and choose, don't I? I mean, I can't very well use people whose absence would be noticed."

She flattened herself against the door. She was beginning to pass out; she tried to fight it but she couldn't; in the distance, fading, she heard Eric say, "You'll make fine bones, duckie. Absolutely first-rate scrimshaw."

I wrote but a small number of short stories compared to the number of novels I produced. It is a form of expression I adopted chiefly when I felt the urge to write but was deprived by obligations or travels of the ten days necessary to write a novel.

In my opinion, short stories offered the advantage of being written at one sitting, in a single morning.

The case of "Blessed Are the Meek" is unique due to rather curious circumstances. The short story was written at Bradenton Beach, Florida, in March 1947 and, to my delight, it received the Ellery Queen's Award when published in the States. However, I kept harboring a feeling that I had not gone to the farthest limits of my subject. So, later on, in December 1947, at Tumacacori, deep in the desert of Arizona, I took it up again in the form of a novel, which I entitled Les Fantomes du Chapelier *or* The Hatter's Ghosts. It is the only time I went back to a subject I had already treated.

Incidentally, two years ago, that is to say thirty-five years later, Claude Chabrol adapted the novel to the screen, under the same title. Speaking of titles, the English title of the short story is the exact translation of the first title I gave it in French before changing it to "Le Petit Tailleur et le Chapelier."

—GEORGES SIMENON

BLESSED ARE THE MEEK

GEORGES SIMENON

(translated by Frances Frenaye)

Blessed are the meek . . .

Kachoudas, the humble little tailor of the Rue des Prémon-trés, was afraid; of this there could be no doubt. A thousand people, ten thousand, to be exact—the entire population of the town except for the very young children—were afraid too, but most of them did not dare to admit it even in the privacy of their own bedrooms.

Several minutes had gone by since Kachoudas had lit the electric light which he pulled by a wire into a position directly over his work. It was not yet five o'clock but the darkness of the November evening had closed in around him. It had rained steadily for a whole fortnight. A hundred yards away, at the cinema festooned with purple lights where a bell sputtered to announce the beginning of every show, a newsreel showed people in other parts of the country navigating the streets in rowboats, and farmhouses cut off by torrents of water which carried along uprooted trees.

These facts were important; they had a bearing on the whole situation. If it hadn't been late autumn with the darkness coming on at four o'clock in the afternoon; if it hadn't rained from morning to night and from night to morning again, to the point where many people didn't have a stitch of dry clothes to put on their back; if there hadn't been gusts of wind whirling down the narrow streets and turning umbrellas inside out as if they were gloves, then perhaps Kachoudas wouldn't have been afraid and, what's more, nothing would have happened.

Kachoudas was sitting with crossed legs on the big table that he had polished with his hind-quarters all day long for the thirty years he had plied his trade as a tailor. He worked on a mezzanine floor with a low ceiling just above his shop. Just across the street an enormous sign in the form of a red top hat hung over the sidewalk in front of a haberdashery. When Kachoudas looked out he could see under the sign into the shop of Monsieur Labbé.

This establishment was badly lighted. The electric-light bulbs were covered with dust and the window had not been washed for a long time. These details are less important, but they played their part. The haberdashery was old and so was the street on which it was situated, which had been the shopping center of the town before the five-and-ten-cent stores and others with glittering showcases had moved in on a thoroughfare five hundred yards away. Now the shops remaining on this dimly illuminated section of the street were so rundown that it looked as if no one ever went into them at all.

Here, then, was another reason for being afraid. And finally, this was the usual hour. At this time every day Kachoudas had the vaguely uncomfortable feeling that meant he must have the glass of white wine which a habit of long standing had made seem absolutely essential.

Monsieur Labbé across the street had exactly the same feeling; for him too this was the usual hour. As a result he would say a few words to Alfred, his red-headed clerk, and put on a heavy overcoat with a velvet collar.

At the same time the little tailor would get down from

his table, knot his tie, put on his jacket, and go down the spiral stairway, calling out behind him:

"I'll be back in fifteen minutes."

This wasn't strictly true. He invariably stayed away for half an hour, but for years now he had announced his return in fifteen minutes.

Just as he was slipping on his raincoat, one which a customer had left and forgotten to call for, he heard the automatic bell ring as the door opened across the street. Monsieur Labbé, his coat collar turned up and his hands in his pockets, was walking close to the walls on the sheltered part of the sidewalk in the direction of the Place Gambetta.

The tailor's bell rang too a moment later, and Kachoudas stepped into the driving rain hardly ten yards behind his neighbor.

The two of them were quite alone on the street, where the gas lamps were spaced far apart, leaving stretches of darkness between them.

With a few quick steps Kachoudas could have overtaken the haberdasher. They were acquainted, exchanged greetings when they shut up their shops at the same time, and spoke to each other in the Café de la Paix where they were both due to arrive in a few minutes. But they occupied quite different ranks in society: Monsieur Labbé was Monsieur Labbé and Kachoudas was only Kachoudas.

Kachoudas, then, was bringing up the rear, and this fact served to reassure him. If someone were to attack him he had only to cry out and the haberdasher would hear him. But what if the haberdasher were to run away? Kachoudas thought this over. The idea sent shivers down his spine, and the fear of being ambushed at a dark corner or alley caused him to walk in the middle of the street. There was not far to go. At the end of the Rue des Prémontrés lay the

213

central square, well lighted and with a certain number of people about in spite of the rain. There a policeman was usually on duty.

The two men, one behind the other, turned to the left. The third building just ahead of them was the Café de la Paix, with its bright lights and comforting warmth. The regular customers were at their tables and Firmin, the waiter, was watching them play cards. Monsieur Labbé took off his overcoat and shook it, and Firmin hung it on the rack. When Kachoudas came in no one helped him off with his raincoat. Naturally, for he was only Kachoudas. The card players and those who were looking on at their game shook the haberdasher's hand, and he sat down just behind the doctor. They gave a curt nod, or perhaps no sign of recognition at all, to Kachoudas who could find no better place to sit than right up against the stove. As a result steam began to rise from his trousers.

The steaming wet trousers led the little tailor to make his discovery. He looked down at them and said to himself that because the cloth was not of very good quality they would probably shrink again. Then, with a professional eye, he examined Monsieur Labbé's trousers to see if their material was better. Of course he did not make Monsieur Labbé's suits. None of the highly respectable people who frequented the café at this hour came to him for their clothes. At most they gave him linings or patchwork to do.

There was sawdust on the floor and wet feet had left irregular marks in it and clumps of mud here and there. Monsieur Labbé was wearing expensive shoes and dark gray, almost black, trousers. On the cuff of his left trouser leg there was a tiny spot of white. If Kachoudas had not been a tailor he would probably never have noticed it. He thought right away that it must be a thread, because tailors are given to pulling threads out. If he had not been such a humble little tailor he would probably not have leaned over to pick it off.

The haberdasher noticed his gesture with some surprise. Kachoudas seized the white spot, which had slid down into the cuff, and it turned out to be not a thread but a scrap of paper.

"Excuse me," he murmured.

The Kachoudases were always excusing themselves. Centuries ago, when they were driven like cattle from Armenia to Smyrna and Syria and other such places, they had acquired this cautious mannerism.

It must be stressed that while Kachoudas was straightening himself up there was not a single thought in his head. Or, to be exact, he thought only: "It isn't a thread, after all . . ."

He could see the legs and feet of the card players, the cast-iron feet of the marble-topped tables, and Firmin's white apron. Instead of throwing the scrap of paper on the floor he held it out to the haberdasher, repeating:

"Excuse me . . ."

He felt that he must apologize because the haberdasher might wonder why in the world he had poked about in his trouser cuff.

But just as Monsieur Labbé took the paper, which was hardly bigger than a piece of confetti, Kachoudas suddenly stiffened and a most unpleasant shiver ran across the back of his neck. The worst of it was that the haberdasher and he were looking straight at each other. For a moment they went on staring. No one was paying them any attention; the players were at their cards and the others were watching the game.

Monsieur Labbé was a man who had been fat and then lost a good part of his weight. He was still fairly voluminous, but there was a flabby look about him. His drooping features were generally expressionless, and on this critical occasion they did not flicker. He took the paper, rolled it between his fingers until it was no bigger than a pinhead, and said:

"Thanks, Kachoudas."

This caused the little tailor any amount of reflection; for days and nights after he asked himself: Was the haberdasher's voice natural? Ironical? Threatening? Sarcastic?

The tailor trembled and almost dropped the glass that he had picked up in order to keep his self-control. He must not look at Monsieur Labbé. It was too dangerous. It was a question of life and death—if, indeed, Kachoudas could hope to hang on to his life at all. He sat glued to his chair, apparently quite still, but with a feeling as if he were jumping up and down. There were moments when he had to hold himself back from running away as fast as he could go. What would happen if he were to get up and shout:

"This is the man!"

He was hot and cold at the same time. The heat of the stove was burning his skin and yet his teeth were on the point of chattering. All of a sudden he remembered how on the Rue des Prémontrés fear had caused him to follow the haberdasher as closely as he could. This was not the first time he had clung to his shadow, and he had done so only a quarter of an hour before. *They had been quite alone in the dark street and now he knew that this was the man!* The little tailor wanted to look at him on the sly, but he did not dare. One look might seal his fate.

Above all he must not run his hand over his neck, as he had a violent longing to do, akin to the temptation to scratch a bad itch.

"Another white wine, Firmin."

A further blunder. Usually he let half an hour go by before ordering a second glass. What should he do? What could he do?

The walls of the Café de la Paix were studded with mirrors, which reflected rising coils of cigarette and pipe smoke. Monsieur Labbé was the only one who smoked cigars and Kachoudas occasionally caught a whiff of them. At the other end of the room, on the right, near the washroom, there was a telephone booth. Under the pretext of going to the toilet, couldn't he slip into it?

"Hello . . . Police? Your man is here . . ."

What if Monsieur Labbé were to push into the booth behind him? No one would hear, for it was always done quite noiselessly. Not a single one of the six victims had cried out. They were all old women, to be sure. The killer had never attacked anyone but an old woman. That was why the men were so bold and did not hesitate to go out on the streets. But there was no reason why the killer should not break the rule.

"The man you're after is here . . . Come and get him . . ."

Twenty thousand francs would be coming to him. This was the reward that everyone was trying to win—so many people, indeed, that the police were at their wits' end with the number of wild clues they were asked to follow. If he had twenty thousand francs . . . But, first of all, who would believe him? He would say:

"It's the haberdasher!"

And they would reply: "Prove it."

"I saw two letters . . ."

"What letters?"

"An *n* and a *t.*"

He really wasn't sure about the *t!*

"Explain exactly what you mean, Kachoudas . . ."

They would talk sternly to him; people always talk sternly to a Kachoudas.

". . . in the cuff of his trouser . . . Then he rolled it into a tiny ball . . ."

Incidentally, where was that tiny ball now, the ball the size of a pinhead? Just try and find it! Monsieur Labbé might have let it drop on the floor where he could grind it with his heel into the sawdust. Or he might have swallowed it.

What did it prove anyhow? That the haberdasher had cut two letters out of a newspaper? Not even that much. He might have picked up the scrap of paper almost anywhere without even noticing it. And what if he *had* had a whim to cut the letters out of a newspaper? It was enough to unsettle a much stronger man than the little tailor, to upset any one of the respectable businessmen sitting about him—shopkeepers, an insurance agent, a wine merchant, all well enough off to spend a good part of the afternoon playing cards and to drink several *apéritifs* every day.

They didn't know. No one knew except Kachoudas. And the man was aware that Kachoudas knew . . . The little tailor was perspiring as if he had drunk hot grog and taken a powerful dose of aspirin. Had the haberdasher noticed his nervousness? Did he look as if he had caught on to the meaning of the scrap of paper?

How could he think over these critical matters without betraying his thoughts, when the other man was smoking his cigar less than six feet away and he, Kachoudas, was supposed to be watching the card players?

"A white wine, Firmin . . ."

He spoke up quite unintentionally, almost in spite of himself, because his throat was so dry. Three glasses of white wine were too many, more than he had ever drunk

at a time except when his children were born. He had
eight children now and was waiting for a ninth. No sooner
was one born than another seemed to follow. It wasn't his
fault, although every time people looked at him accus-
ingly.

How could anyone kill a man with eight children and a
ninth on the way, and probably a tenth after that? Just
then someone, the insurance agent, who was dealing out
the cards, said:

"Queer, he hasn't killed an old woman for three days
now . . . He must be scared . . ."

There was Kachoudas, knowing what he knew, obliged
to listen to this remark without so much as a look at the
haberdasher. Then he had a stroke of his usual bad luck.
As by dint of a tremendous effort he looked straight ahead
of him, he saw Monsieur Labbé's face in a mirror on the
wall. Monsieur Labbé was staring right at him. He was
perfectly at ease, but none the less he was staring and it
seemed to the little tailor as if there were a slight smile on
his lips. He began to wonder if the haberdasher wasn't
going to wink at him, the way he might wink at an
accomplice, as if to say:

"A good joke, eh?"

Kachoudas heard his own voice say: "Waiter. . ."

A very poor idea. Three glasses of wine were enough,
more than enough, especially as too much made him sick.

"Your order, Monsieur?"

"Oh, nothing . . . thank you . . ."

After all, there was one perfectly reasonable explanation. It was a bit hazy in the little tailor's mind, but it did
hold water. There might be two men instead of one: one of
them the killer of old women of whom nothing was
known beyond the fact that he had done away with six of
them in the last three weeks; the other merely someone

who wanted to amuse himself and mystify the town—an eccentric, perhaps, who sent the famous communications addressed to the *Courrier de la Loire* made up of single letters cut out of newspapers. Why not? Such things have been known to happen. There are people who get strange ideas in their heads where crime is concerned. But if there were two men instead of one, how could the second one, who cut out and pasted up the letters, prophesy what the first one would do next?

For at least three of the murders had been announced ahead of time, all of them exactly the same way. The communications came to the *Courrier de la Loire* in the mail and usually the words in them had been cut right out of the *Courrier* itself and carefully stuck one beside the other. For instance:

It was no use to call out a special squad. Another old woman tomorrow.

Some of the communications were longer. It must have taken quite some time to find the right words in the newspaper and fit them together like a puzzle.

Inspector Micou thinks he's smart just because he came down from Paris. But he's only a choir-boy. He's foolish to drink all that brandy; it only makes his nose red.

By the way, didn't Inspector Micou, whom the *Sûreté Nationale* had sent to organize the hunt for the killer, stop in every now and then for a drink at the Café de la Paix? The little tailor had seen him there. It was quite true that he liked brandy, and people would question him quite casually.

"Well, then, Inspector?"

"We'll get him, never fear. Maniacs of his kind are sure to slip up on something. They're too pleased with themselves and they have to boast of what they've done."

Yes, the haberdasher had been right there when the inspector had spoken these words.

Some fools say it's cowardice that makes me kill only old women. What if I simply can't stand old women? I have a right to dislike them, haven't I? But if they go on with this slander I'll kill a man, just to please them. A big, strong man, too. It's all the same to me. That will teach them a lesson!

Kachoudas was small and thin, no bigger than a fifteen-year-old boy.

"You see, Inspector . . ."

The tailor jumped. Inspector Micou had just walked into the café along with Pijolet, the dentist. The inspector was stout and hearty. He turned a chair around and sat astride it opposite the card players.

"Don't bother to move," he said to them.

"How's the hunt going?"

"Getting along, thank you, getting along."

"Any clues?"

Kachoudas could still see Monsieur Labbé starting at him in the mirror, and he had a new and frightening thought. What if Monsieur Labbé were innocent—innocent of the murders and of writing to the newspaper about them? What if he had got the scrap of paper into his trouser cuff by mere chance, as one sometimes gets a flea?

He must put himself in the other's place. Kachoudas had leaned over and picked something up. Monsieur Labbé couldn't know where the scrap of paper had come from. Perhaps the little tailor himself had let it fall and tried to make it disappear on the floor, then nervously picked it up and held it out to his neighbor. Yes, why shouldn't the haberdasher suspect him just as much as he suspected the haberdasher?

"A white wine . . ."

Never mind! He had drunk too much, but all the same he wanted more. There seemed to him to be more smoke than usual in the café; faces were blurred and the card players' table faded away into the distance.

Yes, think of that. If Monsieur Labbé suspected him in exactly the same way . . . Would he too set his mind on the twenty thousand francs reward? People said that he was rich, that it was because he didn't need money that he let his business slide. Otherwise he would clean his windows or even enlarge them, add more lighting, and get in some new stock. He couldn't hope that people would come to buy the hats in the styles of twenty years past that lay on his dust-covered shelves.

Yes, if he were a miser the twenty thousand francs might be a temptation. He had only to accuse Kachoudas, and most people would believe him. For Kachoudas was just the sort of fellow everyone inclines to distrust. Because he hadn't been born in the town, or even in the country, and he had a queerly shaped head which he held a little to one side. Because he lived among an ever-increasing brood of children and his wife hardly spoke a word of French.

But what of that? Why should the little tailor attack old women in the street without bothering to steal even their jewels or their handbags? So Kachoudas reasoned to himself, but the next minute he saw that the same argument held good for the haberdasher.

"Why should Monsieur Labbé, after living sixty years as a model citizen, suddenly feel an urge to strangle old women in dark streets?"

The problem was a complicated one. Neither the familiar atmosphere of the Café de la Paix nor the presence of Inspector Micou was reassuring any longer. Let someone merely suggest to Micou that Kachoudas was guilty and Micou would take him at his word. But if it were a question of Monsieur Labbé . . .

He must think it over seriously. It was a question of life and death. Hadn't the killer announced in the newspaper that he might attack a man next? There was the badly lighted Rue des Prémontrés to walk through, and his shop was just across from that of the haberdasher, who could spy on everything he did. Then there were the twenty thousand francs. Twenty thousand! More than he could earn in six months . . .

"Tell me, Kachoudas . . ."

He felt as if he were coming down to earth from very far away, back among people whose presence he had for several minutes completely forgotten. Because he did not recognize the voice his first impulse was to turn toward the haberdasher, who looked at him as he chewed his cigar. But it was not the haberdasher who had spoken to him, it was the inspector.

"Is it true that you work fast and don't overcharge?"

In a split second he realized what an unexpected piece of good luck this was, and he almost looked over at Monsieur Labbé to see if he had noticed the relief in his face. Kachoudas would never have dared go to the police. And he would have hesitated to write them a letter, because letters go into the files and one can never tell when they may cause trouble. And now the inspector himself, the representative of the law, had practically offered to come to him.

"When it's for mourning I can deliver a suit within twenty-four hours," he said modestly, lowering his eyes.

"Then pretend that I'm going into mourning for the six old women and make me a suit just as fast. I brought hardly anything with me from Paris and the rain has been hard on my clothes. You have some good wool cloth, I hope."

"The best there is."

Good Lord! The little tailor's thoughts were running away with him! Perhaps it was the effect of four glasses of white wine. So much the worse! He ordered a fifth glass, in a more self-assured tone of voice than usual. Something wonderful was going to happen. Instead of going back alone, stricken with fear of Monsieur Labbé at every dark corner, he would get the inspector to go with him, under the pretext of taking his measurements. And once they were in the shop, behind closed doors . . . What a magnificent chance! The reward would be his! Twenty thousand francs! And without the slightest risk!

"If you can come with me for five minutes . . . My place is near by."

His voice trembled. This was luck of the sort a Kachoudas can't count on, not after centuries of having been kicked around by his fellowmen and an unkind fate.

"I could take your measurements and have it ready for tomorrow evening at the same time . . ."

How happy he was to get off to such a good start. All his worries were over, and everything was turning out all right, as if this were a fairy story. Men playing cards . . . good old Firmin (everyone looks good at a moment like this) watching the game . . . the haberdasher, whose gaze he sought to avoid . . . the inspector coming . . . they would go out together . . . he would close the door of his shop and no one would hear . . .

"Listen, Inspector, I know who is the killer . . ."

Then his hopes were dashed to the ground. One little sentence spoiled everything.

"I'm not in that much of a hurry, you know . . ."

The inspector wanted to join in the card game and he knew that someone would give him a place as soon as the hand was over.

"I'll come by tomorrow morning. You're always there, I suppose, aren't you? In weather like this, anyhow . . ."

It was all up. His fine plans had collapsed. Yet the whole thing had seemed so easy. By tomorrow he would probably be dead, and his wife and children would never have the twenty thousand francs which he was entitled to leave them. For he was more and more convinced that he had a right to the reward. He was sure of it, and he rebelled against the sudden obstacle in his path.

"If you were to come this evening, I could take advantage . . ."

No use. The haberdasher must be laughing up his sleeve. The hand was over and the insurance agent gave his place up to Inspector Micou. Detectives had no business playing cards! They should catch on to the slightest hint. Kachoudas couldn't very well beg him on bended knee to come for his measurements.

How was he to go away? Usually he stayed no more than half an hour at the café. This was his only distraction, his one folly. Then he always went home. The children were all back from school by then and they made the most infernal noise. The house smelled of cooking. Dolphine (she had a ridiculously French name in spite of hardly knowing the language) called them in a shrill voice. And he pulled down the light over his work and sewed for long hours, perched on the mezzanine table . . .

He himself smelled, he knew that. He smelled of garlic, which they used abundantly in their cooking, and of the grease in the wool materials that he worked with all day. There were people in the Café de la Paix who drew back their chairs whenever he sat down near the table of the regular customers. Was that enough of a reason why the inspector shouldn't come with him? Every one of the others in the café lived in the direction of the Rue du Palais; they all turned to the left when they went out, while he turned to the right. It was a matter of life and death.

"One more, Firmin . . ."

Another glass of white wine. He had a terrible fear that the haberdasher might follow him out the door. But after he had ordered his wine it occurred to him that if Monsieur Labbé went out ahead of him he might lie in waiting at a dark corner of the Rue des Prémontrés. There was danger if the haberdasher left first, and even more danger if he left second. And yet Kachoudas couldn't stay there all night.

"Firmin . . ."

He hesitated. He knew that he was wrong, that he was going to be drunk, but there was nothing else to do.

"One more of the same . . ."

Everyone was sure to look at him with suspicion.

"How is Mathilde?"

Someone had just asked this question, but who was it? Kachoudas's head was heavy by now; he must have been at his seventh glass of wine. In fact, there was curiosity as to whether he was celebrating the arrival of a new baby. The question he had just heard might have been from Germain, the grocer. It didn't matter much, anyhow. The men were all about the same age, between sixty and sixty-five. Most of them had been in the same class at school; they had started out playing marbles together. Later on they had gone to each other's weddings and all their lives long they spoke to each other in intimate terms. Probably every one of them, when he was fifteen or sixteen years old, had courted a girl who had later married one of his friends.

There was another group of cronies, ranging from forty to fifty years of age, who were ready to step into the shoes of their elders as soon as they left this earthly scene. They played cards at another table, in the left-hand corner of the café. They were a good deal noisier, but they arrived later on, about six o'clock, because they didn't have quite as much leisure.

"How is Mathilde?"

This was a phrase that the little tailor heard almost every day. Someone would say it quite casually, just as if he were saying: "Is it still raining?" For Mathilde, the haberdasher's wife, had long since become a legend. Once upon a time she must have been a young girl like the rest. Perhaps some of the card players had stolen a kiss from her in their younger days. Then she had got married and probably she went in her best clothes to ten o'clock mass every Sunday. For fifteen years she had lived on a mezzanine floor, just opposite to Kachoudas, but her curtains were almost always drawn together. He could only guess at the presence of her motionless white face behind the lace hangings.

"Mathilde's all right . . ."

In other words, she was no worse, but her condition was just the same. She was a paralytic; every morning she was put into a chair and every evening put back to bed. So that the best that could be said for her was that she wasn't yet dead. After Mathilde the players spoke of a number of other things. They barely mentioned the killer, because the customers of the Café de la Paix affected a lack of interest in such things.

Kachoudas had not dared to go away for fear the haberdasher would leave just behind him. And so he went on drinking. Two or three times he noticed that Monsieur Labbé looked at the pale face of the clock hanging between two mirrors, but it never occurred to him to wonder why. This, however, is how he happened to notice that it was exactly seventeen minutes after six when the haberdasher got up and rapped with a coin on the marble table top to summon Firmin.

"How much do I owe you?"

When a man came in he usually shook hands all around, but when he went out he said good-by to everyone together. Some said: "See you tomorrow," and others: "See you later on," which meant that they were coming back for another game after dinner.

"He'll lie in wait at a dark corner of the Rue des Prémontrés and jump out at me as I go by . . ."

If only he could pay for his own drinks in time to follow close on the haberdasher's heels and not let him out of his sight! Kachoudas was the shorter and thinner of the two and probably he could run faster. The best thing to do was to keep a short distance behind and be ready to run at the least sign of suspicious behavior.

The two men went out, one a few seconds after the other. Strangely enough the card players turned to look after the little tailor rather than the haberdasher. There was something uneasy in his manner and a doubt crossed their minds. Someone half murmured:

"Could he be the one?"

Outside the wind was raging. At every corner it struck a man in the face and he either had to bend over double or else be thrown backwards by its impact. It was raining hard. The little tailor's face was streaming and he shivered beneath his light raincoat. Never mind; he was right at the haberdasher's heels. He must keep up the pace, for in this nearness lay his only hope of safety. Three hundred yards, two hundred yards, one hundred yards more and he would be home, where he could lock the door and barricade himself in until the inspector came the next morning to see him.

He was still counting the seconds, when he noticed that the haberdasher had gone by his shop, where the red-headed clerk could still be vaguely seen behind the counter. Kachoudas went by his own place almost unconsciously; a force stronger than himself impelled him to follow on. Just as a little earlier the two of them were alone on the street, they continued to be alone in the more and more deserted section of the town which they were now entering. Each one of them could hear the other's footsteps, besides the echoes of his own. The haberdasher must know that he was being followed.

Kachoudas was half out of his senses with fear. Couldn't he stop, turn around, and go back home? Of course. Perhaps. But this never even occurred to him. Strange as it may seem, he was too congealed by fright. He went on, keeping about twenty yards behind his companion, and from time to time he spoke through the wind and rain to himself:

"If he's really the killer . . ."

Was he still uncertain? Was it in order to satisfy his conscience that he had undertaken this chase? Every now and then the two men passed before a lighted shop window. Then, one after the other, they plunged back into the darkness and could place each other only by the sound of their footsteps.

"If he stops, I'll stop too . . ."

The haberdasher did stop, and the tailor stopped after him. Then the haberdasher went on and the tailor followed him with a sigh of relief.

There were patrols all over the town, at least according

to the newspaper. In order to preserve calm the police had thought up a so-called infallible patrol system. And indeed, as they strode on, one behind the other, they met three men in uniform trudging along in step, and Kachoudas heard them say:

"Good evening, Monsieur Labbé."

When they came to him they flashed a light in his face and said nothing.

There were no old women in the streets. It was enough to make one wonder where the killer ever found his victims. They must all cling to their homes, and go out only in broad daylight, preferably under escort. The two men passed the church of Saint Jean, where a dim light shone at the door. But for the last three weeks the old women must have given up coming to benediction.

The streets were growing narrower and narrower. There were empty lots and fences between the houses.

"He's luring me outside of town to kill me . . ."

Kachoudas was not a brave man, and now he was thoroughly afraid and ready to call for help at the least untoward movement on the part of the haberdasher. If he still followed him, it was not of his own free will.

They had come to a quiet street with new houses along it. He could hear the footsteps, and then all of a sudden there was silence. Kachoudas came to a stop in imitation of the man he was following, sight unseen. Where had the haberdasher gone? The sidewalks were dark. There were only three street lamps, at some distance one from the other. There were a few lighted windows and from one house came strains of piano music. Always the same series of chords—from an exercise, Kachoudas thought, for he was not musical, which a learner was repeating over and over again with the same mistake at the end every time.

Had the rain stopped? In any case he was no longer aware of it. He dared neither go on nor turn back. He was alarmed by the slightest sound and worried lest the piano prevent him from hearing the footsteps that he was listening for.

The chords sounded five, ten times over, then the top of a piano was banged down. Evidently a lesson was at an end. There were loud cries and noise in the house. Probably a little girl, now that she was dismissed, was running to join her brothers and sisters. And someone was putting on a coat and saying to the mother at the door:

"She's made some progress . . . But the left hand . . . She simply must practice with that left hand . . ."

The door opened and the music teacher, who stood for a moment in a rectangle of light, was an elderly maiden lady.

"I promise you, Madame Bardon . . . I've only a hundred yards to go . . ."

Kachoudas could not breathe. It never occurred to him to call out:

"Stay where you are! Whatever you do, don't move!"

And yet he knew. He understood already how things would go. The old lady, who must have been a bit nervous, came down three steps from the door and trotted along close to the wall. It was her own street, after all, and she lived very near by. She had been born on this street and as a child she had played on its sidewalks and doorsteps; she knew every stick and stone of it.

Kachoudas heard her light, quick steps . . . then no steps at all! That was about all he could hear: *the absence of footsteps.* There was complete silence, and then a vague noise like the rustling of clothes. Could he possibly have made himself move? And what good would it have done? If he had called for help, would anyone have had the

231

courage to come out of the house? He leaned up against a wall and his shirt stuck to his back, soaked with perspiration.

"Ah!" Kachoudas was the one to sigh. Perhaps the old lady had sighed too, for the last time. And the killer as well.

He heard steps again, a man's steps, retracing the way. The steps were coming toward Kachoudas. And Kachoudas, who had felt so sure that he could run faster than the haberdasher, could not even raise one foot from the ground! The haberdasher would see him. But didn't he know already that he was there? Hadn't he heard him just behind all the way from the Café de la Paix?

None of that mattered any more. Now the little tailor was entirely at the killer's mercy. This was Kachoudas' very clear impression and he did not argue with himself about it. The haberdasher seemed to take on superhuman proportions and Kachoudas was ready to fall down on his knees, if necessary, and swear to keep quiet for the rest of his life. Hang the twenty thousand francs!

He did not move as Monsieur Labbé drew nearer. Soon they would touch. At the last minute would Kachoudas have the strength to run? And if he did run, wouldn't he be accused of the murder? All the haberdasher had to do was to call for the police. They would run after him and catch him.

"Why were you running away?"

"Because . . ."

"Speak up. Didn't you kill the old lady?"

The two of them were alone on the street, and there was nothing to indicate that one of them was guilty rather than the other. Monsieur Labbé was quicker-witted, and he was a man of a certain position, a native of the town, on intimate terms with the leading citizens and with a cousin in parliament.

"Good night, Kachoudas."

Strange as it may seem, that was all that happened.

Monsieur Labbé must have barely made out his silhouette drawn back into the shadows. To tell the truth, Kachoudas had climbed up onto a doorstep and he had a finger on the doorbell, ready to push it at a moment's notice. And then the killer greeted him quietly as he went by, with a voice that was muffled but not particularly threatening.

"Good night, Kachoudas."

He tried to answer, for the sake of politeness. It seemed to him absolutely necessary to have good manners with a man of this type and to return his greeting. He opened his mouth, but in vain; no sound came out of it. The footsteps were already moving away when he managed to get out:

"Good night, sir."

He heard his own voice, but he had spoken too late, when the haberdasher was already far away. Out of sheer delicacy Kachoudas had not called Monsieur Labbé by name, in order not to compromise him in any way. Exactly!

He was still on the doorstep. He had not the slightest desire to go see the old lady who half an hour before had been giving a piano lesson and who by now must have definitely gone on to another world. Monsieur Labbé was far away by this time. All of a sudden panic overtook him. He mustn't stay in this place. He felt a strong urge to get away as fast as his legs would take him, and at the same time he was afraid of running into the haberdasher. He might be arrested from one minute to the next. Just a short while before a patrol had flashed a light in his face; they had seen and recognized him. How could he explain his presence in this section of the town, where he had no business and where someone had just been murdered? So much the worse! The best thing was to make a clean breast of the whole thing to the police. He started to walk along at a good pace, moving his lips.

"I'm only a poor tailor, Inspector, but I swear on the heads of my children . . ."

The least noise made him jump. The haberdasher might now be lying in ambush for him, just as he had done for the old lady. He took a roundabout way, and wandered through a maze of narrow streets where he had never set foot before.

"He couldn't imagine that I would come by here . . ."

He wasn't a complete fool, after all.

"I'm willing to tell you everything, but you must assign one or two of your men to guard me until he's behind the bars . . ."

If need be, he'd wait at the police station. Not a very comfortable place, but he'd seen worse in the course of his travels. He wouldn't hear his children's whining, that was one good thing. It was not very far from his own house, just two streets beyond the Rue des Prémontrés. Already he could see the red light with the word *Police* across it. There must be an officer right at the door, as usual. He was in no danger. In fact, he was safe at last.

"You'd be making a serious mistake, Monsieur Kachoudas . . ."

He stopped short. A real voice had spoken, the voice of a man of flesh and blood, the voice of the haberdasher. The haberdasher stood there against the wall, with his calm face barely visible through the darkness. Is a man responsible for his actions at such a moment? Kachoudas stammered: "I beg your pardon?"

Just as if he had bumped into someone on the street, or trod on a lady's foot. Then, when nothing more was said and he was let strictly alone, he turned quietly around. He must not look as if he were running away; on the contrary, he must walk like a perfectly normal man. No one was going to follow him right away. He had time to escape. At last he did hear steps behind him, but they were neither quicker nor slower than his own. In other words, the haberdasher wouldn't catch up with him.

Here was his own street, and his shop with a few samples of dark materials and some fashion drawings in the window. And the other shop, across the street. He opened the door, shut it again and turned the key in the lock.

"Is that you?" his wife called down from upstairs.

As if it could have been anyone else at such a late hour and in this weather!

"Be sure to wipe off your shoes."

At this point he wondered whether he was really awake. After all he had lived through, and with the massive shadow of the haberdasher still looming up at the opposite doorway, all she could say was:

"Be sure to wipe off your shoes."

He felt very much like fainting. And what would she have said then?

Kachoudas was kneeling on the floor with his back to the window and just in front of him, only a few inches from his nose, the rotund legs and stomach of a man in an upright position. This man was Inspector Micou, who had not been distracted by the crime of the evening before from coming to have the tailor take his measurements.

The little tailor passed his tape measure around the waist and the hips, wet his pencil on the end of his tongue, and wrote down the figures in a greasy notebook lying on the floor; then he went on to measure the length of the trouser leg and the crotch. All this time Monsieur Labbé stood behind the lace curtains of the window at exactly the same height on the other side of the street. There were no more than eight yards between them. Kachoudas had an empty feeling in the pit of his stomach. The haberdasher would not shoot, he was sure of that. He would not shoot because, first of all, he was not the sort of murderer to go in for firearms. Murderers have their pet ways of doing things, just like anyone else, and they are not easily divorced from their habits. Besides, if he did shoot, he would simply be giving himself up to the police.

In the next place, the haberdasher had confidence in Kachoudas. This was the real point. And yet couldn't the little tailor, from his kneeling position, murmur to the rotund statue whose measurements he was taking:

"Don't move. Pretend nothing has happened. The haberdasher across the street is the killer. He's spying on us right now from behind his window."

But he said nothing at all, and stuck to the part of an innocent and unpretentious tailor. There was an unpleasant odor on the mezzanine, but this did not bother Kachoudas in the slightest degree, for he was quite used to the greasy smell of wool which he carried around with him wherever he went. Probably Monsieur Labbé's shop across the way had the staler and even more unpleasant odor of felt and glue. Every trade has its own stink. If such is the case, what smell is characteristic of a detective? This thought ran through Kachoudas' mind, and goes to show that he had recovered to some extent his aplomb.

"If you can come back late this afternoon for a fitting, I hope I can let you have your suit tomorrow morning . . ."

He went downstairs behind the inspector, then passed in front of him as they walked through the shop, and opened the door, causing the bell to ring automatically. Neither of them had spoken of the killer, or of the elderly maiden lady, Mademoiselle Irène Mollard, whose murder was all over the front page of the newspaper.

And yet the tailor had spent a very restless night, so restless that his wife had wakened him to say:

"Try to lie quietly, will you? You do nothing but kick me!"

After that he could not go to sleep again. He lay awake, thinking hour after hour until his head began to ache. By six o'clock in the morning he had enough of lying in bed and thinking, and he got up. After he had made himself a cup of coffee he went to his workroom and lit a fire. Of course he had to put a light on, for it was not yet day. There was a light across the street too, since for years the haberdasher had got up at half-past five every morning. Unfortunately one couldn't see him through the curtains, but it was easy to guess what he was doing.

Monsieur Labbé's wife would have no callers. Very rarely did a friend penetrate beyond the front door and then for only a short time. She would not receive care even from the hands of the cleaning woman, who arrived every morning at seven o'clock and stayed until night. Monsieur Labbé had to do everything for her himself—dust, put her room in order, bring up her meals, and carry her from her bed to her chair and back. Twenty times a day, when he heard her signal, he rushed up his spiral stairway from the shop to the mezzanine floor. Her signal was a very special one. A cane was placed near her chair and she still had quite enough strength in her left hand to tap with it on the floor.

The little tailor went back to his work, sitting crosslegged on the table.

"Watch out, Kachoudas," he said to himself. "Twenty thousand francs are no joke, and it would be too bad to let them go. But life is worth something too, even the life of a little tailor from the wilds of Armenia. Even if the haberdasher is crazy, he can think faster than you. If he's arrested they'll probably have to let him go—for lack of proof. It's not very likely that he amuses himself by scattering bits of newspaper all over the house . . ."

It was wise to think things over unhurriedly as he sewed. Already a new idea had come to him. Some of the communications sent to the *Courrier de la Loire* were a whole page long. It must have taken hours of painstaking work to find the right words and letters, cut them out, and paste them up in order. Downstairs in the haberdashery shop Alfred, the red-headed clerk, was always about. Behind the shop there was a workshop with wooden head forms where Monsieur Labbé blocked hats, but a peephole with a glass window connected these two downstairs rooms. The cleaning woman reigned over the kitchen and the rest of the house, so that a process of elimination made it clear that the only place where the killer could devote himself to his cutting and pasting was the bedroom shared by his wife and himself, where no one was allowed to enter. Madame Labbé could not move; she could not even talk except by making a succession of weird sounds. What did she think when she saw her husband cutting out scraps of paper?

"What's more, Kachoudas, my friend, if you accuse him now and some proof of his guilt is found, those fellows (he meant the police and even his new customer, Inspector Micou) will claim that they did the whole job and take most of the reward away from you."

Fear of losing the twenty thousand francs and fear of Monsieur Labbé. The tailor was caught between these two fears. But by nine o'clock his fear of the haberdasher had almost gone. In the middle of the night the noise of water flooding the gutters, of raindrops beating on the roof and of wind whistling through the shutters, came to a sudden end. After a long fortnight the storm was miraculously over. By six in the morning there was only a drizzle of rain, silent and almost invisible to the naked eye. Now patches of the sidewalk returned to their natural gray color and people were walking around without unbrellas. It was Saturday, the weekly market day. The market occupied a little old square at the end of the street.

At nine o'clock, then, Kachoudas went downstairs, unlatched his door and started to take away the heavy dark green wood panels that protected the windows of his shop. He was carrying in the third of these panels when he heard the noise of panels of exactly the same sort coming down across the street at the haberdashery. He took care not to look around. He was not too worried because the butcher was talking from his doorstep to the shoemaker. He heard steps coming across the street and then a voice said:

"Good morning, Kachoudas."

With a panel in one hand Kachoudas managed to say in an almost natural tone of voice: "Good morning, Monsieur Labbé."

"Look here, Kachoudas . . ."

"Yes, Monsieur Labbé?"

"Has there ever been anyone crazy in your family"

His first reaction was to dig into his memory, to think of all his uncles and aunts.

"I don't think so . . ."

There was a satisfied look on Monsieur Labbé's face, and he said just before turning around:

"That doesn't matter . . . that doesn't matter . . ."

The two men had made contact, that was all. What they had actually said was of no importance. They had exchanged a few words like the good neighbors they were. Kachoudas had not shown any fear. Wouldn't the butcher over there, who was big and strong enough to carry a hog on his shoulders, have paled if someone had said to him:

"That man looking at you with those grave, dreamy eyes is the killer of the seven old woman."

At the moment Kachoudas could think of nothing but the twenty thousand francs. He went back up to his low-ceilinged mezzanine workroom, climbed up on the table, and sat down to work again.

Across the street Monsieur Labbé was blocking hats. He didn't sell many new hats but his friends at the Café de la Paix had him block their old ones. Every now and then he appeared in a vest and shirt sleeves in the shop. And from time to time, when he heard his wife's signal, he dashed up the spiral staircase.

When Madame Kachoudas came back from the market and began to talk to herself in the kitchen, as she always did, there was a slight smile on the tailor's face. What was it the newspaper had said?

If we go back over the crimes one by one we shall see . . .

First of all, the article went on to say, the crimes were committed not in any particular section of the town, but at its farthest extremities. *Therefore,* the writer concluded, *the killer can go from place to place without attracting attention. This means that he is an ordinary or innocent-looking man. In spite of the fact that his crimes are committed in the dark he has to walk under street lamps or in front of lighted shop windows.*

He's a man who doesn't need money, because he doesn't rob his victims.

He must be a musician, because he surprises his victims from the rear and strangles them with the string of a violin or a cello.

If we look back over the list of the women he has killed . . .

This aroused the interest of Kachoudas.

. . . we shall see that there is a certain connection among them. This isn't very easy to put a finger on. Their social status has varied. The first one was the widow of a retired army officer and

240

the mother of two married children, living in Paris. The second kept a little dry-goods shop and her husband has a job at the Town Hall. The third . . .

A midwife, a clerk in a bookshop, a rich old lady living in a house all her own, a half-crazy woman, rich too, who wore nothing but lavender, and finally Mademoiselle Mollard, Irène Mollard, the music teacher.

Most of these women, the article continued, *were from sixty-three to sixty-five years old and all of them were natives of this town.*

The little tailor was struck by the name of Irène. One doesn't expect an old woman or an old maid to be called Irène, or Chouchou, or Lili . . . One forgets that long before she was old she was a young girl and once upon a time a little child. You see! There was nothing extraordinary about that. But while he worked on the inspector's suit Kachoudas mulled this idea over in his mind.

What went on, for instance, at the Café de la Paix? A dozen or so men met there every afternoon. They were from various walks of life, most of them fairly well off, because it is normal to have attained a certain prosperity after the age of sixty. They all called each other by their first names. And not only did they call each other by their first names, but they spoke in a language all their own, with bits of slang and jokes that nobody outside the group could understand or appreciate. And this was simply because they had all gone to the same school and done their military service together. This was the reason why Kachoudas would always be treated like a stranger, why nobody asked him to take a hand at a card game unless there was no one else available. For months and months he had waited for an empty place at a card table.

"Do you see what I mean, Inspector? I'm sure that the seven victims knew each other as well as the regular customers at the Café de la Paix. It's only because old ladies don't go to cafés that they see each other less frequently. We must find out whether they weren't all friends and how often they called on one another. They were all about the same age, Inspector. Then there's one more detail that comes back to my mind; it was in the newspaper too. Each one of them was described in somewhat the same words as being *well born* and *well educated* . . .

Of course, he wasn't talking to Inspector Micou or to any other member of the police. He had a way of talking to himself, like his wife, especially when he was happy.

"Let us imagine that we know on what basis the killer— I mean, the haberdasher—chose his victims . . .

For he picked them out in advance—Kachoudas had witnessed that. He didn't just stroll around the streets casually in the evening and jump on the first old woman who crossed his path. The proof of this lay in the fact that he had made straight for the house where Mademoiselle Mollard (Irène) was giving a music lesson. He must have acted in the same way on previous occasions. As soon as it could be found out how he laid his plans, on what basis he drew up his list . . . Exactly! Why not? He was proceeding just as if he had drawn up a complete and definitive list. Kachoudas could imagine him coming home at night and scratching off a name.

How many old women were on the list altogether? How many women were there in the whole town between sixty-three and sixty-five years of age, *well born* and *well educated?*

Before the tailor had lunch at noon he went downstairs for a moment to get a breath of fresh air on the sidewalk and to buy some cigarettes at the corner tobacconist's. Monsieur Labbé was just coming out of his door, with his hands in his overcoat pockets. When he saw the little tailor he pulled out one of his hands and gave a friendly wave. This was the way it should be. They exchanged greetings and smiled. Probably the harberdasher had a letter in his pocket and was on his way to mail it. After each murder he sent a communication to the local newspaper. The one which Kachoudas read that same evening in the *Courrier de la Loire* ran as follows:

> *Inspector Micou is silly to enlarge his wardrobe as if he were going to stay here months longer. Two more and I'll have finished. Greetings to my little friend across the street.*

Kachoudas read the newspaper in the Café de la Paix. The inspector himself was there, somewhat concerned about the delivery of his suit when he saw that the tailor had left his work. The haberdasher was there too, playing cards with the doctor, the insurance agent, and the grocer.

Monsieur Labbé found a way of looking at Kachoudas with a smile, a smile with no reservations behind it. Perhaps he really made no reservations, but had a feeling of genuine friendship. Then the little tailor realized that the haberdasher was glad that there was at least one witness of his deeds, someone who had seen him at work. In short, someone to admire him! And he too smiled, in a slightly embarrassed manner.

"I must go work on your suit, Inspector. You can try it in an hour . . . Firmin!"

He hesitated. Yes or No? Yes! Quick, a white wine! A man who's going to make twenty thousand francs can easily afford a second glass.

The little tailor was impressed. First of all by the chimes of the doorbell, whose echoes swelled endlessly through the apparently empty building. Then by the huge gray stone façade, the closed shutters with only a pale light glimmering through them, the heavy varnished door and the polished knob. Luckily, it was no longer raining and his shoes weren't muddy.

He heard muffled steps. A grated peep-hole opened, as in a prison, and one could guess at the pale heavy face behind it by a slight noise which was caused not by chains but by a swinging rosary. Someone looked at him in silence and finally he stammered:

"May I talk to the Mother Superior?"

For a moment he was afraid and trembled. The street was deserted. He had counted on the continuation of the card game. But Monsieur Labbé might have given up his place. And Kachoudas was running a very great risk. If the haberdasher had followed him and was hidden somewhere in the shadows, he surely wouldn't hesitate, in spite of the smile of a short while ago, to add Kachoudas to the list of his victims.

"Mother Saint Ursula is in the refectory. Who shall I tell her is here?"

Good God, if only she'd open the door!

"My name wouldn't mean anything to her. Just tell her that it's something very important . . ."

The nun's muffled steps retreated into the distance and she stayed away an infinitely long time. At last she came back and released three or four well-oiled latches.

"If you'll follow me . . ."

The air was warm, stale, and a trifle sugary. Everything was ivory color except for the black furniture. The silence was such that one could hear the ticking of several clocks, some of which must have been in rooms quite far away.

He did not dare sit down and he did not know how to behave. He had to wait for some time, and then he

244

jumped at the sight of an elderly nun whose approach he had not noticed.

"How old is she?" he wondered, for it is hard to guess at the age of a nun beneath her white cap.

"You asked to see me?"

He had telephoned beforehand from his shop to Monsieur Cujas, the husband of the second victim, who had a job at the Town Hall. Monsieur Cujas was still there, at the "Lost and Found" office.

"Who is calling?" Monsieur Cujas shouted impatiently.

Kachoudas had to screw up his courage before answering:

"One of the detectives with Inspector Micou. Can you tell me, Monsieur Cujas, where your wife went to school?"

To the Convent of the Immaculate Conception was the answer. He might have known that, since the victim had been described as "well educated."

"I beg your pardon, Reverend Mother . . ."

He stammered, feeling more uncomfortable than he had ever felt in his life.

"I'd like to see a list of all your former pupils who might now be sixty-three or sixty-four or . . ."

"I am sixty-five years old myself . . ."

She had a smooth, rosy face and she observed him closely, toying the while with the beads of the heavy rosary that hung from her belt.

"You've had a narrow escape, Reverend Mother . . ."

This was a rather tactless remark. He was panicky. Panicky because he felt surer and surer that he would win the twenty thousand francs reward.

"Mademoiselle Mollard came to school here, didn't she?"

"She was one of our most brilliant pupils."

"And Madame Cujas?"

"Desjardins, she was called as a girl . . ."

"Tell me, Reverend Mother, if they were both in the same class . . ."

"I was in the same class myself . . . That is why, during these past few weeks . . ."

But he could not wait to hear her answer.

"If I could have a list of all the girls who were here at that time?"

"Are you from the police?"

"No, Madame . . . Reverend Mother, I mean . . . But it amounts to the same thing . . . Just imagine, I know . . ."

"What do you know?"

"That is, I think I shall know very soon . . . Do you ever go out? . . ."

"Every Monday, to the bishop's palace."

"At what time of day?"

"At four o'clock."

"If you will be so kind as to make me the list . . ."

What could she be thinking? Perhaps she took him for the killer. No; she was perfectly serene.

"There aren't many of us left from that class. Quite a few have died . . . and just recently . . ."

"I know, Reverend Mother . . ."

"Only Armandine and myself . . ."

"Who is Armandine, Reverend Mother?"

"Madame d'Hauterive. You must have heard of her. The rest have left town and we haven't kept up with them. I have an idea . . . Just wait a minute . . ."

Perhaps a nun, too, enjoys a distraction from her usual routine. After an absence of only a few seconds she came back with a yellowed picture of two rows of young girls, all wearing the same uniform and the same ribbon with a medal attached to it around their necks. And pointing to a weakly looking figure, she said:

"There is Madame Labbé, the wife of the haberdasher. And this one, who's slightly cross-eyed . . ."

Mother Saint Ursula was quite right. Besides the haberdasher's wife there were only two members of the class still alive in the town; Mother Saint Ursula and Madame D'Hauterive.

"Madame Labbé is very ill. I must go call on her next Saturday. That is her birthday and a group of her old school friends have always met in her sickroom."

"Thank you, Reverend Mother."

The twenty thousand francs were his! Or at least they soon would be. Every one of the haberdasher's victims was in the photograph. And the only two still alive, besides Madame Labbé, were obviously those whom the killer had announced as his next victims.

"Thank you again, Reverend Mother. I must go immediately. Someone is waiting for me . . ."

Perhaps his behavior wasn't entirely correct; he wasn't used to convent ways. If they took him for an oaf or a madman there wasn't much he could do about it. He thanked the Mother Superior once more, bowed, backed his way out and started to run down the sidewalk outside so fast that he found it hard to slow up.

Twenty thousand francs! Twenty thousand francs they had promised for the killer, for the killer alone. Wasn't he entitled to more if he brought them a complete list of the victims, both past and future? Thanks to him two of them would survive for some years to come.

"Prove your case . . ."

What if they were to say just that?

"Prove it! Prove that these two persons were to be the

next victims. What right have you to claim that a man like Monsieur Labbé planned to murder Mother Saint Ursula? What? Speak up!"

And yet only a bit of understanding was necessary. An understanding of why the haberdasher had drawn up his list in the first place.

I must go call on her next Saturday, the Mother Superior had said, speaking of Madame Labbé. *That is her birthday and a group of her old school friends have always met in her sickroom.*

Twenty thousand francs. Perhaps fifty thousand, perhaps more . . . Madame d'Hauterive was rich and when she learned that she owed her life to a little tailor with a large family . . .

His wife was waiting at the front door.

"He's upstairs."

"Who's upstairs?"

"The inspector."

"Good!" he cried, with a self-assurance to which she was not accustomed. Never had he wondered whether every man has a chance of living one glorious hour, one hour when he can live up to the best that is in him. And yet just such an hour had come.

"Good evening, Inspector. I'm sorry to have kept you waiting, but I've been very busy . . ."

That was the way! He had spoken in the easy-going tone of voice of the most affluent gentlemen of the Café de la Paix. He had not forgotten the gestures natural to his profession, but he performed them with such grace that he seemed to be juggling with the unattached pieces of the inspector's suit.

"Tell me . . . The twenty thousand francs reward . . . There's no catch to it, is there?"

"Have you a little theory of your own, too?"

A little theory! A little theory, the inspector called it! When Kachoudas had seen the killer at work with his own eyes! When he knew who the next victims would be and had just this minute left the company of one of them . . . Ha! Ha! . . .

"Listen, Inspector . . . If I were quite sure about the reward . . ."

"Well, I can tell you one thing. If you want to win it you'd better hurry up . . ."

They didn't believe him. It was all a joke. They were making fun of him. The inspector added:

"There's someone waiting for me right now in my office . . . A woman . . . Apparently she claims the reward . . . They called me just now at the café."

"What's her name?" Kachoudas asked distrustfully.

"Does it interest you?"

"It isn't a nun, is it?"

"Why should it be a nun?"

"Does her last name have a *de* in it? Is her first name Armandine?"

He had no intention of letting his twenty thousand francs slip away from him.

"If she's neither one of those two, Inspector, she can only be telling you fairy-tales . . ."

Then the inspector let drop: "You ought to know who she is. She works right across the street from you . . ."

Kachoudas listened intently with a hard expression on his face.

"She's the cleaning woman of your friend the haberdasher . . ."

For at least two minutes the inspector was left trussed up in an unfinished suit, which had only one sleeve and no collar, while the little tailor strode nervously up and down the room, and every now and then his mouth was twisted into a sarcastic smile. It was impossible. It wasn't right. He had thought of everything except that old cleaning woman. What credit did she deserve for the fact that she had access to the house and could spy on everything. She hadn't thought of the Convent of the Immaculate Conception, had she? She didn't know the names of the next victims. Well, then . . .

"Look here, Inspector . . . Supposing I tell you right away . . ."

But what about proofs? Always that confounded matter of proofs! And to think that the cleaning woman *might* have proofs, even if they were only scraps of paper she had picked out of the garbage can.

"It's only fair, when all's said and done, that the first-comer should have the reward, isn't it?"

"Of course."

The light was on across the street, as it always was at this hour. It made only a vague circle behind the lace curtains, but one could guess at the shape of Madame Labbé's chair and her motionless white face.

"Saturday is her birthday . . ."

"What's that?"

"Never mind . . . Saturday the sixty-three to sixty-five year old survivors are scheduled to meet in her sickroom and . . ."

This was not Kachoudas' hour of glory, it was his exact minute. He must hurry, on account of the cleaning woman.

"Listen, my man . . ."

"Twenty thousand francs, then?"

"Yes, if you . . ."

If he could prove it, of course.

"Look here . . ."

Kachoudas picked up the heavy scissors with which he

250

had cut the cloth that was now draped so strangely around the inspector. He opened the window and made a desperate gesture, hurling the scissors straight at the window on the other side of the street.

Then he stood perfectly still, quivering inside. The glass had shattered with a tremendous noise. He had to catch his breath before a smile came over his face, a triumphant smile that a little tailor of his kind can afford only once in a lifetime. Across the street he and the inspector could see in the chair of the haberdasher's invalid wife only a wooden head on top of a pile of rags.

"Tell me, Madame . . ."

"Mademoiselle, if you please . . ."

A sour old thing, Monsieur Labbé's cleaning woman! They had brought her over from the police station and as soon as she saw her employer in handcuffs she knew that she was too late.

"You knew that Madame Labbé was dead, did you?"

"I was sure of it."

"For how long a time?"

"Months and months. I was sure, that is, without really knowing . . ."

"What do you mean?"

"Well, mostly on account of the fish . . ."

"What fish?"

"All kinds of fish, herrings, halibut, cod . . . She couldn't eat fish."

"Why not?"

"Fish upset her. Lots of people are like that. I had to be very brave, I can tell you. If I don't get at least a share of the twenty thousand francs, then there's no justice . . ."

Kachoudas stirred in his corner, but the inspector made a reassuring sign in his direction.

251

"What was that about the fish?"

"Well, one day when I had cooked some fish for him and I wanted to send up some meat to his wife, he told me that I needn't bother. He took all her meals to her, you know, and kept her room in order. Then there was the string . . ."

"What string?"

"The string I found last week when I was cleaning up his workshop. He never wanted me to go in there, but I made up my mind to do it while he was away, because there was such a bad smell. Back of the hats I found a string hanging from the ceiling. He pulled on that to make the same noise that his wife used to make when she tapped with her cane on the floor. As for the twenty thousand francs, I'm going to see a lawyer . . ."

Kachoudas almost rose again. Monsieur Labbé gave a dignified smile.

"So first of all you killed your wife . . ."

He shrugged his shoulders.

"You strangled her the same way you did the others . . ."

"Not the same way, Inspector. With my hands. She was suffering too much . . ."

"Or rather, you were tired of looking after her . . ."

"As you like . . ."

"Then you began to kill off your wife's friends. Why? And why in such rapid successions?"

Kachoudas raised his hand as if he were at school.

"Because of the birthday!" he shouted.

"Quiet, please," said the inspector. "Let Monsieur Labbé talk . . ."

Monsieur Labbé nodded approvingly at the little tailor.

"Exactly. He's quite right. They all had to be killed by next Saturday . . ."

And he winked at Kachoudas. There was no doubt about it: he winked at him as if he were an accomplice. It was just as if he were saying:

"They'll always blunder along. But we two—we understand each other . . ."

And the little tailor, who had just won his twenty thousand francs, could not help smiling back.

. . . for they shall inherit the earth.

I am especially fond of "The Purple Is Everything" for two reasons: It is a story of nonviolent violence and it was a gift. In the days when MWA headquartered on West Twenty-fourth Street, a group of us "girls" used to lunch at the long-passed Guffanti's Restaurant on Sixth Avenue. We called it Guffy's Tavern and we called ourselves The Literary Ladies' Chowder and Marching Society. We met to eat, drink and make mysteries we hoped would sell. And some did.

On this day Margaret Manners, may she rest in peace, confided that she knew how a painting might have been stolen from the Museum of Modern Art. I fell in love with the idea. I no longer remember where Margaret's idea ended and my extrapolations began. I do remember how strongly I argued that it must not be a crime story in the conventional sense: The violence committed should be against the heart. I don't suppose I groveled, or slithered in the sawdust, but the moment came when Margaret said, "Ah, love, you take it. I'd only muck it up." I knew she wouldn't muck it up, splendid writer that she was, but I never looked back.

I do now. With enduring thanks.

—DOROTHY SALISBURY DAVIS

THE PURPLE IS EVERYTHING

DOROTHY SALISBURY DAVIS

You are likely to say, reading about Mary Gardner, that you knew her, or that you once knew someone like her. And well you may have, for while her kind is not legion it endures and sometimes against great popular odds.

You will see Mary Gardner—or someone like her—at the symphony, in the art galleries, at the theater, always well-dressed if not quite fashionable, sometimes alone, sometimes in the company of other women all of whom have an aura, not of sameness, but of mutuality. Each of them has made—well, if not a good life for herself, at least the best possible life it was in her power to make.

Mary Gardner was living at the time in a large East Coast city. In her late thirties, she was a tall lean woman, unmarried, quietly feminine, gentle, even a little hesitant in manner but definite in her tastes. Mary was a designer in a well-known wallpaper house. Her salary allowed her to buy good clothes, to live alone in a pleasant apartment within walking distance of her work, and to go regularly to the theater and the Philharmonic. As often as she went to the successful plays, she attended little theater and the experimental stage. She was not among those who believed that a play had to say something. She was interested in "the submerged values." This taste prevailed also in her approach to the visual arts—a boon surely in the wallpaper business whose customers for the most part prefer their walls to be seen but not heard.

In those days Mary was in the habit of going during her lunch hour—or sometimes when she needed to get away from the drawing board—to the Institute of Modern Art which was less than a city block from her office. She had fallen in love with a small, early Monet titled "Trees Near L'Havre," and when in love Mary was a person of searching devotion. Almost daily she discovered new voices in the woodland scene, trees and sky reflected in a shimmering pool—with more depths in the sky, she felt, than in the water.

The more she thought about this observation the more convinced she became that the gallery had hung the picture upside down. She evolved a theory about the signature: it was hastily done by the artist, she decided, long after he had finished the painting and perhaps at a time when the light of day was fading. She would have spoken to a museum authority about it—if she had known a museum authority.

Mary received permission from the Institute to sketch within its halls and often stood before the Monet for an hour, sketchbook in hand. By putting a few strokes on paper she felt herself conspicuously inconspicuous among the transient viewers and the guards. She would not for anything have presumed to copy the painting and she was fiercely resentful of the occasional art student who did.

So deep was Mary in her contemplation of Claude Monet's wooded scene that on the morning of the famous museum fire, when she first smelled the smoke, she thought it came from inside the picture itself. She was instantly furious, and by an old association she indicted a whole genre of people—the careless American tourist in a

foreign land. She was not so far away from reality, however, that she did not realize almost at once there was
actually a fire in the building.

Voices cried out alarms in the corridors and men suddenly were running. Guards dragged limp hoses along
the floor and dropped them—where they lay like great
withered snakes over which people leaped as in some
tribal rite. Blue smoke layered the ceiling and then began
to fall in angled swatches—like theatrical scrims gone
awry. In the far distance fire sirens wailed.

Mary Gardner watched, rooted and muted, as men and
women, visitors like herself, hastened past bearing
framed pictures in their arms; and in one case two men
carried between them a huge Chagall night scene in which
the little creatures seemed to be jumping on and off the
canvas, having an uproarious time in transit. A woman
took the Rouault from the wall beside the Monet and
hurried with it after the bearers of the Chagall.

Still Mary hesitated. That duty should compel her to
touch where conscience had so long forbidden it—this
conflict increased her confusion. Another thrust of smoke
into the room made the issue plainly the picture's sur-
vival, if not indeed her own. In desperate haste she tried
to lift the Monet from the wall, but it would not yield.

She strove, pulling with her full strength—such
strength that when the wire broke, she was catapulted
backward and fell over the viewer's bench, crashing her
head into the painting. Since the canvas was mounted on
board, the only misfortune—aside from her bruised head
which mattered not at all—was that the picture had jarred
loose from its frame. By then Mary cared little for the
frame. She caught up the painting, hugged it to her, and
groped her way to the gallery door.

She reached the smoke-bogged corridor at the instant

the water pressure brought the hoses violently to life. Jets
of water spurted from every connection. Mary shielded
the picture with her body until she could edge it within
the raincoat she had worn against the morning drizzle.

She hurried along the corridor, the last apparently of
the volunteer rescuers. The guards were sealing off the
wing of the building, closing the fire prevention door.
They showed little patience with her protests, shunting
her down the stairs. By the time she reached the lobby the
police had cordoned off civilians. Imperious as well as
impervious, a policeman escorted her into the crowd, and
in the crowd, having no use of her arms—they were still
locked around the picture—she was shoved and jostled
toward the door and there pitilessly jettisoned into the
street. On the sidewalk she had no hope at all finding
anyone in that surging, gaping mob on whom she could
safely bestow her art treasure.

People screamed and shouted that they could see the
flames. Mary did not look back. She hastened homeward,
walking proud and fierce, thinking that the city was after
all a jungle. She hugged the picture to her, her raincoat its
only shield but her life a ready forfeit for its safety.

It had been in her mind to telephone the Institute office
at once. But in her own apartment, the painting propped
up against cushions on the sofa, she reasoned that until
the fire was extinguished she had no hope of talking with
anyone there. She called her own office and pleaded a
sudden illness—something she had eaten at lunch though
she had not had a bite since breakfast.

The walls of her apartment were hung with what she
called her "potpourri": costume prints and color litho-
graphs—all, she had been proud to say, limited editions or
artists' prints. She had sometimes thought of buying
paintings, but plainly she could not afford her own tastes.

On impulse now, she took down an Italian lithograph and removed the glass and mat from the wooden frame. The Monet fit quite well. And to her particular delight she could now hang it right side up. As though with a will of its own, the painting claimed the place on her wall most favored by the light of day.

There is no way of describing Mary's pleasure in the company she kept that afternoon. She would not have taken her eyes from the picture at all except for the joy that was renewed at each returning. Reluctantly she turned on the radio at five o'clock so that she might learn more of the fire at the Institute. It had been extensive and destructive—an entire wing of the building was gutted.

She listened with the remote and somewhat smug solicitude that one bestows on other people's tragedies to the enumeration of the paintings which had been destroyed. The mention of "Trees Near L'Havre" startled her. A full moment later she realized the explicit meaning of the announcer's words. She turned off the radio and sat a long time in the flood of silence.

Then she said aloud tentatively, "You are a thief, Mary Gardner," and after a bit repeated, "Oh, yes. You are a thief." But she did not mind at all. Nothing so portentous had ever been said about her before, even by herself.

She ate her dinner from a tray before the painting, having with it a bottle of French wine. Many times that night she went from her bed to the living-room door until she seemed to have slept between so many wakenings. At last she did sleep.

But the first light of morning fell on Mary's conscience as early as upon the painting. After one brief visit to the living room she made her plans with the care of a religious novice well aware of the devil's constancy. She dressed more severely than was her fashion, needing herringbone for backbone—the ridiculous phrase kept running through her mind at breakfast. In final appraisal of herself in the hall mirror she thought she looked like the headmistress of an English girls' school, which she supposed satisfactory to the task before her.

Just before she left the apartment, she spent one last moment alone with the Monet. Afterward, wherever, however the Institute chose to hang it, she might hope to feel that a little part of it was forever hers.

On the street she bought a newspaper and confirmed the listing of "Trees Near L'Havre." Although that wing of the Institute had been destroyed, many of its paintings had been carried to safety by way of the second-floor corridor.

Part of the street in front of the Institute was still cordoned off when she reached it, congesting the flow of morning traffic. The police on duty were no less brusque than those whom Mary had encountered the day before. She was seized by the impulse to postpone her mission— an almost irresistible temptation, especially when she was barred from entering the museum unless she could show a pass such as had been issued to all authorized personnel.

"Of course I'm not authorized," she exclaimed. "If I were I shouldn't be out here."

The policeman directed her to the sergeant in charge. He was at the moment disputing with the fire insurance representative as to how much of the street could be used for the salvage operation. "The business of this street is business," the sergeant said, "and that's my business."

Mary waited until the insurance man stalked into the building. He did not need a pass, she noticed. "Excuse me, officer, I have a painting—"

"Lady . . ." He drew the long breath of patience. "Yes, ma'am?"

"Yesterday during the fire a painting was supposedly destroyed—a lovely, small Monet called—"

"Was there now?" the sergeant interrupted. Lovely small Monets really touched him.

Mary was becoming flustered in spite of herself. "It's listed in this morning's paper as having been destroyed. But it wasn't. I have it at home."

The policeman looked at her for the first time with a certain compassion. "On your living-room wall, no doubt," he said with deep knowingness.

"Yes, as a matter of fact."

He took her gently but firmly by the arm. "I tell you what you do. You go along to police headquarters on Fifty-seventh Street. You know where that is, don't you? Just tell them all about it like a good girl." He propelled her into the crowd and there released her. Then he raised his voice: "Keep moving! You'll see it all on the television."

Mary had no intention of going to police headquarters where, she presumed, men concerned with armed robbery, mayhem, and worse were even less likely to understand the subtlety of her problem. She went to her office and throughout the morning tried periodically to reach the museum curator's office by telephone. On each of her calls either the switchboard was tied up or his line was busy for longer than she could wait.

Finally she hit on the idea of asking for the Institute's Public Relations Department, and to someone there, obviously distracted—Mary could hear parts of three conversations going on at the same time—she explained how during the fire she had saved Monet's "Trees Near L'Havre."

"Near where, madam?" the voice asked.

"L'Havre." Mary spelled it. "By Monet," she added.

"Is that two words or one?" the voice asked.

"Please transfer me to the curator's office," Mary said and ran her fingers up and down the lapel of her herring-bone suit.

Mary thought it a wise precaution to meet the Institute's representative in the apartment lobby where she first asked to see his credentials. He identified himself as the man to whom she had given her name and address on the phone. Mary signaled for the elevator and thought about his identification: Robert Attlebury III. She had seen his name on the museum roster: Curator of . . . she could not remember.

He looked every inch the curator, standing erect and remote while the elevator bore them slowly upward. A curator perhaps, but she would not have called him a connoisseur. One with his face and disposition would always taste and spit out, she thought. She could imagine his scorn of things he found distasteful, and instinctively she knew herself to be distasteful to him.

Not that it really mattered what he felt about her. She was nobody. But how must the young unknown artist feel standing with his work before such superciliousness? Or had he a different mien and manner for people of his own kind? In that case she would have given a great deal for the commonest of his courtesies.

"Everything seems so extraordinary—in retrospect," Mary said to break the silence of their seemingly endless ascent.

"How fortunate for you," he said, and Mary thought, perhaps it was.

When they reached the door of her apartment, she paused before turning the key. "Shouldn't you have brought a guard—or someone?"

He looked down on her as from Olympus. "I am some-one."

Mary resolved to say nothing more. She opened the door and left it open. He preceded her and moved across the foyer into the living room and stood before the Monet. His rude directness oddly comforted her: he did, after all, care about painting. She ought not to judge men, she thought, from her limited experience of them.

He gazed at the Monet for a few moments, then he tilted his head ever so slightly from one side to the other. Mary's heart began to beat erratically. For months she had wanted to discuss with someone who really knew about such things her theory of what was reflection and what was reality in "Trees Near L'Havre." But now that her chance was at hand she could not find the words.

Still, she had to say something—something . . . casual. "The frame is mine," she said, "but for the picture's protection you may take it. I can get it the next time I'm at the museum."

Surprisingly, he laughed. "It may be the better part at that," he said.

"I beg your pardon?"

He actually looked at her. "Your story is ingenious, madam, but then it was warranted by the occasion."

"I simply do not understand what you are saying," Mary said.

"I have seen better copies than this one," he said. "It's too bad your ingenuity isn't matched by a better imitation."

Mary was too stunned to speak. He was about to go. "But . . . it's signed," Mary blurted out, and feebly tried to direct his attention to the name in the upper corner.

"Which makes it forgery, doesn't it?" he said almost solicitously.

His preciseness, his imperturbability in the light of the horrendous thing he was saying, etched detail into the nightmare.

"That's not my problem!" Mary cried, giving voice to words she did not mean, saying what amounted to a betrayal of the painting she so loved.

"Oh, but it is. Indeed it is, and I may say a serious problem if I were to pursue it."

"Please do pursue it!" Mary cried.

Again he smiled, just a little. "That is not the Institute's way of dealing with these things."

"You do not *like* Monet," Mary challenged desperately, for he had started toward the door.

"That's rather beside the point, isn't it?"

"You don't *know* Monet. You can't! Not possibly!"

"How could I dislike him if I didn't know him? Let me tell you something about Monet." He turned back to the picture and trailed a finger over one vivid area. "In Monet the purple is everything."

"The purple?" Mary said.

"You're beginning to see it yourself now, aren't you?" His tone verged on the pedagogic.

Mary closed her eyes and said, "I only know how this painting came to be here."

"I infinitely prefer not to be made your confidant in that matter," he said. "Now I have rather more important matters to take care of." And again he started toward the door.

Mary hastened to block his escape. "It doesn't matter what you think of Monet, or of me, or of anything. You've got to take that painting back to the museum."

"And be made a laughingstock when the hoax is discovered?" He set an arm as stiff as a brass rail between them and moved out of the apartment.

Mary followed him to the elevator, now quite beside herself. "I shall go to the newspapers!" she cried.

"I think you might regret it."

"Now I know. I understand!" Mary saw the elevator door open. "You were glad to think the Monet had been destroyed in the fire."

"Savage!" he said.

Then the door closed between them.

In time Mary persuaded—and it wasn't easy—certain experts, even an art critic, to come and examine "her" Monet. It was a more expensive undertaking than she could afford—all of them seemed to expect refreshments, including expensive liquors. Her friends fell in with "Mary's hoax," as they came to call her story, and she was much admired in an ever-widening and increasingly eso-teric circle for her unwavering account of how she had come into possession of a "genuine Monet." Despite the virtue of simplicity, a trait since childhood, she found herself using words in symbolic combinations—the lan-guage of the company she now kept—and people far wiser than she would say of her: "How perceptive!" or "What insight!"—and then pour themselves another drink.

One day her employer, the great man himself, who prior to her "acquisition" had not known whether she lived in propriety or in sin, arrived at her apartment at cocktail time bringing with him a famous art historian.

The expert smiled happily over his second Scotch while Mary told again the story of the fire at the Institute and how she had simply walked home with the painting because she could not find anyone to whom to give it. While she talked, his knowing eyes wandered from her face to the painting, to his glass, to the painting, and back to her face again.

"Oh, I could believe it," he said when she had finished. "It's the sort of mad adventure that actually could happen." He set his glass down carefully where she could see that it was empty. "I suppose you know that there has never been an officially complete catalogue of Monet's work?"

"No," she said, and refilled his glass.

"It's so, unfortunately. And the sad truth is that quite a number of museums today are hanging paintings under his name that are really unauthenticated."

"And mine?" Mary said, lifting a chin she tried vainly to keep from quivering.

Her guest smiled. *"Must* you know?"

For a time after that Mary tried to avoid looking at the Monet. It was not that she liked it less, but that now she somehow liked herself less in its company. What had happened, she realized, was that, like the experts, she now saw not the painting, but herself.

This was an extraordinary bit of self-discovery for one who had never had to deal severely with her own psyche. Till now, so far as Mary was concerned, the chief function of a mirror had been to determine the angle of a hat. But the discovery of the flaw does not in itself effect a cure; often it aggravates the condition. So with Mary.

She spent less and less time at home, and it was to be said for some of her new-found friends that they thought it only fair to reciprocate for having enjoyed the hospitality of so enigmatically clever a hostess. How often had she as a girl been counseled by parent and teacher to get out more, to see more people. Well, Mary was at last getting out more. And in the homes of people who had felt free to comment on her home and its possessions, she too felt free to comment. The more odd her comment—the nastier, she would once have said of it—the more popular she became. Oh, yes. Mary was seeing more people, lots more people.

In fact, her insurance agent—who was in the habit of just dropping in to make his quarterly collection—had to get up early one Saturday morning to make sure he caught her at home.

It was a clear, sharp day, and the hour at which the Monet was most luminous. The man sat staring at it, fascinated. Mary was amused, remembering how hurt he always was that his clients failed to hang his company calendar in prominence. While she was gone from the room to get her check book, he got up and touched the surface of the painting.

"Ever think of taking out insurance on that picture?" he asked when she returned. "Do you mind if I ask how much it's worth?"

"It cost me . . . a great deal," Mary said, and was at once annoyed with both him and herself.

"I tell you what," the agent said. "I have a friend who appraises these objects of art for some of the big galleries, you know? Do you mind if I bring him round and see what he thinks its worth?"

"No, I don't mind," Mary said in utter resignation.

And so the appraiser came and looked carefully at the painting. He hedged about putting a value on it. He wasn't the last word on these nineteenth-century Impressionists and he wanted to think it over. But that afternoon he returned just as Mary was about to go out, and with him came a bearded gentleman who spoke not once to Mary or to the appraiser, but chatted constantly with himself while he scrutinized the painting. Then with a "tsk, tsk, tsk," he took the painting from the wall, examined the back, and rehung it—but reversing it, top to bottom.

Mary felt the old flutter interrupt her heartbeat, but it passed quickly.

Even walking out of her house the bearded gentleman did not speak to her; she might have been invisible. It was the appraiser who murmured his thanks but not a word of explanation. Since the expert had not drunk her whiskey Mary supposed the amenities were not required of him.

She was prepared to forget him as she had the others— it was easy now to forget them all; but when she came home to change between matinee and cocktails, another visitor was waiting. She noticed him in the lobby and realized, seeing the doorman say a word to him just as the elevator door closed off her view, that his business was with her. The next trip of the elevator brought him to her door.

"I've come about the painting, Miss Gardner," he said, and offered his card. She had opened the door only as far as the latch chain permitted. He was representative of the Continental Assurance Company, Limited.

She slipped off the latch chain.

Courteous and formal behind his double-breasted suit, he waited for Mary to seat herself. He sat down neatly opposite her, facing the painting, for she sat beneath it, erect, and she hoped, formidable.

"Lovely," he said, gazing at the Monet. Then he wrenched his eyes from it. "But I'm not an expert," he added and gently cleared his throat. He was chagrined, she thought, to have allowed himself even so brief a luxury of the heart.

"But is it authenticated?" She said it much as she would once have thought but not said, Fie on you!

"Sufficient to my company's requirements," he said. "But don't misunderstand—we are not proposing to make any inquiries. We are always satisfied in such delicate negotiations just to have the painting back."

Mary did not misunderstand, but she certainly did not understand either.

He took from his inside pocket a piece of paper which he placed on the coffee table and with the tapering fingers of an artist—or a banker—or a pickpocket—he gently maneuvered it to where Mary could see that he was proffering a certified check.

He did not look at her and therefore missed the spasm she felt contorting her mouth. "The day of the fire," she thought, but the words never passed her lips.

She took up the check in her hand: $20,000.

"May I use your phone, Miss Gardner?"

Mary nodded and went into the kitchen where she again looked at the check. It was a great deal of money, she thought wryly, to be offered in compensation for a few months' care of a friend.

She heard her visitor's voice as he spoke into the telephone—an expert now, to judge by his tone. A few minutes later she heard the front door close. When she went back into the living room both her visitor and the Monet were gone . . .

Some time later Mary attended the opening of the new wing of the Institute. She recognized a number of people she had not known before and whom, she supposed, she was not likely to know much longer.

They had hung the Monet upside down again.

Mary thought of it after she got home, and as though two rights must surely right a possible wrong, she turned the check upside down while she burned it over the kitchen sink.